Vindicated

Sharon C. Cooper

Dedication

To my thrill-seeking sister-friend, Tanya Stanley.
Thanks for making my life adventurous!

Chapter One

Dakota Sherrod regulated her breathing as the production crew double-checked her harness. The intention had been to shoot this scene in one take, but three attempts later, they were still trying to get it perfect.

"You need to land in the center of the mark once you get to the second rooftop," the movie director insisted, frustration lacing his words, as if it was Dakota's fault he couldn't get the shot they desired. "The target has been moved to the right a few inches. There's no reason you shouldn't be able to stick the landing once you're over the ledge."

Dakota nodded, trying like hell to hold her tongue to keep from telling him where he could stick his target. If she had to do this scene one more time, she was definitely going to hurt somebody.

Anxiousness thumped through her body as she mentally prepared herself despite the physical impact the scene was having on her. This had to be the last take. Her knees couldn't handle another landing. Each time her feet connected with the roof, her joints screamed from the blunt force.

As the body double for the lead actress, doing all of the stunts for the highly anticipated action flick was an amazing opportunity. Dakota had been a stand-in for the A-list actress on a number of projects, but this one could catapult her career to the next level. Her only concern was that the movie included more intense and dangerous scenes than usual. The effect they were already having on her body had her thinking about changing careers. But besides stunt work and sex, there was nothing else she enjoyed doing that would offer the same excitement and adrenaline rush.

Audrey, the stunt coordinator, tugged on the cables that Dakota was hooked up to and nodded to the director. It was almost time. Time to show them that despite some of the unconventional methods used to film some of her scenes, she could handle anything they threw her way. Camera and crew members were set up on both rooftops and there were a few below intending to capture every angle of the action. And she planned to give them what they wanted.

Dakota shivered. The thin T-shirt and skintight jeans did nothing to shield her from the cold breeze that seemed to come out of nowhere. The wind had calmed since they arrived on the rooftop, but she could feel it stirring up again.

"How does this harness feel?" Audrey asked. Dakota had mentioned that the first one she'd been wearing was too big and probably was the cause of the failed landing the day before.

"It feels fine." They'd been checking and rechecking everything for the past twenty minutes. Moviegoers would be amazed at the details that went into a sixty-second shot. She appreciated the extra care taken to make sure she was safe with each stunt, but it was time to get this scene over with.

"Ready?" Audrey asked.

"Yes." Dakota was more than ready. Prepping to leap from one rooftop, six stories high, to another one, amped the rhythm of her heartbeat, sending excitement pulsating to every cell in her body. Yeah, she was a little anxious, but this was the rush that kept her coming back for more.

The crew moved away from her and gave the director a thumbs-up. Dakota readied herself.

"Aaaaand action!"

Dakota took off in a sprint. Pumping her arms in sync with her legs, she weaved around air conditioner units and pipes as she dashed across the roof. Her booted feet ate up the blacktop, kicking up gravel in the process. Adrenaline soared through her veins the closer she got to the roof's edge, and she pushed harder. The wind kissing her heated cheeks did nothing to slow her pounding heart and the burn in her joints. Leaping to the next roof at top speed was her main focus.

You. Can. Do. This.

The sounds of birds, traffic, and the production crew faded into the background. The only sound penetrating her brain were helicopter propellers. The whirring of its blades flying overhead fueled her speed in a need to outrun the machine, adding an extra layer of excitement to the process.

Three.

Two.

One.

Leap!

Dakota flew through the air, her arms and legs, like the blades of an airplane propeller, thrust her forward and over the narrow street below.

"Oomph!" she grunted when the bottom of her black combat boots made contact with the second roof. She winced when the impact jarred every bone in her body.

She didn't stop.

She couldn't stop.

Dakota sprinted across the second rooftop as if her life depended on it—which it did, according to the script. The same momentum drove her to another ledge. With one palm on the rough surface of the ledge, she swung her legs over the top and hurdled over the building.

Yes! She had hit every target perfectly.

She dropped ten feet below onto another roof and landed on a twelve-inch thick cushion that helped soften her fall.

"Cut!"

Dakota's legs, feeling like limp noodles, gave out and she collapsed onto the mat, arms and legs spread as she struggled to catch her breath. There was no way the director didn't have what he needed from her for the scene.

Homer Parland, a well-known director in the business, had been riding her tail for the past two weeks. He kept making her do and then redo stunts, and then claimed a problem with one aspect of it or another. This was her first time working on a project with him and based on his snide remarks spoken under his breath in passing, it was clear he didn't like her.

As long as she did her job and got paid, Dakota didn't give a damn whether he liked her or not. It wouldn't be the first time she'd had to deal with jacked-up attitudes on a set. Hearing stupid comments like: *Are you going to send your daddy after me since we changed the scene?* Or, *Give her whatever she wants. The last thing I need is Wesley Bradford showing up on set.*

Early in her career, she had made the mistake of having her father, Wesley, represent her. One of the leading talent agents in the business, he had guided her career successfully for the first two years. He also made tons of enemies along the way. A *whatever-I-have-to-do* kind of guy, his clients always ended up with lucrative contracts. It didn't matter who he had to step on to make that happen.

But Dakota had fired him twelve years ago. Rarely had they seen eye-to-eye, often disagreeing more often than not on pretty much every subject. It didn't take long to figure out they couldn't have a father/daughter relationship and an agent/client relationship at the same time. Still, however, she had to put up with people in the industry who dealt with him at one time or another.

"You okay?" a production assistant asked, pulling Dakota out of her thoughts. He dropped down beside her.

"Yeah," she panted. Seconds ticked by as her breathing slowly went back to normal. She sat up with their help. They couldn't remove the cables or her harness until the director gave the word. Dakota inhaled and released slow even breaths, praying that was the last take.

Once she was back on the ground, she spotted Homer heading their way.

"That was better, but I want to run it one more time."

"What? Are you kidding me? Damn it, Homer! That shot was perfect and you know it!" Dakota seethed, getting in his face. She had never confronted a director like this before, but between her body aching and frustration nipping at her nerves, she couldn't stop herself.

The crew that was around moments ago eased away, leaving her and Homer alone.

"I don't know what your beef is with me, but I've given you a hundred percent every day. I've done *everything* you've asked of me. If any of those shots were off, it wasn't because of me. Yet, I'm the one out here busting my ass because you guys can't get it right!"

Homer stared at her for the longest minute. Dakota thought she saw a flicker of a smirk on his lips, but it was gone so fast she couldn't be sure.

"Are you done?" he finally asked.

Still fuming and holding back what she really wanted to say, Dakota kept her mouth shut but continued to glare. She should just throat-punch him. That would ease the irritation thumping through her veins. Having a black belt in karate, she knew just where to hit him without killing him. Inflict pain so he could feel what her body was experiencing at the moment. But the last thing she needed was a lawsuit or to lose this job. Being known for punching a director wouldn't go over well in the industry.

"Now that I have your attention, you can either be back here in forty minutes, or I'll find someone else for this project. Your choice." Without a backward glance, he headed over to the camera crew.

"Sorry, Dakota. If it helps, I thought the last shot was on point," Audrey said as she quickly unhooked the gear Dakota was still wearing. "Hang in there."

"Thanks," Dakota said and headed to the trailer that she shared with several other stunt people. Just as she reached the structure, she spotted a familiar face and her sour mood started to shift. Justin Crosby walked toward her holding up a cup of coffee, and a cute little boy followed close behind him.

Justin owned a rigging construction company that movie producers in Atlanta often used. His team was charged with the responsibility of installing and overseeing rigging gear like scaffolding, cranes, and cables, as well as building sets and scenery structures among other tasks.

He was also fine as hell, with a fun personality that could brighten her irritated mood. Dakota would have made a play for him when they first met, but he was dating a woman for the last two years, and they were now engaged to be married.

"Hey. Thought you could use a pick-me-up," he said, handing her the cup.

"You thought right. Thank you. So, who is this handsome young man?" She bent down to the boy's height.

"This is my nephew, Dominic. He's the best cure for a rough day. Oh, and he's the one I was telling you about who wants to be a stuntman. Dom, this is Dakota Sherrod."

"Hi," he said, grinning hard.

"It's nice to meet you. That's awesome that you want to be a stuntman."

"I saw you running on that building. It was cool when you jumped!" Dominic said, his enthusiasm palpable as he recounted part of her stunt and told her about a car chase scene that he'd seen earlier.

"When I get older, I might do some of that stuff, but I don't know if I can run through fire. Do you jump out of airplanes and fall down stairs like stuntmen?" Dominic asked, his eyebrows drawn tight as if they were having a deep conversation.

Dakota couldn't hold back a laugh. He was too cute. She glanced at Justin and he grinned and shrugged.

"Like I said, he's the best cure for a rough day."

"Actually, I have jumped out of planes as a skydiver, but not for a stunt."

"Oh…have you ever met Wonder Woman?"

Dakota chuckled. "I've met the actress who played her and her body double."

For the next ten minutes, Dominic lobbed one thought-provoking question after another at her.

"How old are you, Dominic?"

He shuffled from one foot to the other. "I'm nine, but I'm going to be double-digits in a couple of months."

Dakota smiled and listened as he talked about what he planned to do for his birthday and what presents he wanted. The kid dominated the conversation, entertaining her and Justin as he leaped from one topic to the next.

When there was a slight lull in the conversation, Dakota turned to Justin. "What else are you planning to show him today?"

Justin glanced at his watch. "This is probably it since my brother will be here soon to pick him up."

"My dad has to take me to taekwondo today."

"Guess what, Dom. Dakota is a black belt in karate," Justin said.

Dominic's eyebrows arched in surprise. "*For real?*"

Dakota loved his energy and enthusiasm.

Dominic sighed. "I'm only a yellow belt."

"Well, work hard, and I'm sure you'll eventually get your black belt."

He nodded, that serious expression back on his face when he said, "Can I have your telephone number?"

"Dom!" Justin thundered. Dakota's lips twitched, trying to hold back a laugh. "What the heck, man? You know that's not appropriate."

"What? I may have some more questions," Dominic explained before he stared down at his shoes. Then he glanced up at Justin. "Plus…Uncle Laz said if you meet a pretty girl, get her telephone number."

Dakota burst out laughing and Justin struggled to keep a straight face as he explained why a kid shouldn't ask a grown woman for her telephone number. She didn't know who Uncle Laz was, but Dakota had a feeling he'd be hearing from Justin.

While they argued good-naturedly, Dakota noticed a tall man glancing around as he slowly headed in their direction.

He must be Dominic's dad.

Over six feet tall, low haircut with a perfectly trimmed goatee, he had the same cinnamon skin tone and build as Justin, but the guy appeared more intense. And mouth-watering gorgeous.

Sipping her coffee, she tried not to stare, but it was hard not to. Sexy walk. Powerful build. The closer he got, she could even see his dark, penetrating eyes. Now, this was a man she wouldn't mind getting to know.

Dominic looked over his shoulder and then took off running. "Dad!" he yelled.

"I see good looks run in the family," Dakota murmured to Justin, noting that his brother was even more handsome than she originally thought. "I just want to know why you never introduced me to him, and please tell me he's single."

A crooked grin tilted the left corner of Justin's mouth. "He's single, and I thought about introducing you two, but he wasn't ready."

Dakota's brows dipped. "What the heck does that m—"

"Dakota, this is my dad!" Dominic announced proudly.

"That's Ms. Dakota to you," his father corrected. His gaze did a slow glide down her body before returning to her eyes. "Or is it Mrs.?"

"Uh…it's Miss," she said, thrown by the unabashed way he checked her out and the deep rumble of his voice.

Though his gaze had thoroughly appraised her, Dakota had a feeling he saw way more than what was on the outside. Observant. Intimidating. Fit. Probably military or maybe he was in law enforcement. The way he'd been glancing around when she had first spotted him, he had clearly been taking in his surroundings. As if preparing himself just in case something jumped off and he had to leap into action.

"Dakota Sherrod, this is my brother Hamilton Crosby."

"His name is Hamilton, but you can call him Ham. That's what my uncles and godfather call him. He used to be a policeman. Now he's a...a security specialist," Dominic shared proudly. Clearly, he thought nothing of putting Hamilton's business out there to a perfect stranger.

His father shook his head. "You must have made some impression on my son. It's nice to meet you." He extended his hand and she shook it.

Her pulse leaped. Every nerve in her body was on high alert at the thrilling current that shot through her body.

Well damn.

This was a first. Lately, she hadn't had much of a social life, thanks to a busy schedule; but the few men she allowed to get close never made her body tingle. And heck, all Hamilton had done was touch her hand. What would happen if his brawny hands skimmed over the rest of her body?

Just the thought sent a delicious shiver through her.

Dakota eased her hand from his grip and swallowed. Her palm still prickled as she glided it down the side of her jean-covered leg.

"I see Ted trying to get your attention," Justin said nodding his head toward where one of the crew members was standing near a trailer. He had both hands up, and each finger spread, signaling she needed to be on set in ten minutes.

Dakota sighed. "Sorry, fellas. Duty calls. It was nice meeting you guys. Unfortunately, I have to get going. But first..."

She handed her coffee to Justin. "You didn't even finish it," he said.

"Hold it for a second." She snatched the pen sticking out of his shirt pocket and reached for Dominic's hand. Dakota scribbled her telephone number in his palm as he giggled and squirmed under her touch.

"Call me sometime, and um…give your dad my number."

Dominic's wide grin lit up his face. "Okay."

Dakota returned Justin's pen, thanked him before reaching for her coffee cup, then turned and walked away. She put a little extra hip action into her walk since she could feel Hamilton's gaze on her.

Justin had been right. Dominic was the perfect cure for a crappy day. The renewed energy was just what she needed to get through more filming. Now, hopefully, his father would take the hint and give her a call.

Then again, she couldn't help wondering what Justin meant by that comment about Hamilton when he said, *He wasn't ready.*

Chapter Two

Hamilton's gaze followed the leggy beauty, surprised by her blatant flirtation. His whole body had come alive the moment their hands touched. The electrifying charge that shot through him couldn't be hidden and he was sure she saw the reaction when his brows shot up. That had been a first.

Damn, she looks good.

He hadn't been able to ignore her lithe, curvaceous body in the snug T-shirt, and the tight jeans cupping her butt perfectly. To say Dakota Sherrod was fit would be an understatement. She had a face like an angel and a body that should be on the cover of a fitness magazine.

But it had been her intriguing honey-brown, almost golden, eyes that had totally blown his mind.

"She's pretty, isn't she?" Dominic said grinning, reminding Hamilton that his son and brother were standing next to him, watching him gawk at the woman. "And she's a stuntwoman. You shoulda saw her jump off the top of the building. It was so cool!" With the awe in his son's voice, it was obvious that he was captivated by the woman.

Hamilton couldn't much blame him, and he had to agree with his son's assessment. Dakota was definitely pretty, but she looked a little young. Maybe late twenties, early thirties with a short pixie haircut and skin the color of sun-kissed bronze.

"I take it you're interested," Justin said close to Hamilton's ear.

Hamilton had been around plenty of beautiful women in his life, but it had been a long time since one had immediately sparked his interest.

"Maybe," he said to his brother as they all headed toward the exit. "Thanks for showing Dominic around today. Was he any trouble?"

"Not at all. As a matter of fact, he was perfect for cheering up Dakota."

"Why did he have to cheer her up?" Hamilton asked as they watched Dominic skip ahead like only an excited kid could do while they trailed behind him.

"It's crazy, man. The director's been riding her ass since the project started, and he hasn't let up. It's amazing that she's been able to put up with his shit."

"Is he harassing her?"

"Not exactly. He's just being a jerk. Almost like he's trying to get her to quit, but I wouldn't call it harassment...exactly. Dakota thinks he wants or had wanted someone else in her role, but she's not sure what his problem is. So far, he hasn't thrown anything at her she can't handle. Today, I saw her having words with the guy, and though I wasn't close enough to hear the exchange, it looked pretty heated."

Hamilton wanted to ask more questions but didn't. If Justin had the smallest hint that he was interested in the woman, his brother would be quick to play matchmaker.

"Are you done for the day?" he asked Justin.

"Not yet. I have a few more hours of work. We need to erect twenty-foot scaffolding and build a few temporary walls for a set that's needed by the end of the week."

After working in his degreed field of mechanical engineering, five years ago Justin announced to the family that he planned to start his own rigging construction company. Hamilton had jumped at the opportunity to invest in the venture, and the business had exceeded the five-year projections.

Hamilton looked up to find Dominic running back to them. "Dad, there's a food truck," he pointed toward the exit. "Can I have some money to buy a sandwich?"

"I'll walk out with you guys," Justin said.

The food truck was parked on the street a few feet from the gate. Cast and crew members huddled near it, some eating while others stood in line to order.

Hamilton handed Dominic a ten-dollar bill and started to follow him to the truck.

"Dad, I'm not a baby. I can go by myself."

Hamilton stopped and huffed out a breath. He'd been hearing those same words more often than not lately.

Justin chuckled. "That boy is a trip."

"You don't know the half of it."

Instead of irritating his kid by following behind him, he and Justin stood off to the side where they could still see him.

Hamilton's heart swelled at the thought that his child was growing up and becoming more independent. Some days he found it hard to believe he had a nine-year-old. The kid was sprouting up like a weed on a daily basis, making him realize he didn't have a baby anymore. At forty-one, Hamilton had planned to be married with at least three kids by now, but that hadn't been in the cards for him.

"So, what did you think of Dakota?" Justin asked.

Hamilton glanced at his brother who was trying to look nonchalant after posing the question. His family and friends had been attempting to fix him up with one woman after another, especially lately.

After leaving the police force and then ending his engagement to Jackie, Dominic's mother, Hamilton hadn't been interested in getting involved in another serious relationship. He'd been suffering through a string of one-night stands, but lately, he'd been thinking about settling down with one woman. Maybe his family sensed that change in him, prompting them to butt into his social life even more.

"Damn, Ham." Justin frowned and folded his thick arms across his chest. "It wasn't a hard question. Hell, you either like her or you don't."

"Why do I have a feeling running into Ms. Sherrod wasn't a coincidence?"

Justin rolled his eyes. "She's good people, man. And it's time for you to get off of that self-inflicted…punishment that you put yourself on. Shit happens. Time to get over that mess from the past and move on."

"I'm not on a *punishment*. I just haven't been interested in getting involved in anything serious. Besides, my number-one focus right now is raising Dom. Outside of work, that doesn't leave much time for anything else."

"That's bullshit. You can lie to me but stop lying to yourself. I know…hell, we all know why you hook up with women who you have no intention of having a relationship with."

Hamilton glanced back at the line that was slowly moving and watching Dominic observe the people around him. He was such an astute, intuitive kid, rarely missing much.

Sighing, Hamilton thought about his brother's words. Had he been punishing himself for something that happened years ago? He hadn't looked at it like that. He had lost faith in happily-ever-afters. To him, his unwillingness to trust women or let one get too close stemmed from the need to protect himself against the women who meant him no good.

"Listen, man. You and Dakota are perfect for each other."

Hamilton narrowed his eyes at his brother. "Why? What makes her so perfect for me?"

"For one, did you see that woman? She's hot as hell."

Hamilton laughed. "No argument there, but I meet beautiful women all the time. There has to be more to her than a cute face and gorgeous body to keep my interest."

Overseeing security at Club Masquerade, the hottest nightclub in Atlanta, brought him into contact with some of the sexiest women alive. The same was the case as a managing partner at Supreme Security Agency. On a daily basis, he came face to face with models, actresses, and all types of women who needed and could afford their security services.

"Secondly, she's smart, funny, and one of the nicest people I've ever met," Justin continued. "Besides all of that, she's the one person I know could put up with your prickly ass."

Hamilton had to laugh at that. Both of his brothers were always saying that he was too serious and too hard on people. Truth was, he had a low tolerance for bullshit.

"Call her man. You won't be disappointed, and I promise you two are going to hit it off."

"How old is she?"

"Around thirty-four or thirty-five, and don't even go there about robbing the cradle. A six-year difference is nothing."

Hamilton looked up as Dominic approached them carrying a sandwich and a drink, a frown marring his face.

"What's wrong?" Hamilton asked and accepted the change he was given.

"That guy in the truck had a picture of Dakota...I mean Ms. Dakota."

"And?" Hamilton questioned, wondering what bothered his son about that, but a little surprised himself by the information.

"It was stuck on the wrapper." He held up his sandwich. "I saw it before he grabbed it, and I asked what he was doing with her picture."

"What did the man say?" Justin asked.

"He said she was his woman." Dominic spat the words as if they were a bitter taste on his tongue. "I know he was lying."

Hamilton didn't speak and Justin stopped laughing. Dominic might've only been nine, but he was a sharp kid and very intuitive. He was also a good judge of character.

"How do you know he was lying?" Justin asked before Hamilton formed the words.

"Uncle Laz told me what to look for when someone is lying," he said absently as he handed Hamilton his drink and then started unwrapping his sandwich. "That guy had shifty eyes and when he laughed, he sounded like Woody in *Toy Story*."

On that, Justin fell out laughing, as if Steve Harvey himself had told him the funniest joke.

Hamilton couldn't hide his own smile, especially considering how serious Dominic looked. His Uncle Laz—Hamilton's best friend Lazarus Dimas—was a police detective with Atlanta PD and Dominic's godfather. Laz treated him like his own, and they talked on a daily basis. Normally Hamilton was okay with their conversations, but occasionally he had to remind Laz that Dominic was only a nine-year-old kid. Laz's argument was always that it was never too early to teach his godson life lessons.

"Man, Dom, I've said it before and I'll say it again. You are truly your father's son," Justin said to Dominic before he turned to Hamilton. "Now I know why he wants to be a cop. He's even more suspicious than you."

"Uncle Jay, I changed my mind, remember? I'm going to be a stuntman."

"Oh yeah, that's right."

Still thinking about the photo, Hamilton said, "Dominic, maybe the guy has a picture of Ms. Dakota because she's an actress. A lot of people get autographed photos of people they…admire, especially if—"

"It didn't have her name on it, and she's not an actress. She's a stuntwoman. You don't see the stuntpeople's face in the movies," Dominic said and took a bite of his sandwich.

Justin looked at Hamilton, his left brow raised as if to say *good point.*

Like in many conversations with his son, Hamilton didn't have a comeback.

"I think I'm going to have Uncle Laz check it out," Dominic said, sounding like a cop before he reached for his drink which Hamilton had still been holding.

"Dom, look," Hamilton started, trying to pick his words carefully. "It's none of our business whether that guy was lying or not. Who knows, he might've been telling the truth."

Dominic shook his head. "No, he wasn't," he said with conviction. "Ms. Dakota wouldn't like him. He looked...creepy."

Hamilton frowned. "And how would you know what she'd like or not like? Exactly how much time did you guys spend together?" he asked and then glanced at his brother, who threw up his hands.

"I just know. And because she likes you. I saw the way she looked at you."

Justin laughed again. "This kid is too much. I almost hate I have to get back to work." He pulled Dominic into a headlock and hugged him tightly. "Later, little dude. Thanks for the laughs today. It's been real."

"Thanks for letting me come to work with you, Uncle Jay. It was a lotta fun."

"No problem, kid." Justin turned to Hamilton, grinning. "I agree with my nephew. Dakota was feeling you, man. Call her."

As Hamilton walked the two blocks to his truck with Dominic by his side, he thought about his son's observation. Was Dakota seeing the guy who had the food truck? She had openly flirted, even telling him to give her a call sometime. Would she have done that if she was involved with someone else?

Probably.

Hamilton knew from experience that some women couldn't be trusted. What if Dakota was one of those women? Dating a man while flirting with another. Then again, maybe the guy had been lying. But why?

17

Hamilton shook the thoughts free as they approached his truck. He didn't have time to try and figure out a woman he knew nothing about. If their paths crossed again, fine. If not, that was cool, too. No matter what his brother said, Hamilton wasn't sure if he was ready to put his heart out there again anyway.

But he couldn't deny that there was something about Dakota that piqued his interest. Question was—what to do about it?

Chapter Three

Hamilton tapped his pen against the top of the large mahogany table that served as his desk, his thoughts on Dakota again. It had been several days since he'd seen her, but a day hadn't gone by that he didn't think of her. Yet, he still hadn't picked up the phone and called.

Why? He couldn't pinpoint what it was about this woman that gave him pause. His initial impression of her ticked off numerous qualities he looked for in a woman. Attractive. Physically fit. Adventurous.

The fact that Dominic hadn't stopped talking about Dakota was a plus. His son meant everything to him, so whoever Hamilton settled down with would have to be able to get along with his kid.

Noting the time at the bottom right corner of his laptop screen, Hamilton pushed back from the table. He had fifteen minutes to get downstairs to his meeting with Atlanta's finest—the nickname they had given their security specialists. The bodyguards, comprised of over thirty men and a few women, worked out of the Atlanta office and most were former cops or had served in other areas of law enforcement. Once a week, he and Mason met with the team, updating them on new assignments and discussing any issues.

Hamilton grabbed the half-full cup of black coffee he'd been nursing for part of the morning and snatched up his tablet before heading out of his office.

"Oh Ham, I'm glad I caught you," Egypt Durand, their executive assistant said as she hurried into the main area of the office suite carrying several file folders. Dressed in a pink jacket with a skinny black belt around her narrow waist, and a short black skirt with bold white and pink flowers, she looked professional and stylish at the same time. How she managed to flutter around the office in her sky-high heels always mystified Hamilton, but she did it without missing a step.

"Mason said he won't be back until later this afternoon. Are you able to cover his agenda items?"

"Sure, not a problem."

"Great, I need to add two things to his section of the agenda, though." She pulled a file folder from one of the drawers. Hamilton waited patiently as she jotted notes onto a slip of paper.

Unlike the security specialists hired by Supreme Security Agency-Atlanta, Egypt didn't have a law enforcement or military background. She was the sister of one of their team members and had worked in corporate America for fifteen years before seeking employment with their agency.

She pushed her long dreadlocks over her shoulder as she wrote feverishly. Hamilton didn't even want to think about how chaotic the office would operate without her. For the last four years, she had supported him and Mason Bennett, one of the owners who was in charge of the Atlanta office and never complained. As far as Hamilton was concerned, she could ask anything of him and he'd get it done.

Egypt handed him the slip of paper. "Okay, I think that's everything. Oh, and don't forget you have two interviews. One at eleven, and the other at two this afternoon."

"Yes, ma'am. Got it."

He left for the first-floor meeting room, his black Stacy Adams shoes clicking against the polished concrete floor as he walked past the set of elevators, opting for the stairs. The ten-thousand-square-foot renovated warehouse housed everything they needed and then some. The luxuries included a state-of-the-art gym, indoor shooting range, crash rooms, a huge well-stocked kitchen, and a helipad on the roof.

Hamilton couldn't ask for a better place to work. After leaving Atlanta PD ten years ago, and despite having a degree in criminology, he hadn't been sure what he'd do with the rest of his life. All he knew was that he had a young son on the way and he wanted a safer and more flexible job. He had started with overseeing security for Club Masquerade, owned by Mason's family. Now, as a new managing partner at Supreme, Hamilton didn't spend as much time at the club and his professional life had exceeded his expectations.

Once Hamilton reached the second-floor landing, he heard Angelo, one of their specialists talking before he came into view.

"Ham, don't start without me. Give me two minutes," he said, a cell phone plastered to his ear as he darted past him and up the stairs, taking them two at a time.

"All right but hurry up."

Hamilton strolled into the meeting room where most of the team was sitting or standing around talking.

"What's up, Ham?" Kenton, another specialist, said as he approached. "What did I ever do to you and Egypt that you guys would stick me with the diva from hell?"

Hamilton grinned; not because he didn't sympathize with Kenton, but because the 'diva from hell' moniker fit the hip-hop singer perfectly. She was a nice enough woman, but most of her demands were so unrealistic that a few of the team members refused to guard her.

"Sorry, man. Last hired typically get what others don't want." Hamilton shrugged.

Kenton was a former undercover FBI agent and had moved from DC to be closer to his family. He was an ideal security specialist with brains, an impressive professional background, and at thirty-five years old, he was movie-star handsome—according to Egypt. Since their client base was

Sharon C. Cooper

mostly comprised of wealthy entertainers and socialites, they often wanted their bodyguards to fit into the image the client wanted to portray. There were even some who wanted their security specialist to serve double duty as their date for the evening. Their clients had an option of seeing photos of the team member they were interested in using as their security detail, and many of their clients often chose Kenton on looks alone.

"All right guys, settle down so we can get started. We have a lot to cover this morning. Let's start with the movie premiere taking place at Atlantic Station in a few weeks."

An hour after starting the meeting, Hamilton fielded a few questions.

"Ham, with the movie premiere coming up, you said you wanted at least ten of us there for five hours handling crowd control before and after, correct?" Myles, one of their full-timers, asked.

"That's right."

"What about the after party in Buckhead? Will it be the same team members, or are you pulling in a different group?"

"Ha! Look at him trying to come up with a way to rub shoulders with the rich and famous," Angelo cracked, eliciting laughter from others in the room.

"Man, be quiet. Acting like you ain't interested, too." Myles laughed.

"Damn straight I am."

"All right, all right," Hamilton chimed in. "It'll be the same team, and I'm waiting for confirmation on how much additional personnel is needed. Those who are guarding individuals won't be included in that count."

After answering a few more questions, Hamilton ended the meeting. He sent a few people to see Egypt for new assignments, while he talked to some of the guys who had additional questions.

Once he finally left the room, his cell phone vibrated in his pocket. He glanced at the screen and saw that it was his

22

ex-fiancée Jackie, Dominic's mother. Apparently, she finally saw fit to return his call.

For the second time in weeks, Dominic had asked to move in with him. According to his son, he didn't like his mother's new boyfriend, calling him fake and telling Hamilton that the guy was only nice to him when Jackie was around. Hamilton hadn't said much during that conversation. He had met the boyfriend and hadn't cared much for him either.

"Hey, Jackie."

"Hey. Can you please talk to your son when you pick him up from school? He's been mouthing off again and disrespecting my new friend."

Funny how Dominic was *his* son whenever he did something wrong, but she took credit for his excellent grades and accomplishments.

"Disrespecting him how?" Hamilton moved down the hallway out of the earshot of others. Instead of going back to his office, he headed outside to the back deck that overlooked a small fenced-in yard, and a parking lot on the side.

"Does it matter, Ham? He knows better than to disrespect anyone, especially an adult, and I'm not having it. As it is, he can barely get off of one punishment before I have to put him on another because of his smart mouth."

He agreed that Dominic could go too far with talking back or questioning their decisions, but he never disrespected someone for no reason.

"This is partly what I wanted to talk to you about when I called earlier. I thought you were returning my call."

"I...um...I haven't checked my messages. What did you want to talk about?"

"Your friend. Are you still seeing the same dude, Braeden?"

"Yes, but who I date is none of your business," she retorted.

"It is if he's spending the night in my house when Dominic is there. You and I had an agreement, Jackie."

"Oh, so now Dom is telling you everything that goes on here? You have him spying on me and my man?"

"No, actually he didn't tell me your man spent the night. What he said is that the guy told him he'd better take out the trash. Considering that conversation took place *before* I picked Dom up to take him to school, it doesn't take a detective to figure out Braeden probably stayed the night. So, no. Our son did not rat you out."

Seconds ticked by before she said, "Oh."

"Jackie, I don't care who you date, but Dominic is my number-one priority. He should be your number-one priority too. I'd prefer you not bring one guy after another around him, especially when you don't know these people well."

"You act as if I'm with someone new every other week when that's not the case. Dominic has only been introduced to a couple of the men who've been in my life. But this isn't about him at all, is it? You're never going to forgive me, are you? You're going to continue holding it against me that I didn't stand by you when—"

"Don't!" Hamilton growled, gripping the phone tighter, trying like hell to hold back from saying something he might regret. "This has nothing to do with the past. This is about *our* son. We had an agreement. No overnight guests when he's there."

"I have needs, Hamilton. You can't tell me that you don't have women coming and going from your place when Dominic is there!"

"Never! I have never brought a woman around our son."

"What about your stuntwoman girlfriend that he keeps talking about? You tryin' to tell me she isn't spending time at your house?"

"That woman is someone Dom met on the movie set with my brother. I'm not sure what he's been telling you, but that was my first time meeting her and I haven't seen or talked to her since."

"Well, it doesn't matter either way to me." Some of the initial bitterness in her tone moments ago had died down. "You can see whoever you want, just like I can. I don't butt into your business and I expect you to stay out of mine."

"Jackie, it's getting clearer by the minute that you're not maintaining our agreement. I don't want my kid in that house when you're screwing around with every Tom, Nick, and Jerry."

"I'm not having this conversation with you, Ham. I'm a grown-ass woman. As long as I'm taking care of Dominic and making sure he's fed, clean, and happy, I can do whatever the hell I want."

"You're right, you can. But that's my house. *My* house, *my* rules. If you don't like it, get out!"

"If I leave, I'm taking Dominic with me, and you won't ever get to—"

"Be careful, Jackie. Be very careful in what you say next." Hamilton's voice went low and lethal as he barely managed his anger. "This is the second time in recent months you threatened to keep my kid from me. I don't know what that boyfriend of yours is whispering in your ear, but if you even think about depriving me time with Dom, you'll regret it."

The silence on the other end of the phone was as thick as a cinder block. They had never gone to court to battle about child support, visitations, or anything regarding Dominic. They had their own agreement that was in the best interest of all of them.

Hamilton saw Dominic whenever he wanted. In exchange, Jackie got to live in a home he owned, rent-free, and he paid more child support than any court would ever require. She already knew that once that agreement didn't work for either of them, he'd be the one going to court and would fight like hell for full custody.

"Fine. Whatever, Ham. Anything else?"

He debated on whether to mention that Dominic no longer wanted to live with her, but he held off. For the most part, Jackie had done a great job with their son, and Hamilton actually thought she was a good mother. A little high-strung at times, but there was no doubt in his mind that she loved Dominic.

"Listen, if you need me to get him more often, that's not a problem." Hamilton understood having needs and though he spent several days a week with Dominic, Jackie was the one who had him the majority of the time. "Also, my parents would love to see him more often. Just let me know if you need more time to yourself."

"Thanks, Hamilton, and sorry about the way I acted. You're right. Dominic's happiness should come first, and I'll abide by our agreement."

"I appreciate that and I'll continue to do the same. We've never put certain...*needs* before the well-being of our kid. I don't want either of us to start now."

"I don't either," she said quietly.

"As for Dominic being mouthy, I'll talk to him tonight."

"Thanks."

Hamilton ended the call, still thinking about the conversation. He wouldn't mind Dominic living with him, especially since his son was getting older. Maybe he would still bring up the topic to Jackie soon.

In the meantime, Hamilton planned to investigate the new boyfriend.

Normally, Jackie dated decent guys, but after meeting Braeden a few weeks ago, he hadn't been impressed. Now that Dominic had brought up his issues with the man, that was a good enough reason for Hamilton to do a little digging. He just hoped he didn't find anything incriminating.

Chapter Four

A rush of adrenaline pumped through Dakota's veins as she shifted gears, pushing her 650-horsepower Mustang Shelby GT harder. She grinned and watched the speedometer needle inch to ninety and then to ninety-five as her car floated along as if being carried by a cloud.

"Would you slow down?" her roommate Tymico screamed, her eyes wide as she gripped the edge of her seat with one hand and the door with the other. "What is wrong with you? You're going to get us killed!"

"Relax. You're perfectly safe with me."

"I should've just went straight to the airport, but no. Stupid me agreed to go for a ride with you," her friend grumbled, mumbling a few more words under her breath. As a flight attendant, Ty spent more time in the air than on the ground, especially lately. They might share an apartment but with their work schedules, until this morning, they hadn't hung out in weeks.

Dakota glanced in her rearview mirror and laughed out loud. The Mustang owner in the other vehicle—the same one who dared to race her up Interstate 20—trailed behind, probably wondering what type of engine she had in her car. They had weaved in and out of the uncharacteristically light traffic for the last three miles, uncaring whether cops were on the lookout.

"Later, sucker!" Dakota called out before easing her foot off the gas and letting the engine drop down to a mere sixty miles per hour. She rarely traveled that highway, but it never failed that when she did, someone would pull alongside her and provoke her into racing them. The adrenaline junkie within her never passed up the opportunity.

"You need psychiatric help! One of these days, your stupid stunts and driving like a maniac are going to get you killed. Then I'm going to have to find a new best friend."

Dakota laughed, only making Tymico scowl deeper. "Now you know I'm irreplaceable. No one can bring this much excitement to your life."

"Yeah, whatever. Just get me to the airport in one piece."

After breakfast, they had driven out to Conyers, a suburb of Atlanta, to drop off old clothes to a friend whose church was collecting items for the homeless. Dakota was always up for any excuse to go for a long drive.

"I'm glad you finally talked to your dad," Tymico said. "He sounded pretty desperate to speak to you when he called late last night."

"Everything is always an emergency with him. And he knows that I'm still mad at him for calling that director *on my behalf* before I left Los Angeles last month."

"Get over it. Some of us wish we had a father who loved us as much as yours loves you." Tymico had been an only child raised by her mother. Her father wasn't in the picture and she rarely mentioned him. "Besides, I think Wesley means well with his overprotectiveness and he's such a sweetheart."

"Well, you can have him. When he starts breaking promises, lying to you, and then tries to control your life, don't bother trying to give him back."

Tymico shook her head and laughed. She and Ty had been friends forever, and her friend always defended Wesley, saying he was probably doing the best he could. Maybe he was, but Dakota wished he'd remember that she was a grown woman, capable of taking care of herself and fighting her own battles. Which was partly why she agreed to have lunch with him after she dropped off Tymico. The other reason why they were meeting was to discuss some threatening letters he had received recently.

"Okay, enough about me. How's it going with what's his name...the new guy? Brad?" Dakota asked as she headed to Atlanta's Hartfield-Jackson airport. They usually told each other everything, but with this guy, her friend wasn't saying much about him. Only making Dakota more curious about what she was hiding.

"It's going well," Tymico finally said and smiled. "Dee, I *really* like this guy. He's nice, well established, loves traveling, and he's a real sweetheart."

"Then why are you so closed mouth about him?"

"I know we usually talk about our men, but...I guess I just don't want to jinx this. And he's a little older than me and I don't want you judging."

Dakota glanced at her friend before returning her attention back to the road. "How much older?"

"Only a few years. I guess I'm just trying not to get my hopes up and trying not to think about getting married like I usually do when I first meet a guy. Right now, we're just having a good time and letting the relationship play out."

"So, when can I meet him?"

"Um...soon. We're still getting to know each other."

Dakota narrowed her eyes at her friend. "Please don't tell me he's married."

"Of course not!" Tymico snapped, and Dakota regretted the words the moment they slipped out of her mouth. "Dee, I can't believe you. You know how I feel about cheaters!"

"Okay, okay, I know. I'm sorry. I shouldn't have implied that; it's just that you've been acting funny about this man."

"Because I'm trying to grow the hell up and not fall in love too fast. You know how I am when I start dating someone new."

29

Dakota nodded. She did know. Tymico fell in love with anyone who showed her an ounce of attention. Often, she professed her love way too soon, and she usually ended up being the one who got hurt. Her friend was cover-model beautiful, inheriting her Chinese mother's eyes, hair, and bone structure. She had her African-American father's height and caramel skin-tone. Guys often saw her pretty face, not realizing she was also super-smart because that wasn't the side that Tymico showed.

"Okay, I'll let it drop. For now." Dakota would just have to trust that Tymico was using good judgment.

But who was she to pass judgment or give any pointers on dealing with the opposite sex? Lately, she either attracted idiots, man-children, or men who weren't interested in anything serious. She was ready for marriage and a family and had vowed not to waste her time on men who weren't looking for the same thing. Now, all she had to do was find her Mr. Right.

*

An hour later, Dakota neared the Midtown area and followed the GPS instructions that would take her to the restaurant. Her father had texted the address while she was in Conyers but failed to include the name of the establishment.

Dakota glanced around as she drove through West Midtown, passing a few art galleries and numerous small eateries along the way. She hadn't been in that community for a while and was surprised to see the number of condos and apartment complexes that had sprung up in the last eight to twelve months. That was happening all over the city. Clearly, builders knew something she didn't know.

"Oh crap!"

She slammed on her brakes and checked her rearview mirror, thankful no one was close behind her. Caught up in her thoughts, she had missed a turn.

So much for following the GPS instructions.

Grumbling, she circled the block to get to her destination and wondered if she had the wrong address. The area didn't have many restaurants, only lofts and houses.

She turned on her wipers as the pitter-patter of rain tapped the windshield and slowed when the street name came into view. Dakota made a right turn and crept along the narrow street until she found the address. Her father's BMW was parked in front of a large brick structure that looked as if it might've been some type of warehouse at one point.

Supreme Security Agency.

"So much for lunch. Another lie," she mumbled to herself.

Dakota remained in her car, her fingers tapping against the steering wheel as she debated on whether to find out what her father was up to or just take off. Before she could decide, Wesley Bradford climbed out of his luxury vehicle, and as usual, his cell phone was plastered to his ear.

Dakota released a frustrated growl, shut off the Mustang and tried to tap down her negative attitude. She exited her car. Now it was only sprinkling outside, but if the clouds in the sky were any indication, a storm was brewing. A storm that could easily match the frustration swirling within her knowing that her father had lied to her. Again.

"I thought we were meeting for lunch," she snapped instead of giving a more appropriate greeting when they met in the tight spot between their vehicles.

"Hold on a sec," Wesley told the person he was talking to on his cell. With a hand over the mouthpiece, he turned to Dakota.

"Hey, sweetheart." He leaned in to kiss her on the cheek, but she pulled back, forcing him to kiss the air.

"You lied…again. I don't know why I thought you were serious about lunch. It's getting to the point that I don't know what to believe when it comes to you. This isn't a restaurant." She pointed at the building.

"Inviting you to lunch was the only way to get you here," he said as if lying to her was fine.

"You're admitting to lying to me…manipulating me?"

"I'll explain everything, and then we'll go to lunch as promised. Please, sweetheart. This is serious."

Dakota huffed and folded her arms across her chest, not caring if she was behaving childishly. She went through the same crap with him over and over and it was getting old.

But there was something in his voice that made her take a good look at him. Concern radiated in his eyes, letting her know that maybe whatever was going on was serious.

"Just give me a minute to finish up this call and…actually, you go on in before it starts raining again. I'll be in shortly. We're meeting with Mason Bennett. He's expecting us."

Moments later, Dakota entered the building, taken aback on how different it looked on the inside than the outside. Despite the lack of windows in the front, the space was light and airy. The architectural details were stunning. The glass block windows on the side walls with exposed brick gave the building plenty of privacy without sacrificing natural light. From the painted concrete floors to the brightly painted walls and glass dividers that sectioned off various spaces, the environment was modern, fresh, and classy.

"Hi, may I help you?" A receptionist stood behind the long counter. Tall and slim with an athlete's build, she was pretty with an air of confidence and authority. Dakota hadn't even noticed the woman when she first walked in.

"Actually, I'm waiting for my father." Dakota pointed her thumb over her shoulder and toward the door she had just walked through. "I guess we have a meeting with a Mason Bennett."

"Your name?"

"Dakota Sherrod. My father—"

The receptionist's ringing phone interrupted. "I'm so sorry. Give me one minute," she said apologetically to Dakota.

"No problem. Take your time." Dakota roamed around the waiting area, stopping in front of a large framed photograph. The seascape piece with its bold vibrant colors depicted the perfect setting of the sun sliding down behind the deep blue sea. Whoever had taken the photo captured the essence of a sunset. Or was it a sunrise?

Dakota glanced at the gold plate on the lower right-hand side of the photo. *Photographer: Olivia Miller. Title: Joy in the A.M.*

Ah, a sunrise.

Voices nearby snagged Dakota's attention and she turned as two men came around the corner and headed to an elevator. Her heart thudded against her chest when she recognized one of them.

Hamilton.

As if sensing her staring at him, his steps slowed and his conversation came to a halt. His actions reminded her of a movie scene, reeling in slow motion as he turned slightly before glancing over his shoulder.

Their gazes collided and held.

Dakota couldn't believe she was actually seeing him. Only thirty feet away stood the man she hadn't been able to stop thinking about. Warmth soared through her when she realized he was looking at her, seeming to be as shocked as she was, and her skin tingled at his lengthy appraisal.

It had been a long time since a man had turned her on like this. But it was when the corners of his mouth lifted into a sexy-as-sin grin did Dakota's knees go weak.

Dimples? How the heck did I miss those the other day?

She had always been a sucker for a good-looking man with dimples. Add that feature to his height and the power he exuded without even trying, he was the perfect leading man. Now that she thought about it, the dimples had gone unnoticed before because he hadn't smiled the other day. She'd had a feeling then that flashing his straight white teeth wasn't something he did often.

What made today different?

Caught up in her thoughts, she hadn't realized he was moving toward her until he was less than five feet away.

"Dakota?"

She gave an awkward wave. "Hi. We meet again." The huskiness of her own voice surprised even her. Her pulse kicked up and that attraction she felt deep in her soul the other day had returned with a vengeance, making her tremble with need.

Damn, he looked good.

Hoping she wasn't drooling, she ran her thumb and forefinger over her mouth just in case because he looked absolutely delicious.

She loved seeing a man in a suit. And Hamilton was sexier than any man had a right to look. Today there was a sophistication about him that she hadn't picked up on the other day. Then he had looked cool and confident. Now, he displayed a power and strength that she found seriously attractive. She'd always been drawn to danger...and excitement. There was no doubt that Hamilton could provide the latter.

Normally, Dakota wasn't one of those loose women who dropped her panties on the first date or for a man she just met. Yet, it had been a long time since she'd wanted a man as much as she wanted this one. It was as if she could already feel his rock-hard body rubbed up against hers with the ability to please her like no other.

Oh, for goodness' sake. Get yourself together, girl. He's just a man. A strong, virile man, but a man nonetheless.

Straightening her shoulders, she planted on her most flirtatious smile, prepared to make this man squirm the way he was doing to her.

"It's good seeing you again," he finally said, his voice smooth and deep as his intense perusal took her in slowly, desire radiating in his eyes. "What are you doing here?"

"Actually, my father got me here on false pretenses...sorta. I was under the impression I was meeting him for lunch. Imagine my surprise when I pulled up out front and didn't see a restaurant. He's outside and mentioned that we're meeting with Mason Bennett."

Hamilton nodded, now looking at her with the same intensity as the other day. "I assume that means that one of you is having some trouble," he said it as a statement, but Dakota heard the question within the comment.

"Yes, he told me earlier that he's been receiving some threatening letters." She tilted her head as another thought came to her. "Dominic mentioned that you used to be a cop and that you were now a security specialist. What does that mean?"

"Why don't I take you upstairs where you can wait," he said instead of answering her question. "Mason is currently out of the building, but should be back shortly, especially if he's scheduled to meet with you and your father."

Hamilton glanced at the receptionist who placed her hand over the mouthpiece of the telephone while he instructed her to escort Dakota's father upstairs once he came inside. She gave a thumbs-up without interrupting her call. Before Hamilton could move away from the desk, another man about his size and build, looking like a defensive lineman for the Atlanta Falcons stopped him. Dakota only heard a little of the conversation, but it was safe to say that Hamilton was the boss.

"Sorry about that. Let's head up." He escorted her to the elevator, one of his large hands at the small of her back, sending sparks of desire shooting through her body. To her regret, he dropped his hand and pushed the up button for the elevator.

"So, what is it that you do, Hamilton?" she asked again as they stepped into the elevator. Drawing in a deep breath, she held it before releasing it slowly in hopes of calming her pounding heart. Being in such close quarters with him had her wiping her sweaty palms down the side of her legs. Could the man be any more enticing? And what the hell was wrong with her? She was acting as if she hadn't been near a man in, like, forever.

He pushed button four, the top floor. Dakota zoned in on his large hands and his long, tapered fingers. All types of inappropriate thoughts raced through her mind. She cleared her throat and averted her gaze, releasing a shaky breath to calm herself.

"I'm a managing partner here at Supreme and I do some personal security work."

"Like a bodyguard?"

He nodded. "Yes."

"And you used to be a cop."

A smile lit his face and those damn dimples winked at her.

"I can't believe I didn't know you had dimples." The words flew from her mouth before she could pull them back, but they were true. The dimples enhanced his handsome features.

"After you," he said, chuckling when the elevator stopped and the doors opened. He extended his arm so that she could precede him out of the claustrophobic box. "As for you being here, did your father tell you anything else about what's going on?"

Dakota shook her head. "Not much. He mentioned receiving some threats, but this isn't the first time."

"No?"

Dakota shook her head. "Unfortunately, no. It seems he has a hard time getting along with people."

Hamilton nodded. "I see," he said as they walked into a large glass-enclosed office and waiting area. There was a woman with gorgeous dreadlocks and skin the color of milk chocolate at a desk talking on the phone. She smiled and nodded at Dakota. The gold nameplate on the desk read Egypt Durand.

"Ham, wait," Egypt called out when he started to direct Dakota down another hallway. "Mason said he'll be here in ten minutes."

"Okay, I'll show Ms. Sherrod to the conference room. Her father should be up shortly."

"This is a beautiful building," Dakota said as Hamilton led her down a short hallway, passing several pieces of artwork hanging on the walls. "Who did the paintings?" They made it to a room that was just as warm and inviting as the rest of the building. Whoever had overseen the warehouse renovations had done an exceptional job.

"Olivia Miller. She's the wife of one of the owners, Cameron Miller, who works out of the Chicago office. Once Wiz," Hamilton stopped when Dakota looked at him, confused. "I mean Cameron. They call him Wiz because he's a genius when it comes to computers. Anyway, once she found out they were opening an Atlanta location, she got to work on all of the decor, including the artwork and photographs."

Hamilton and Dakota sat at the conference table, their conversation flowing easily. Minutes ticked by without her father or Mason showing up, and the burning question Dakota wanted to ask from the moment she'd run into Hamilton on the first floor dangled on the tip of her tongue.

"So, why haven't you called me?"

Chapter Five

Hamilton smiled at Dakota's directness as he pondered her question. Apparently, this appointment must have come up suddenly since he was usually made aware of meetings with potential new clients. But it didn't matter in this case. He was just glad Mason was running behind schedule.

Dakota was even more stunning than he remembered. Her skin glistened under the fluorescent lights, and her confident gaze held a bit of humor. It was as if she was waiting to see what type of nonsense he was going to come up with. He didn't know much about the woman, but there was something in the way she stared back at him with a bold confidence that intrigued him.

But Hamilton took his time responding, preferring to admire her sense of style which matched her adventurous nature. Wearing a short brown leather jacket over a low-cut tan button-up blouse that hugged her full breasts and flat stomach, he hadn't been able to stop staring when he spotted her downstairs, even more so now. Tan skinny pants and tall brown thigh-high suede boots rounded out the sexy attire.

"Are you trying to come up with a good lie on why you haven't called?" Dakota asked, interrupting his thoughts, a wicked smile gracing her tempting lips.

Hamilton sat back in his seat and rubbed a hand down his goatee. "One thing you should know about me, Dakota, is that I will never lie to you. As for me not calling, I've been meaning to. Things have been crazy busy, and—"

"And you really don't have a good excuse," she added. A twinkle of mirth radiated in her honey-brown eyes. Eyes he could stare into until the end of time.

Hamilton smiled. "Direct. I like that, and you're right. I don't have a good excuse."

"Someone once told me that we always make time for what we *really* want to do. So maybe you *really* didn't want to talk to me."

"That's definitely not it. I did plan to call. I just hadn't taken the time to do so. But while we're on the subject, Dominic has been on me to call you as well."

"You have a great kid."

"I agree. He's the best, even if he is a pain in the ass sometimes. Oh, and he's been concerned about you."

Dakota's perfectly arched eyebrows dipped into a frown. "Concerned about me? Why?"

"He saw a photo of you in the food truck that was parked outside the movie set the other day. The guy working in it told Dom that you were his woman."

"What? Are you kidding me? That's ridiculous! The guy…Lester is a little too…too creepy. Trust me, I've never even considered hooking up with him. As for the photo, I have no idea where he got a picture of me. I'll have to talk to him about that."

Warning bells blasted inside of Hamilton's mind at the thought of this guy having her picture and claiming they were an item while she vehemently denied it. But Hamilton's attention immediately shifted when Dakota slipped out of her leather jacket and hung it on the back of her chair, giving him a perfect view of her full, perky breasts pushing against the thin blouse.

"Wait. Is that why you haven't called me?" Dakota asked as if putting two and two together. "You actually think something's going on with me and Lester?"

Hamilton shrugged, knowing that wasn't the reason he hadn't called. He actually didn't have what she would consider, a good reason for not calling. He couldn't deny that he was interested, but there was something about her that gave him pause and he couldn't put his finger on it. Rarely did he go against his gut instinct. Yet, he was seriously thinking about making an exception.

"Lester owns the food truck," she said. "And though he's told me that he's in love with me and plans to make me his wife, there is *absolutely* nothing going on between us. I just figured it was his way of flirting."

Hamilton nodded, seeing how that could be the case.

"And besides that, there is no way I would've suggested you call me if I was involved with someone else. I don't know what type of women you roll with, but that's not who I am."

Hamilton studied Dakota and heard the conviction in her voice. He might not have called her, but he hadn't been able to stop thinking about this woman. She had even invaded his dreams the night before. Yet, he still couldn't shake whatever was holding him back. He'd always been selective about the women he spent time with, but whatever this vibe was that he was picking up from Dakota was something different.

He glanced at his watch.

"Well, even though it's clear that you're not as interested in me as I am in you, if I need a bodyguard will you take on the assignment?"

A slow smile crept across Hamilton's mouth. He liked this woman more and more. "Nope. I couldn't."

She leaned forward and placed her forearms on the table as she narrowed her gorgeous eyes at him. "You mean to tell me that you dislike me so much that you wouldn't even take me on as a client?"

Hamilton mirrored her move and lowered his voice. "That's not what I'm saying at all. If I were to take you on as a client, then I wouldn't be able to invite you out for dinner. It wouldn't be professional."

She stared at him for the longest time before the beginning of a smile tipped the corners of her mouth. "Is that right?"

Hamilton nodded.

"Mason is grabbing something out of his office, but you and your daughter will be meeting with him in here," Hamilton heard their executive assistant say as the conference room door opened. He stood just as Egypt stepped into the room.

"Hey Hamilton, this is Wesley Bradford," she said of the man who followed her in.

Shocked with disbelief, a slow burn of anger swirled inside Hamilton's gut at the sight of the man who had almost ruined his life.

"What the hell are you doing here?"

Chapter Six

"I could ask you the same thing!" Wesley roared. "Where the hell is Mason Bennett? Has he stooped to hiring has-been cops to work as bodyguards?"

An anxious surge swept through Dakota. She uncrossed her legs and scooted her chair back. Stunned, she watched the man she had hoped to get to know better and her father square off like two bulls preparing for battle.

"There's no way I'm dealing with some lowlife like you who gets his thrills by—"

A low growl came from Hamilton and he moved past his chair, knocking it over as he stomped across the room.

"Whoa, wait!" Dakota jumped from her seat, tripping over the leg of the chair and winced when her hip hit the edge of the table as she hurried after Hamilton. She jumped in front of him and pushed against his hard chest, struggling to stop him from attacking her father.

Hamilton stepped away from her and glared, looking as if he wanted to rip her apart. "*This* asshole is your father?" he growled, a lethal chill hanging on the edge of his words.

"Yes, and I take it you two know each other," Dakota said, breathing hard, her hands planted on her hips. She didn't know what had transpired between him and her father, but she had no intention of shrinking under his heavy glare.

Earlier, his eyes held a bit of desire and mischief, but now his dark gaze was hard and unyielding. His stance, stiff and combative. Anger bounced off of him in waves, as if he would pounce at any moment.

Dakota's attention went to the door where Egypt stood, her worried gaze darting back and forth at them. Next to her was a tall immaculately-dressed man who matched Hamilton's height and build.

"What's going on in here?" the man asked.

"That's what I want to know," Dakota said. She turned to Hamilton whose chest rose up and down as he continued to fume.

"I'll tell you what's going on!" Wesley yelled and approached Mason. "If this is the man I have to work with, I'm taking my business somewhere else."

"No need," Hamilton finally spoke.

Dakota remained clueless as to what had happened between him and her father. She didn't really know Hamilton, but no doubt her father had made yet another enemy.

"As for me offering you protection," Hamilton said, backing away from Wesley and heading toward the door, "there isn't enough money in the world that would make me want to protect you."

"Hamilton, wait," Dakota said and touched his arm, effectively halting him and forcing him to look at her.

"Goodbye, Dakota." He eased out of her hold and proceeded to the door but slowed and said something to Mason before leaving. Egypt followed, closing the door behind her.

Dakota whirled around, getting right in her father's face. "You care to tell me what that was all about? First, you get me here under false pretenses, and then you rile up a man who could squash you with little effort."

Her father was no slouch standing almost six feet tall, but he was no match for Hamilton's muscular build or his youth. Dakota would put him in his late thirties, early forties and two hundred and twenty pounds of solid muscle.

"Start talking, Dad or I'm out of here. And start with what that was I just witnessed between you and Hamilton."

Her father sighed and turned away from her, running his hand over his low-cut hair and letting it drop to the back of his neck.

"We had a run-in a long time ago when he worked for Atlanta PD. I haven't seen or had to deal with him in years and I plan to keep it that way. That's all I'm saying on the subject."

Dakota folded her arms across her chest. "So what hap—"

"The subject is closed, Dee Dee. If you want to discuss the threats that I told you about earlier, we can do that, but I'm done discussing Hamilton Crosby."

"Dakota, I'm Mason Bennett. Sorry for my delay," he said.

"No problem." Dakota shook his hand, glad that he hadn't arrived sooner, giving her a chance to get to know Hamilton. Not that it mattered now. After what she just witnessed between him and her father, it was safe to say he'd want nothing to do with her.

"What the hell type of circus are you running here, Mason?" Wesley snapped.

Dakota rolled her eyes and reclaimed her seat while her father stood next to her, glowering at Mason. Her mind was still spinning at the sudden change of events in the past few minutes, yet Mason looked calm and collected.

"First you show up late for our meeting, then I find out you have that ass—"

"That's enough, Wes!" Mason thundered and Dakota's brows shot up. "You're the one who called me for my help this afternoon. If you have a problem with the way I run my business and who I employ, then show yourself out."

Dakota's gaze volleyed between the men, making her wonder even more what the heck was going on. Very few people stood up to Wesley Bradford, but she had a feeling he had met his match with Mason. At least she hoped.

For most of her life, she had watched her father act as if he was some type of king, expecting people to bow down to his every whim. It drove her nuts and used to embarrass her when she was growing up. Now, his behavior only irritated her.

"I assume you and my father are friends," Dakota said to Mason.

"No. We're not." Instead of sitting at the head of the table, Mason sat across from her in the chair Hamilton had vacated. "Wesley is an associate of my brother's and called in a favor this afternoon. Unfortunately, I'm not sure if I can grant it since I have no clue as to what I just walked in on." Mason speared her father with a hard look.

"Yeah, me either," Dakota mumbled, still thrown by Hamilton's behavior. One minute they were having a great conversation with him almost asking her out for dinner. The next minute, he was behaving like a totally different person.

Dakota studied her father. Considering he was in his mid-sixties, he didn't look a day over forty-five. Always dressed to perfection, today was no different. The dark gray suit with faint pinstripes, a crisp white shirt and expensive paisley tie was only a small example of the wealth he had amassed.

He had worked hard over the years, often sacrificing relationships to make the next buck. It didn't matter that he had several homes around the country, dated some of the prettiest women on the face of the planet, and could probably financially support a small country. He was alone most of the time, and Dakota couldn't be sure that he was happy.

"Since you're not willing to share what the beef is between you and Hamilton, tell me why I am here?" Dakota asked, more than ready to leave. Maybe if she was lucky, she'd run into Hamilton before she left the building.

"I'm afraid your life might be in danger," Wesley said to her and then turned to Mason. "I really need to hire security for both of us."

Dakota shook her head. "I'm not agreeing to have someone follow me around, especially since this might be a whole lot of nothing. Why is this time different than the other times people threatened you?"

Wesley huffed, not looking too pleased with her.

"Let's see the letters you told me about on the telephone," Mason said.

Wesley pulled several folded pieces of paper from the inside pocket of his suit jacket before claiming the seat at the head of the table. He handed the documents to Mason.

"You said that the police weren't able to pull prints from them, right?"

"That's correct. The cops have been useless, as usual. They claim there's nothing they can do since the guy hasn't actually done anything. They kept the envelope and original letters to see if they could pull some DNA from them. Then they asked me a few questions and after that they left my office."

"How do you know these came from a guy?" Mason asked as he skimmed the documents.

Besides tall and good-looking, clearly, he was good at what he did because Dakota hadn't caught that her father referred to the person as a *guy*.

"I have no idea who it is. It could be anyone."

"Considering the letters don't look the same, could it be more than one person having issues with you?"

Dakota snorted, but quickly covered her mouth, knowing a loaded question when she heard one.

"May I?" she asked Mason, nodding at the letters he set on the table. He handed them to her. "I'm not sure if my father has mentioned this, but this isn't the first time someone has threatened him. Seems every couple of years he pisses someone off."

She ignored her father's scowl as she read the letters.

You will pay for what you did to me.

Your day is coming.

That last letter was what probably freaked her father out, prompting him to seek protection and insist on her getting some too.

No one associated with you will be safe.

Each letter was different in that two were hand-written and the last was done with words clipped from a newspaper or magazine. Dakota could see why Mason had asked if it was possible that two people could be involved.

She had tuned back into the conversation between the two men just as her father said, "This situation feels different, which is why I think we each need a bodyguard."

"Unless I missed it, you still haven't said why this feels different. You've received a few prank notes before and I've actually heard people threaten to kill you to your face, but nothing ever came of those situations."

Her father remained silent as she and Mason looked on, waiting for him to say something that would enlighten them. Dakota hated seeing him so concerned. Though their relationship was rocky at best, she knew he had a good side. Her dad could be a nice, giving man when he wanted to be. Unfortunately, most people didn't get to see that side of him. They were usually privy to the arrogant and entitled behavior he so often portrayed.

"Listen, Wes, I think it's a good idea that you're taking these seriously. Better to be prepared and safe. We can set you and Dakota up with bodyguards. I'll just need some details. Like how many do you want? Do you need 24/7 service? If you want to move forward with this, I can have Egypt pull the paperwork together, and—"

"Wait. Dad, you still haven't said why this time is different."

"I don't know, Dakota. It just feels different. I'll admit over the years no one has ever followed through with their threats, but in those cases, I knew when I had pissed someone off. "With these," he held up the papers, "I have no clue why I'm getting these threats."

His voice grew louder with each word and his hands shook until he set the papers on the table. Dakota had sensed his concern during their phone call earlier and when she arrived outside. But there had been plenty of times when his overprotectiveness toward her was unwarranted.

"Also, I've never received handwritten threats. These showed up at my office, making me think it's someone in the industry. Maybe a former client, or someone I fired, or someone who I didn't sign. Hell, it could be anyone."

"Have you considered hiring a private detective?" Mason asked.

Wesley nodded. "It's crossed my mind and it's something I'm seriously considering, but I'm a private man and would prefer not to have someone poking around in my business."

Dakota and Mason shared a look and she wondered if he was thinking the same thing she was thinking.

He's hiding something.

If Mason had the same thought, he kept it to himself.

"Listen, Dad. I can tell you're worried, but I'm not convinced that I need a bodyguard. I haven't had any issues with anyone that I can't handle, and more importantly, I can take care of myself."

Wesley shook his head. "Dakota, please don't start with that nonsense. Despite what you think, just because you risk your life every day in that perilous career, you're not invincible."

"What do you do for a living?" Mason asked.

"She's a stuntwoman," Wesley supplied before she could respond.

Mason grinned. "Nice. Can't say that I've ever met a stuntwoman before. I would imagine it's pretty exciting work."

Dakota smiled. "Never a dull moment."

"Oh, please. Don't encourage her. Every day she goes out and risks her life, and for what? Those measly pennies they pay you is nothing compared to what you could be making as an actress."

"Dad, we're not having this conversation. Despite what you might think, I'm grown, and I can make my own decisions. And I've decided that I don't want someone tagging behind me all because of you being overprotective. I appreciate you looking out for me, but thanks and no thanks."

"Dakota."

She stood and turned to Mason. "Mason, thanks for your time. And since I'm sure my father won't be apologizing for his rudeness earlier, please accept my apology on his behalf."

"Knock it off, Dakota. I can apologize for myself, and though you might be grown, you're still my baby. I would die if..." He stopped and cleared his throat and for the first time, Dakota heard real fear in his tone. "It would kill me if anything happened to you. I already lost your mother. I can't lose you, too."

That was the first time in a long time that he had mentioned her mother. Was he really afraid that he'd lose her too?

A stab of guilt punched Dakota in the gut. Lately, she'd been thinking about how it was just the two of them now. They really did need to figure out how to get along, especially since her grandmother, who was the buffer between them, had died months earlier.

Dakota had lost her own mother in a car accident when Dakota was five, and her grandmother, Wesley's mother, had come to live with them.

Dakota glanced at Mason, wondering what his take was on her father and the threats.

After a long hesitation, she dropped back down in her seat.

"I want to know that you're safe," Wesley continued.

Maybe this was more serious than she first thought. If it wasn't, this was the first time he had gone this far to hire an agency to protect them. Maybe she could bend a little.

"Okay. I'll agree to a bodyguard."

He released a shaky breath. "Thank you, sweetheart." Wesley regained his composure, rubbing the back of his neck the way he'd been doing earlier.

"There is one condition," Dakota said.

Wesley threw up his hands. "Of course there is. What's the condition?" he grumbled, probably feeling the effects of having a daughter who was as stubborn as him.

Again, Dakota glanced at Mason who met her gaze. He'd been quiet for the last few minutes, listening without comment as her and her father hash out their differences.

"I want Hamilton. Or no deal."

Wesley slammed his palm hard against the wood table. "Damn it, Dakota! I don't have time for this nonsense."

A slight grin lifted the left corner of Mason's lips, but he remained quiet. Dakota had a feeling he had already known what she was going to say.

"No! I won't have it. I don't trust him, especially with you."

Dakota studied her father. He was the most stubborn person she'd ever had to deal with, but his behavior was stranger than usual. This situation had him rattled. Or was it Hamilton that had him so flustered?

"Why not? You either tell me what you have against him, or I'm sticking to what I want." She didn't want a bodyguard, but if something really was going on that could cause her harm, she wanted to be prepared.

"Dee Dee, you're the most important person in my life, and I will not allow a man like Hamilton Crosby to look after you. I don't even want you talking to him. Better yet, I think we need to look for another agency."

Dakota glanced at Mason to find him staring at her father. If Hamilton was so bad, why wouldn't her father just tell them what the issue was?

Mason stood and buttoned his suit jacket before picking up the file he had walked in with. "I agree, Wesley. I think it best you seek protection from another company.

Unfortunately, you won't find one better than mine. As for Hamilton, I'm not sure what you have against him, or how your paths have crossed, but I can assure you, he's the best at what he does."

"I beg to differ!" Wesley snapped.

Mason shrugged. "That's your right, but if you're really concerned about your daughter, I'd think you'd want the best." He turned his attention to Dakota and handed her a business card. "If at any time you decide you need a security specialist, give us a call."

He opened the conference room door. "My assistant will see you both out. Enjoy the rest of your day." Within seconds, Egypt appeared.

"I'll be happy to show you out," she said.

Wesley stormed out without a backward glance. His attitude only made Dakota more curious about the threats, and his behavior toward Hamilton had her puzzled.

"Egypt, I'm so sorry for all of this. I don't know what's gotten into my father."

"No need to apologize. I'm sorry to hear how the meeting turned out, but Mason made it clear that if you need our services, feel free to give us a call."

"What can you tell me about Hamilton?"

Egypt smiled, but was slow to speak, and looked at Dakota as if deciding on whether she was worthy of a man like Hamilton. "He's a sweetheart. Kind, loyal, and protective of his family and friends. He's super nice...until he's not. Screw him over and you'll regret the day you ever met him. He has a very low tolerance for bullshit."

Dakota nodded. "I see."

She silently walked with Egypt to the set of elevators. Twisting her lower lip between her teeth, Dakota debated on voicing her next request. "Um...is it possible for me to speak to him before I leave?"

Egypt gave her a sympathetic look. "I'm sorry, but he's unavailable." She glanced over her shoulder and moved in closer. "But I'll let him know you want him to call you."

Dakota smiled, feeling as if she had an ally when it came to Hamilton. "Thank you. That would be great."

She didn't know what happened between him and her father, but she had every intention of finding out. She also planned to cash in on that dinner he almost promised.

Chapter Seven

Sweat dripped into Hamilton's eyes. His angry breaths came in short spurts as he sent a left hook, then a right uppercut to the hundred-pound punching bag that hung from a wood beam on the ceiling. He didn't bother wiping his face. All he could do was keep sticking his punches and moving his feet.

The last person he had expected to see today was Wesley Bradford. Hell, he hadn't even planned to run into Dakota, but the pleasant surprise hadn't thrown him off-kilter as much as the shock of seeing her father.

Her father.

Damn.

His jaw tightened and the rhythm of his punches increased, sending shock waves through his arms each time his fists connected with the bag. Hatred descended on him like a three-ton boulder at the maddening realization that the two were related.

How could that be?

How had he not known that Wesley had a daughter?

Hamilton grunted and growled, putting his full weight behind each strike he threw. He hadn't bothered putting on boxing gloves, wanting to feel the burn. Now his knuckles were probably close to bleeding and his fists and arms throbbed as his punches came faster and harder. He didn't care.

He'd been in the company's fitness center for the past half-hour, finding little peace in pummeling the punching bag. The workout was supposed to tamp down the hate and anger pulsing through him. It wasn't working. Nothing was working. But each time he made contact with the bag, he imagined he was connecting with Wesley Bradford's face. The man who had almost destroyed him.

"Rough day?"

Hamilton heard Mason before he saw him. It wasn't until his friend stood on the other side of the bag, holding it in place did Hamilton lighten up on his jabs. But he kept moving.

"I don't hate many people. As a matter of fact, I can't think of anyone I hate more than Wesley," Hamilton said, his punches growing harder again. Mason could take it. Former marine sniper, the guy was fit and built like a damn truck. Hamilton was no slacker, but the body conditioning Mason had done in the military was still a part of his routine. The guy worked out daily as if his life depended on it.

"What's up with you and Wes? I can't ever remember seeing you snap like that before," Mason said, his voice rattling each time Hamilton's fist connected to the bag.

Hamilton knew the questions were coming, but he wasn't ready to discuss that time in his life. A time that had rocked his whole world. A time he wished he could wipe from his memory. A time that had almost cost him his son.

His heart raced and he fought the urge to scream with rage. Instead of responding, he kicked the bag, one long kick after another until his legs felt like limp noodles.

Mason laughed and stepped away from the bag. "Hmm...now I'm really intrigued. You know, as your boss, I could threaten to fire your ass if you don't come clean."

"You won't fire me," Hamilton breathed, still unable to stop moving, though he did stop the kicks.

Mason pulled one of his gourmet lollipops from his pocket. A big man over six feet tall and two hundred and thirty pounds sucking on a lollipop looked crazy, but Hamilton figured it was better than smoking. Mason had been trying to stop indulging in them for years, especially now that he had a wife and children. After he left the military, the sweet treat had been like a crutch, a source of comfort for him. Now, four years later, he was down to only one a day instead of three.

Hamilton softened his punches against the bag. He and Mason had been friends a long time. He knew it would take a lot more than keeping quiet for Mason to fire him. However, as his boss, his friend deserved an explanation.

"You know, we all have things in our past we'd rather not discuss," Mason started, "and I respect your privacy, but I have to ask. Will whatever transpired between you and Wesley hinder you from doing your job? Will it bring negative attention to Supreme Security?"

"No," Hamilton said after a short hesitation. He had vowed years ago when he told the story that took place late in his career with Atlanta PD, that it would be the last time. Yet, he felt obligated to give Mason something.

"You know me better than most. You know my character and what I'm capable of. Let's just say Wesley, years ago, accused me of something so heinous, I almost got fired from Atlanta PD. Actually, the backlash of what went down had a lot to do with my decision to quit the force."

"Sounds serious."

"It was beyond serious. I will never forgive that asshole for what he did. As for his daughter, I don't know her well and if she's anything like her father, I want nothing to do with her."

Mason narrowed his eyes, removed the lollipop from his mouth and pointed it at Hamilton. "I'm usually the cynic. I'm the one who is hard on people whether I know them or not. But this doesn't sound like you."

Between the two of them, Hamilton had always been considered the patient and understanding one. But when it came to Wesley, there had been times when Hamilton hadn't even recognized himself. He behaved out of character every time the guy was around.

"So, what happened between you and Dakota Sherrod?"

That stopped Hamilton, and he placed his hand against the boxing bag to stop it from moving. His head hung low as he struggled to get air into his lungs.

"What do you mean, what happened between her and I? I barely know the woman. Considering who her father is, she's probably some privileged spoiled liar who takes advantage of people."

"Maybe, but that's not how I read her. She seems nothing like Wesley. But that's beside the point. Her life might be in serious danger, and she's refusing a bodyguard."

Hamilton, still breathing hard, grabbed a towel that he had set on a weight bench nearby. Running it over his upper body haphazardly, he dropped it back down on the bench and snatched up his discarded T-shirt.

In the short time he'd known Dakota, he could already tell she had a stubborn streak. As for her refusing a bodyguard, that probably had more to do with her adventurous nature. Maybe she could protect herself, but her ability to leap tall buildings wouldn't help in a gun fight.

"What does her refusal have to do with me?"

"I doubt it has anything to do with you, but she's not taking the threats against her father seriously. She seems to be under the impression that it's just another day in Wesley's drama-filled world."

Hamilton cringed each time he heard the man's name, but the thought of Dakota getting caught up in her father's mess didn't sit well with him.

"Do you need me to talk to her? Tell her how important it is to take threats seriously?"

"No. I want you to take the assignment of guarding her, should it come to that. Besides, she said you're the only person she wants."

Hamilton's brows lifted.

"Needless to say, that didn't go over well with Wes, who refused our services by the way."

"No surprise there since he has a low opinion of me."

Mason shrugged. "His loss. I had only offered our services as a favor to my brother, despite knowing what an ass Wes is. Now that I know you and he have a bad history, we won't be able to work with him."

Hamilton shook his head. "Just because I won't work with him doesn't mean you can't assign someone else."

"Nah, I'm done with him. As for Dakota, I figured you must've put that famous Crosby charm on her. Clearly you said or did something to make her feel like you're the shit." Mason's mouth twitched as if trying to fight a smile.

Hamilton grunted. Instead of commenting on Mason's observation, he said, "Do you really think she's in danger?"

Hamilton took long gulps of water from his water bottle while Mason recapped the brief meeting, including Dakota and Wesley's disagreement. It sounded like the two didn't get along well, but that didn't change his mind about her. He was staying clear. It didn't matter that she had dominated most of his thoughts since meeting her the other day.

Even as he thought that last part, he couldn't deny the sizzling connection each time he was in her presence. And maybe he was crazy, but listening to Mason rattle off the threats had Hamilton's protective instincts kicking in. Could he guard Dakota without letting his attraction to the tempting beauty get in the way?

He hoped he didn't have to make that decision. If luck was on his side, she'd be right about Wesley's threats being nothing at all.

"Whether or not she's really in danger," Mason continued, "is hard to say. But Wesley seems to think she might be a target. That they might use her to get to him.

Hopefully, he's being overprotective, but better safe than sorry. If that is the case, this could be an easy assignment for you. Then again, Dakota is a very beautiful woman. Keeping a professional distance from her might prove to be your hardest assignment to date."

"I'm always professional."

"Yeah, you are, but the stuntwoman seems to have a thing for you. You might have your hands full and I mean that literally."

Hamilton chuckled. "Duly noted, but I don't think I'm your man." He didn't want anything to happen to her, but he'd rather keep his distance and not tempt fate. "We have plenty of others who can guard her. You don't need me."

"Well, when Wesley called me earlier this afternoon about his situation, he had mentioned that he wanted the best security specialist we had to protect his daughter. You're the best."

Hamilton would admit that he had a lot of experience in security and protection detail, but he wouldn't kid himself in assuming that he was the best.

"Flattery will get you nowhere. Get someone else."

"Oh, so you'll think about it. Great," Mason said, as if not hearing Hamilton. He headed to the door. "I'll let you go ahead and get cleaned up. Egypt told me to remind you that you have an appointment at four-thirty."

As the door closed behind his friend, Hamilton glanced at the clock on the wall. He had an hour to get himself together. His workout and the talk with Mason had calmed him some, but it would probably take a stiff drink and a good night's sleep to help him forget Wesley. And it would take a lot more than that to get Dakota out of his mind.

*

Days later, Hamilton approached his assistant's desk waving a yellow sticky note she had left for him. "Hey, Egypt. You wanted to see me?"

"Yes, can you do me a favor?"

"Anything for you." He balled up the slip of paper and tossed it into the trash can next to her desk.

"You're such a sweetie, but you might change your tune when you find out what I want."

Hamilton glanced at the jacket she was holding up and shrugged. "What?" And then it dawned on him.

Brown leather.

Dakota.

"Ms. Sherrod left this here the other day. I hadn't realized it because we haven't used that room since then. Anyway, I told her someone would drop it off before the day was over."

Hamilton just stared at their assistant, knowing what she was up to. Anyone could have dropped that jacket off, or Dakota could've picked it up herself.

Egypt had been trying to fix him up with some of her single friends for the past year, but Hamilton always shot her down. Not that he wasn't interested in dating, he just hadn't been interested in dating any of her friends. The last thing he needed was for something to go wrong in the relationship, and then their friendship would be trashed.

"Before you say no," she continued, "I think you owe Ms. Sherrod an apology."

Hamilton leaned back and frown. "For what?"

"For snapping. I heard you all the way down the hall that day, and then you walked out."

"Come on, Egypt." Hamilton moved from the desk, feeling like a kid being reprimanded. "You weren't in there, and you—"

"Here's the jacket, her telephone number and address. Go. Oh, and Ham…give her a chance. I like her."

Chapter Eight

Dakota stood in her living room, her gut churning in trepidation at the thought of seeing Hamilton again. Earlier, when she first heard his voice on the phone, she'd been cautiously optimistic that he was still interested. But when he made it clear he was just dropping off the jacket that she'd left at their office, that bit of hope fizzled. A little.

The conversation had been short, but she wasn't ready to let the intense vibe between them go. She needed him to know she wasn't her father.

Dakota took another quick glance around the apartment. Besides the moving boxes, stacked three-high in the corner, everything was in place. Her and Tymico's lease was up at the end of the month and they both felt it was time for the next chapter in their lives. Dakota couldn't imagine her life without her friend. Which was why moving out of their current apartment and into their own places would be weird. Even so, nothing could break their sisterly bond.

Dakota huffed out a calming breath before stepping into the hallway, locking her apartment door behind her. With any luck, she could talk Hamilton into coming back to her place and hearing her out. She hadn't gone two feet before her pain-in-the-butt neighbor stepped out of his apartment.

"Well, well, well. Tonight must be my lucky night."

Dakota rolled her eyes and folded her arms across her chest. "Sonny, I don't have time for your nonsense. I need to get to the lobby."

"Why do we have to go through this every time we run into each other? I don't know why you insist on playing hard to get."

He reached out to touch her face and she leaned back. He might've smelled good, but she didn't want his hands anywhere on her. As it was, his closeness alone made her uncomfortable. Lately, he'd been coming on stronger, getting a little too touchy-feely. It was like that when she had stupidly agreed to go out with him a few months ago.

"I *am* hard to get," she finally said. "Now back off!"

She stepped around him and headed for the lobby, but he grabbed her butt and squeezed.

Dakota whirled around, catching him off guard. She clipped him in the jaw with her elbow and swept her right leg out, tripping him to the floor.

"Don't you ever put your hands on me again," she ground between gritted teeth. It had been a long time since a man's touch made her want to stomp the crap out of him.

Sonny leaped up quickly, and she got into a ready stance. He had no idea that with her training, she could kill him with one perfectly placed jab.

Stunned, Sonny stood with his hand holding his cheek…and then he smiled.

It was as if the fog had been lifted and she was snapped out of a temporary trance. Instead of speaking, Dakota turned and stormed away.

Yet again she had chosen wrong. For a person who was hoping to meet a nice guy and get married sometime in the very near future, she'd been lousy at picking men, especially lately.

"Dakota, wait up. I'm sorry. You're right. I was way out of line." Sonny jumped in front of her, slowing her pace, but stayed back a couple of feet, his hands raised. "I shouldn't have put my hand on you. I had a couple of drinks tonight and I'm not thinking straight. I promise, it'll never happen again...unless you want something to happen."

"Sonny, just move." She glanced around him through the glass door to see if Hamilton had arrived but didn't see him.

"Okay, one more thing. You owe me. How about you and me go out Friday night?"

"Clearly you have lost your mind. I don't owe you a damn thing. When I *finally* agreed to go to dinner with you, your ass took me to some shit-hole house where an orgy was going on."

He chuckled and licked his lower lip. A sly grin, one that he probably thought was sexy, spread across his mouth. He looked more like a slimy predator than the handsome man who had first started asking her out almost a year ago. Now, Dakota wished she had stuck with turning him down. Her thought back then had been not to date someone who lived within walking distance of her. But he had worn her down with his persistence.

"Come on, baby. I already apologized for that," he said. "And that was almost three months ago. You can't still be holding that against me. Besides, I thought it was just going to be a house party. I had planned on us getting our eat on, and then doing a little bumpin' and grindin' on the dance floor. Then I tho—"

"Sonny, just stop. You blew it. That was your one shot. Besides, I'm seeing someone," she lied but thought about Hamilton. It would be perfect if he'd show up at any second. With his unknown help, she could nip this nonsense with Sonny in the bud tonight.

*

Hamilton glanced at the address that he had scribbled on a slip of paper. He was having second thoughts about dropping off Dakota's jacket, but it was the least he could do. The way he left her in the conference room without an explanation had been a punk-ass move. Granted, it was in the best interest of all of them that he'd left when he had, knowing it wouldn't have taken much for him to haul off and punch Wesley.

Just as Hamilton exited highway 85, his phone rang through the truck speakers and his best friend Lazarus's name popped up on the radio screen.

He pushed the phone button on his steering wheel. "What's up, Laz?"

"Not much. I was taking a break and figured I'd check in."

Hamilton and Lazarus had been college roommates while attending Georgia State and were closer than most brothers. Back then, some even referred to them as Ebony and Ivory. These days, they practically lived in two different worlds. Hamilton had opted for a safer career, while Laz lived for his job as an Atlanta police detective.

Recently, there had been rumors swirling around that he was a dirty cop. Hamilton knew better. Sure, his friend pushed the limits and skated on the edge of the law, but Laz was committed to ridding the city of scum. He was also the best damn detective in Atlanta. Lazarus got the job done, not caring that many of his arrests resulted in internal affairs investigation.

"How's my godson?" Laz asked of Dominic.

"It's scary how much that kid reminds me of you," Hamilton said as they discussed Dominic's latest antics. Laz only laughed while listening to one story after another.

"Man, I love that kid. He's a quick study and will make a helluva cop when he grows up."

"Oh, I didn't tell you. He wants to be a stuntman now."

Hamilton gave him a quick recap of Dominic's trip to the movie set, realizing that Laz had heard about parts of the visit from Dominic.

Discussing the movie set brought up thoughts of Dakota Sherrod or Dakota Bradford. Whatever the hell name she went by. Hamilton had the shittiest luck. Of all the women who could have caught his attention, it had to be Wesley's daughter. Talk about a buzzkill.

"Well, tell Dom we're still on for laser tag this weekend."

"Okay." Hamilton slowed down across the street from Dakota's building. He frowned when he spotted her inside the glass doors in what appeared to be a heated discussion with a man.

"He'll be at my parent's house. You can pick him up from there."

"That works for me. I'll get a home-cooked meal. It's been awhile."

Irene Crosby, Hamilton's mother, lived to cook for her husband and three boys as well as Laz. She treated him like one of her own, and he rarely missed an opportunity to dine at her table.

"So, what's up with you and your woman?" Hamilton asked.

After a slight hesitation, Laz asked, "What woman?"

"The woman whose name you usually work into every conversation. Is that gorgeous prosecutor still giving you hell?"

Hamilton laughed when Laz released a string of curses. His friend didn't want to admit it, but he was in love with attorney Journey Ramsey. It didn't matter that she was a state prosecutor who challenged most of Laz's cases.

Hamilton parked his truck in the first available spot up the street and grabbed Dakota's jacket from the passenger seat. Before shutting off his truck, he switched to his cell phone to continue the conversation.

"That woman will forever be a gorgeous thorn in my side. Giving me hell is putting it mildly."

Hamilton started to tease him but noticed a dark vehicle creeping up the street with its lights out.

"Are you still there?" Laz asked. "What are you doing?"

"Stay on the line, man," Hamilton said as he eased around to the other side of his vehicle, slipping the handgun he usually carried from his ankle holster. Some things he did out of habit, like checking out his surroundings and noting when something seemed out of order. Then there were other times when an ominous feeling licked at his nerves—that's when he got into protection mode and armed himself. Right now, his intuition was screaming that something was about to go down.

He glanced at Dakota's building. He could barely see her behind the guy with the wide shoulders, but the way her arms were flopping around, it was safe to say they were still in a heated discussion.

Hamilton's heart rate amped up. He had been a cop long enough to know that as slow as the car was moving, whoever the passengers were, they were definitely up to no good.

He remained out of sight and close to his truck until the vehicle crept past him. Then on a whim, he glanced at the license plate.

"Laz, I have a plate for you. Queens, Nora, Tom, 9705." Hamilton rattled off the license plate number, his police training kicking in. "A dark four-door Chevy with tinted windows just past me with no headli—"

Hamilton flinched when gunshots pierced the quietness of the night.

"Shots fired!" he ground into the phone and jerked back to the other side of his truck as the individuals in the vehicle opened fire on Dakota's building.

He could barely hear Laz calling his name when screams erupted. A car going in the opposite direction slammed on their brakes. People on the sidewalks scattered. Within seconds, the hit car peeled away.

Hamilton took off in a sprint toward the building. He yelled the address to Laz, knowing he'd heard the gunshots.

"A black and white is on the way," his friend said into his ear. "And I'll be there shortly."

A sense of foreboding crawled through Hamilton's body, unsure of what he would find when he reached the building. Still holding Dakota's jacket, he pocketed his cell phone and kept his gun at his side as he slowed. Maybe Wesley's fear for his daughter's life wasn't as far-fetched as she thought.

Another scream came from inside the building once he neared the entrance. Shards of glass from the double doors littered the sidewalk, as well as inside the lobby.

Hamilton eased his gun into the back waistband of his pants, making sure his jacket covered the piece as he entered the building. Foreboding inched through him when he spotted a body. The man Dakota had been arguing with lay lifeless, bullet holes in the back and blood painting part of the floor around him.

Some of the neighbors had ventured into the hallway, one with a phone to his ear sounding as if he was talking to a 911 operator, and another woman screaming for someone to do something. Both were standing in the middle of the staircase, keeping their distance.

Hamilton's heart kicked against his ribcage as his gaze darted around the space, the pressure in his chest mounting.

Where the hell was Dakota?

He quickly checked the unmoving man for a pulse.

"Is he...is he dead?" the frantic woman asked, not as crazed as she'd been a moment ago. The man on the phone looked as if he was waiting for Hamilton's response as well.

"Yeah. Everyone stay back. I already called this in, and the cops are on the way," he said. He still had no idea what had happened to Dakota, but he did see blood smudges that started near the victim's body and got thinner a few feet away.

He eased away from the body while the man and woman standing on the stairs weren't paying attention and followed the trail. It stopped at the edge of a narrow hallway that curved around.

Hamilton pulled up short and his body tensed.

Hunkered down in a small area beneath the stairs, Dakota sat, blood covering her arms, hands, and the front of her sweater. Before Hamilton could say anything, her gaze shot up. She jerked back and bumped the wall. Her light honey-brown eyes were wide with alarm, and her face paled.

But then she recognized him.

Dakota opened her mouth to speak, but only a slight whimper came out as her chest heaved up and down rapidly. Her bloody hands and sweater stood out like a beacon of fire sitting on a hill.

He swallowed hard, scanning her body as he eased toward her. The sounds of people coming out of their apartments and sirens in the distance faded to the background. At the moment, she was his only concern.

Stooping down he moved his large body closer into the tight space, careful not to hit his head on the low ceiling. He kneeled next to her and set the jacket he'd been holding onto the floor.

"Where are you hit?" he asked quietly.

"I—I don't...I—I'm not. Son—Sonny's blood. So—so much blood." Her voice cracked.

Dakota lifted her shaking hands toward her face, but Hamilton stopped her by grabbing both wrists. He didn't want her to get someone's else's blood on her face. He also still wasn't convinced that she wasn't hurt considering the amount of blood on her clothes.

"I—I need to get to my apartment. They might come back."

Hamilton doubted they were coming back, at least not today, but he didn't like the idea of her being in the open. Although hiding in the tight space beneath the stairs did give some cover.

"Let me make sure you weren't hit. I'm going to lift your sweater a little. Okay?"

She nodded and shivered, her breathing increasing.

"Does anything hurt?"

"My butt. Can you check to see if I have a bruise?"

Hamilton's left brow arched as he looked down at her. When his hands stilled on her sweater, those long lashes shielding her eyes lifted, and she glanced up at him. Each time he stared into those gorgeous eyes, his pulse kicked up. He could almost hear the blood rushing from his brain to the lower part of his body, but now wasn't the time for lustful thoughts. Dakota had said the words about her butt with a straight face, but he couldn't determine if she was serious.

Serious or not, there was no way in hell he was checking out her ass. He'd already had a hard time trying to block thoughts of her out of his mind. Considering she seemed to be sitting just fine, maybe she'd made the comment to get a rise out of him. It worked. He knew people who used humor to take their mind off of serious situations. Either way, he wasn't going to torture himself any more than he had to.

Still concerned about the blood covering her clothes, he made quick work of checking her for wounds, running his hands gently down her sides, hips, and legs. She winced a little when his hand grazed her left hip, but considering the amount of blood on her, he was shocked he didn't find any bullet wounds.

"What happened?" Hamilton asked and let her lean against him, noting that the adrenaline she'd been high on was probably subsiding. He had no idea how she'd been able to get to the back of the stairs.

"S—Sonny and I had been arguing and then…shots rang out, like—like machine guns or something. Glass shattering and people screaming was all I heard. Hell, that's all I'm still hearing." She shook her head as if trying to shake the sounds free.

"Did Sonny say anything?"

Seconds ticked by and she didn't speak but shivered again, her hands shaking slightly, and he cradled her against him fearing that she was going into shock.

"He, um…grunted when he got hit and his eyes grew big." Her voice cracked. "Sonny's body jerked a few times, and…and he crashed into me and I fell hard on the floor. I—I was pinned under him," her voice shook and she stared down at her hands before rubbing them on the thighs of her jeans. "I should've…I should've done something."

"Baby, there was nothing you could've done." The endearment slipped through before he could stop it. She still had to talk with the cops and he didn't want her to lose it yet by blaming herself for not doing more. "The shooting took place within ten seconds. You—"

"I freaked when he was on top of me. I just knew I had to get away. I pretended it was a scene. I just kept pushing against him enough to get free, and...and then you came."

An overwhelming feeling Hamilton couldn't describe came over him. He was glad he was there. Glad she wasn't alone. He had seen enough dead bodies to know it could screw with your mind.

Dakota glanced up at him and his breath hitched as tears filled her eyes, but then she quickly looked away.

"I—I need to go. All of this...this blood. I need to get to my apartment," she mumbled.

Hamilton was thinking the same thing, but not for the same reasons as her. He was pretty sure those guys weren't coming back, but if she'd been the target, the gunmen would find a way to determine if she was dead. And if she hadn't been the target, she was still a witness.

"Where's your apartment?" It wasn't a good idea to move her from the scene, but Hamilton planned to treat her like he'd treat one of his charges that he was guarding. His number-one priority in those situations was to make sure his client was safe.

"Down the hall." Dakota lifted a trembling finger and pointed to the left. "Apartment 105."

Hamilton heard more frantic voices nearby and sirens getting closer. He needed to move her now before it got too crowded.

"Let's go." He lifted her from the floor before she could protest and eased down the hall.

Chapter Nine

Hamilton leaned against Dakota's kitchen counter watching as Laz and his partner, Detective Ashton Chambers, questioned her. So much for just dropping off a jacket and leaving. This evening hadn't turned out the way Hamilton anticipated. It just went to show that it didn't matter how much you planned, your life could change or end in a heartbeat.

Considering Dakota had witnessed a murder and could have easily been a victim, she was holding up pretty good. After she showered, he had given her a glass of scotch to help calm her nerves. Now her eyes were partially open and it probably wouldn't take much for her to fall asleep.

Hamilton pushed away from the counter and walked across the open space to the living room. "Guys, how about giving her a little break?" he asked and nodded his head toward the kitchen, hoping they'd follow.

"Actually, that's a good idea. I need to return a call. Be back in a few," Ashton said and headed for the door.

Laz followed Hamilton to the kitchen. "You all right?" he asked, looking at him with concern.

"Yeah, I'm fine." Hamilton reclaimed his position next to the counter and Laz stood partially in front of him. It was clear he wanted to talk without Dakota hearing.

"What were you even doing here?" he whispered. With the open floor plan, it didn't give much privacy for conversation.

"I met her the other day. Justin introduced us on the set of—"

"Wait. Is this the stuntwoman?" Laz asked and Hamilton frowned. He couldn't remember mentioning her. "Dom told me about her and that he got her telephone number for you."

Hamilton shook his head. "That kid talks too damn much. Does he tell you everything?"

"Yep, as he should."

Laz and Dominic's relationship had been like that from the day the kid started talking. Hamilton wasn't an insecure man, but the bond between those two could've given him a complex. Instead, he was glad Dominic had several strong men in his life.

"We happened to run into each other the other day at Supreme," Hamilton explained.

"Is she a client?"

"No. She's Wesley Bradford's daughter."

Laz's mouth dropped opened and Hamilton almost laughed. His friend was rarely at a loss for words, but he listened as Hamilton gave him the short version of that day in the conference room. He hadn't been the only one to suffer at the hands of Wesley. His family and closest friends had gone through hell right along with him. Laz was one of few who knew what happened years ago and had no love for the man.

Laz narrowed his eyes and then glanced at Dakota before returning his attention to Hamilton.

"That gorgeous woman is that bastard's daughter?" he said in a loud whisper. "You're shitting me."

"Nope. When I ran into Wesley the other day, I thought I'd be calling you to bail me out of jail. All the hate I felt for him years ago came to the forefront and I wanted to wrap my hands around his neck and squeeze."

"Glad you refrained from killing the guy. What's up with her dad?"

"He's been receiving threatening letters and wants Dakota protected. He thinks she might be in danger, but she refused a bodyguard. According to her, Wesley being threatened is nothing new. Go figure."

Hamilton had a feeling Dakota would change her mind about getting some type of protection after what happened tonight.

"Damn." Laz glanced into the living room again. "Well, there is a way you can fuck with old Wes and really make him sorry for the shit he put you through."

Hamilton was almost afraid to ask. "And that is?"

"Marry his daughter."

"Yeah, right. That's *never* going to happen."

"Why not? You're finally ready to settle down, and I can already tell by the way she's been stealing glances at you that she's interested."

"Man, quit. She was almost killed tonight. Whatever look you think you saw was probably fear."

"Nah, man. Any other woman would have totally freaked out and would probably be bawling their eyes out, but not her. She hasn't shed a tear."

Hamilton sighed, not bothering to respond because he thought the same thing. She might've been a badass stuntwoman, but what she'd just gone through would've made a grown man cry. The fact that no tears had dropped could've meant she lacked feelings and she was probably heartless just like her father, but Hamilton didn't believe that. For some reason, he had a feeling Dakota was a fearless woman who walked to her own beat.

"Are you telling me you're not attracted to her?" Laz asked.

"I'm not saying that at all. She's a beautiful woman, but nothing is going to happen between us. So, you might as well lose that—"

"Because she's Wesley's kid."

"Well, yeah, Laz. I can't believe you even have to ask. That man made my life a living hell. I don't want anything to do with him or anyone related to him."

"Yeah you say that, but I'm picking up a different vibe from you. You're feeling this woman."

Hamilton didn't respond. What could he say? Everything Laz had said was true. He hadn't even planned to still be at her apartment, but he couldn't deny that the longer he was around Dakota, the more he wanted to be near her.

And that was a problem.

*

Dakota sat quietly, numbed by the night's events, or maybe it was the scotch that she had recently downed. Sitting on her leather sofa, she tried to process what happened. One minute she'd been talking to Sonny, and the next thing she knew, gunshots rang out.

Each time she closed her eyes, a vision of his shocked expression after being shot in the back filled her mind. Had he not been standing there, she would be...

Dakota couldn't finish the thought. Shivers gripped her and she held the blanket that was around her shoulders tighter. Even her ears were still ringing. Normally, she could compartmentalize everything in her mind, but this... This was something that didn't make sense.

She shifted and brought her legs up on the sofa, but pain shot through her hip and tailbone, radiating through her body. She drew in a breath and bit her bottom lip, forcing back a groan as she lowered her feet back to the floor.

Her body had taken a beating over the years, but the aches she experienced now, mixed with the mental anguish clogging her mind was more than she could handle at the moment.

Just relax.

Forcing her body to listen to the words floating around in her mind, her breathing slowed and the pain eased somewhat.

Dakota glanced across the room and her gaze slammed into Hamilton's. Heat rose to her cheeks. He'd been staring at her for the past hour but had kept his distance once they had gotten her into the apartment.

She could've kissed him for talking the detectives into giving her a short break. As a matter of fact, Dakota didn't know what she would've done had Hamilton not showed up when he had. No way would she have been able to hold herself together without having his calm presence there.

Dakota rubbed her eyes, fighting to keep them open as she yawned. It had been a long day, and considering the detectives and Hamilton were still there, it didn't seem the night was going to end anytime soon.

Even before she looked back across the room, she could feel Hamilton's attention on her.

Yep. Still looking.

He watched her while he talked to the cutie-pie detective who he referred to as his brother. She figured he meant brother in blue since they had been on the police force together a few years back. But they seemed closer than just friends. They clearly weren't biological brothers. Sure, they were both handsome, but it was safe to say they had different parents. Laz was white with the most startling hazel-green eyes she'd ever seen before. He also had a swagger that could capture any woman's attention.

Dakota released a long sigh and dropped her head back against the sofa and closed her eyes. Technically, Sonny had saved her life. She didn't even want to think about what would've happened if he hadn't been standing in front of her.

"Dakota?"

Her eyes popped open and she lifted her head, surprised to see Detective Dimas sitting on the sofa next to her. Hamilton stood next to him, his arms folded across his broad chest and concern written across his face.

Had she dozed off? How hadn't she felt the sofa dip or feel Hamilton's presence? Especially since her body vibrated whenever he was near.

"Laz—I mean Detective Dimas—has a few more questions. Are you up for it?"

Dakota studied *Laz* for a moment as something dawned on her. "Are you *Uncle* Laz?" Her conversation with Dominic came to mind.

Laz flashed a sexy grin that went well with his hypnotic eyes. "That depends on who you've been talking to."

"Dominic told me that you instructed him to always get a pretty girl's telephone number."

Laz chuckled and Hamilton cursed under his breath. "In my defense, I was referring to girls his own age."

"Damn it, Laz. He shouldn't be asking for anyone's telephone number. He's too young," Hamilton said.

"I actually thought it was good advice," Dakota said, looking at Laz. "Maybe you can share some of your wisdom with Dominic's father." She yawned again as Laz burst out laughing.

"Yeah, I'll do that." Laz chuckled.

She didn't bother glancing at Hamilton, knowing he was probably glaring at both of them.

Once the detective sobered, he asked Dakota, "How well did you know Sonny?"

"Not well. He moved into the building almost a year ago. I don't see him every day. Well...I didn't see him every day."

"Were you two dating?"

"No," Dakota said quickly, her gaze connecting with Hamilton's again. She didn't know why it mattered that he knew that, but it did. "I went out with Sonny once, but he and I aren't...weren't compatible. He was a little too rough around the edges for me, if you know what I mean."

Detective Dimas nodded. "He was a street captain with the 4-1 gang."

"Really?" She shouldn't be surprised. Sonny hung out with some bad seeds if the "party" he had taken her to was any indication.

"What we need to figure out," the detective said, "is if that hit was intended for him...or for you."

*

This was the first time tonight that Hamilton had witnessed any vulnerability from Dakota.

He shoved Laz in the shoulder. "You really need to work on your tact," he mumbled before taking the seat on the other side of Dakota. She'd had a quick shower and her light floral scent smelled fresh and clean, drawing him to her like a hummingbird to wildflowers.

"You think they were shooting at me? I thought it was some random shooting." Her voice faded to a muted whisper. "My father. Surely you don't think—"

"Before you start jumping to conclusions, the cops are not sure what the shooting was about or who—"

"It had all the signs of a hit," Laz said matter-of-factly. Hamilton wanted to punch him, especially seeing that Dakota's breathing had increased and she was holding the blanket around her shoulder with a death grip.

She turned startled eyes to Hamilton. "Is that what you think? You think that was a hit?"

He suddenly wanted to wrap her in his arms and provide some sense of comfort. He couldn't lie to her but didn't want to frighten her either. Dakota needed to be diligent in taking care of herself. That wouldn't happen unless he was honest.

"Yes."

"Oh my, God." She leaped off the sofa, but winced and gasped, her hand flying to her hip as her knees buckled.

Hamilton was out of his seat before he realized it, and Laz flanked the other side of her.

"I think you need to go to the hospital," Hamilton said as they led her back to the sofa. Dakota had refused to go earlier, claiming she was fine, but he wasn't so sure.

She shook her head and didn't speak right away.

"At least get checked out. It's better to be safe than sorry," Laz added.

"No. I just need a good, long soak. I've been banged up worse than this and survived." Dakota reclaimed her seat.

"Do you have someone you can stay with for a couple of days?" Laz asked.

Hamilton glanced around the room at the ton of boxes. Dakota had explained that she would be moving in a few weeks to a place she was leasing in Brookhaven, a suburb of Atlanta. He wondered if she and her roommate were parting on good terms. After the shooting, he wasn't ruling anyone out as possible suspects.

"Can you go to your father's house?" Hamilton asked past the lump in his throat. Wesley might be a lot of things, but at least he had the means to keep her safe.

Why'd she have to be related to the guy? Had she been anyone else, Hamilton believed they could be good together.

"My father and I are not on good terms." She snuggled deeper under the blanket and blew out a breath. "I like you, Hamilton. I wish we could have met under different circumstances." It was as if she'd been reading his mind. "Just so you know, I'm not my father. I don't know what happened between you two, but please don't hold his issues against me."

After a slight hesitation, he said, "Fair enough. So, what do you want to do? I don't think it's a good idea for you to stay here. At least not until the police know more." Her roommate was out of town and wasn't expected back for a couple of days.

"I think I need to hire some protection."

Dakota spoke so quietly, Hamilton barely heard her. She might not have shown fear earlier, but she was clearly scared. It was like a punch in the gut. He liked the fearless side of her better but damned if a wave of possessiveness didn't seep into his bones. He didn't want anything to happen to her.

"I want to hire you."

Hamilton shook his head. "You can't hire me."

"Ham, she does need some protection. At least until we determine who the target was," Laz interjected.

Hamilton stood and ran his hand down his goatee. His friend was right. They could hope all they want that she wasn't the target, but until Laz and Ashton found the shooters, Dakota could be in danger.

"Pack a bag. I'm taking you to a safe house."

Laz looked at him with raised eyebrows. Hamilton tried to ignore him but could hear the unspoken words.

I know you want her, but are you sure this is a good idea?

This was absolutely not a good idea. Yes, she needed to be somewhere safe with someone to protect her.

Him being that someone was a disaster waiting to happen.

Chapter Ten

Ohmigod, ohmigod.

Breathing hard, Dakota stared into Sonny's lifeless eyes, fear like nothing she had ever experienced charging through her body.

"*Sonny,*" *she cried, shaking him. Feeling a stickiness on her hands, she knew without looking it was blood. She still called his name, still shook him several times, hoping, praying...*

He's gone.

I have to get out of here.

Heart pounding double-time, she wiggled beneath his heavy weight as tears pricked her eyes. Come on, move...move! She told herself trying to squeeze from beneath him.

She was trapped and the gunman was coming back.

I can't let them get me. I have to get out of here. I have to get out of here.

"*Dakota.*"

She jerked when someone touched her arm. With her heart thumping wildly, she started punching and kicking, but something restrained her.

He was back. The gunman had come back. She needed to get away.

Her breaths came in short spurts, and she jabbed her fists back and forth in quick succession, making contact with a hard body.

"*Shit.*" *A low growl followed. "Dakota." Strong hands gripping her arms ignited her will to fight harder.*

"Get back. Get off me!" she yelled and kept throwing punches, connecting with soft flesh and maybe a jaw.

"Dammit, Dakota!" Her name pricked the deep fog in her mind as the grip on her arms grew tighter. "Dakota, wake up."

Breathing hard, she blinked several times, her eyes adjusting to the darkness. Her gaze landed on Hamilton standing to her right.

"You're safe. Okay? You're safe." He said the last words quietly. The calm in his voice washed over her like a gentle breeze, cooling the heat that had engulfed her.

He slowly loosened his grip on her arms, and Dakota sagged against the seat. Her heart rate slowed as she glanced around the dark interior of the huge truck. The events of the evening coming back to her.

Sonny.

Gunshots.

Blood.

Hamilton.

"I won't bother asking if you're okay," he said, his voice deep but low, just above a whisper.

Dakota ran her hands down her face as she straightened in the front seat. She must have fallen asleep on the ride to the safe house. Clearly, she'd been knocked out if she missed the whole ride. They were in a garage and Hamilton was out of the truck, standing on the passenger side of the vehicle with the door open.

Hamilton rubbed a hand over his left jaw. "You pack a mean right hook. Now I know not to get too close if ever I have to wake you again."

Dakota grimaced. "I—I'm sorry. I was dre…I dreamed about the shooting." She chanced a glance at him and hated to see that look in his eyes. The look of pity. A look she rarely saw from anyone. She wasn't some weak, insecure woman, but damn. Right now, she was having a hard time keeping it together. "I can't stop seeing Sonny's face when, after..."

80

"That's probably going to happen more often than not over the next couple of days." He leaned in, a hand on the headrest of her seat and the other on the dashboard. "I've seen grown men on the police force lose the contents of their stomach after seeing a dead body. It's not something you get over quickly. It's going to take time. If you need to talk," he shrugged, "I'm here."

Dakota was quickly learning that Hamilton had way more than good looks going for him. He wasn't a big talker, but the man was undeniably a listener. He had also been extremely patient from the moment he showed up at her place. Even when she balked at the idea of being sequestered in a safe house, he listened, but calmly told her—more than once—to pack a bag. Dakota had always been attracted to take-charge men who weren't intimidated by her independent hear-me-roar attitude. Tonight was no different.

Hamilton's light touch on her hand snagged her attention. "Come on. Let's get you inside."

A short while later, he showed her around a three-bedroom, two-bathroom ranch home in the Alpharetta neighborhood that was twenty-five miles outside of Atlanta. According to him, the place was one of several safe houses the agency owned and had been remodeled to include all of the comforts of home, including a state-of-the-art alarm system and bulletproof windows. Decorated with contemporary furnishings and warm colors, it was beautiful; not at all what Dakota had expected when he first suggested her going to a safe house.

She followed Hamilton into one of the bedrooms. He set her backpack and small suitcase on a bench at the foot of the queen-sized bed. "This is the bedroom you'll be using while you're here. It has a bathroom with any toiletries you might need."

The blinds were closed and instead of turning on the overhead light, he illuminated the space with the two lamps sitting on the side tables. Decorated in coral, brown, and gray, the room wasn't very big but, like the rest of the home, it was warm and inviting.

As Hamilton roamed around the space pointing out the television remote, bathroom and closet, Dakota leaned against the wall just inside the room. She inhaled a steadying breath before releasing it slowly while half listening to him. When she woke up that morning, she saw her day going way different than it had. She didn't have to work for the next three days and had looked forward to vegging out in front of the television, especially since Tymico was scheduled to be out of town.

Thinking about Ty, Dakota knew she needed to call her. She probably should call her father as well, but he was the last person she wanted to deal with right now.

She rubbed her tired eyes, suddenly feeling the weight of what had happened in the last few hours. An overwhelming sense of defeat engulfed her like a dark cloud weighing her down. There was a shooter roaming around the city and tonight she might've been his target.

A vision of Sonny's lifeless body came to mind again, and a shiver gripped her body. How would she ever be able to erase that sight?

Dakota stepped away from the wall and wrapped her arms around herself as if that would keep all bad thoughts and memories away. Still trembling, she was going to have to do some serious praying, meditating, or whatever else it took to get her mind right.

She kept her head down and rubbed her hands up and down her arms, trying to shake the imagery. "I need to call Ty and let her know, um…let her know what happened."

"I have a burner phone you can use while you're here." Hamilton had insisted she leave her cell phone at the apartment. He said they didn't know what they were dealing with and didn't want to take a chance on someone being able to track her whereabouts through the phone.

When Hamilton didn't say more, Dakota glanced up to find him watching her. She had never felt so vulnerable in her life, and the way he was looking at her again stirred something inside. It wasn't the lust and desire she'd experience each time before when they were near. No, right now she just wanted to be wrapped in his strong embrace and pretend the last few hours hadn't happened. Pretend she hadn't almost lost her life tonight. Pretend that watching Sonny die was just a bad...very bad dream.

Dakota wasn't sure what Hamilton saw on her face, but his dark intense eyes softened. She swallowed hard and tried to keep in check the emotions threatening to burst free. It wasn't working. She glanced away, refusing to let this man see her fall apart.

"You're safe here," he said when he moved closer. One of his large hands cupped her cheek, the pad of his thumb caressing her heated skin. "I'm not going to let anything happen to you."

Dakota bit her bottom lip as tears filled her eyes. Why'd he have to be so damn sweet? Despite whatever her father had done to him, Hamilton had been nothing but kind. That said a lot about his character. In her experience, people who hated her father usually disliked her as well.

She couldn't remember the last time she cried, as she blinked several times to keep the tears at bay. Maybe the melancholy feeling was because of how gentle Hamilton was being, or maybe it was due to the events of the evening. Heck, it could have even been because she was so exhausted that she could barely see straight, but whatever the reason, she didn't want to cry in front of him.

"Thank you," she choked out, horrified by the way her voice cracked. She quickly swiped away an errant tear.

Hamilton huffed out a breath and before Dakota realized what he was doing, he pulled her into his strong arms. She didn't resist. She couldn't. All the fight had left her.

She buried her face into his muscular chest and looped her arms around his waist, soaking up his strength. He had no idea how much she needed the hug. Still feeling emotional, she wasn't ashamed to wave an invisible white flag and say uncle at the realization that the night had brought her to her knees. Not literally, but her equilibrium was off and fatigue had seeped deep into her bones.

They stood holding each other for the longest time with Hamilton whispering reassuring words. She would get through this.

Dakota's body tingled from the light kiss he brushed against the side of her head. Peace settled around her and some of the sadness that had consumed her just minutes earlier washed away.

This type of closeness was what she missed in her life. This was what she'd been craving. Someone significant to share her life with. Someone to talk to about her troubles. Someone to make her feel as if all was well with the world, even when she knew it wasn't. Hamilton was reminding her of what she'd been missing.

Dakota trembled against his hard body. *Damn, he felt good.* Hugged up against him made her aware of just how long it had been since she'd been with a man. She breathed in. The woodsy scent of his cologne surrounding her fanned the lust that had been ignited the first time they'd met. Considering how their last meeting had gone, them being there together like this seemed surreal.

When Dakota turned slightly, the side of her forehead brushed against Hamilton's chin and she sucked in a breath. The light stubble sent a tingle of awareness through her body. Being this close to him did wicked things to her, and she wanted nothing more than to press her lips against his.

"Dakota," Hamilton said roughly close to her ear, as if pained. He brought his hands up and cupped her face, forcing her attention to his eyes. He shook his head looking conflicted. "Damn, you do something to me."

The feeling was mutual, but before she could utter a word, he lowered his head and his mouth covered hers.

Dakota's heart pounded harder in her chest and her eyes drifted closed as she devoured the sweetness of his soft lips. The kiss started slow and gentle. Him nipping at her top lip and then her lower one. Soon the caress of his mouth on hers grew harder, more demanding. He pulled her closer, his body molding against hers. A flare of excitement engulfed Dakota when he nudged her lips apart and slipped his tongue inside her mouth.

It was as if they did this all the time. The intensity reminded her of the powerful connection she felt between them days ago. Every stroke of his tongue had her blood pressure rising, only emphasizing what she already knew.

They clicked.

Hamilton backed her to the wall and the low rumble of a growl started in his chest and worked its way up. He sounded like she felt—out of control. His hands slid from her face and did a slow trail down the side of her body, caressing every dip and curve. The way he held her, the taste of his sweet lips and the power behind every thrust of his tongue made her forget everything else. She moaned, savoring the feel of his hard body against hers.

Dakota gasped into his mouth when he palmed her butt. Gripping. Caressing. Kneading. Electric jolts charged through her body. Right now, he could ask anything of her and she'd willingly give it. With them both breathing hard, Hamilton possessed her mouth, taking total control and she yearned for so much more.

She wanted him. God, she wanted him more than she had wanted any man in a long time.

"Hamilton." His name slipped out as her hands did a slow crawl up his rock-hard torso, his muscles contracting beneath her touch. Hungry for so much more and unable to control herself, Dakota lifted her right leg, and wrapped it around his hip, needing to feel all of him. "I want you," she whispered.

Hamilton's mouth froze on her lips. His hands stilled on her butt. Hell, Dakota couldn't even tell if he was still breathing. She wanted to kick herself. Her words had clearly ruined the moment.

She lowered her leg and released a frustrated breath as she dropped her hands. Maybe she should have kept quiet, but she meant every word. She wanted him.

He was just as affected and didn't move away. His palms settled against the wall on either side of her. Chests heaving up and down as they gazed into each other's eyes, neither spoke for the longest moment until he broke the silence.

"I was out of line. Way out of line. You and me…can't happen."

Dakota heard the words and he figured that he probably meant them, but his actions said something altogether different. Like the way his gaze dropped to her lips longingly, and the way he still hadn't pulled away from her.

He wanted her. He wanted her as much as she wanted him.

"You keep telling yourself that if you want to," Dakota said close to his ear, nipping at his earlobe, and loving the way he visibly shivered. Desire sparked in his eyes, or maybe that was just her imagination. Either way, she knew she had left an impression on him. "You and I are going to be amazing together."

Dakota slipped under his arm, leaving him near the wall as she grabbed her backpack and headed to the bathroom. Her body craved him…and maybe a long, hot soak in the tub, but right now only a cold shower would do.

Chapter Eleven

I have clearly lost my damn mind.

Hamilton released a frustrated breath as he pushed away from the wall and stood upright, adjusting himself in the process. She had him so turned on, he was tempted to do something really stupid like strip out of his clothes and wait on the bed for her fine ass.

He ran his hand over his head and down to the back of his neck, struggling to recall any woman having this type of effect on him. Granted he hadn't been officially hired to guard her, and the agency didn't have a policy on sleeping with clients—yet—but still... He had his own rules about not sleeping with someone on his watch. Not only was it unprofessional, it could be dangerous. No personal security specialist wanted or needed that type of distraction when they needed to be alert at all times.

And Dakota was a distraction. A gorgeous, sexy, intoxicating distraction.

What had he been thinking? Why the hell had he kissed her? The moment their lips touched, Hamilton knew he had screwed up. But damned if he hadn't wanted to get her naked. If the way she stomped off was any indication, she wanted that, too.

He glanced at the closed bathroom door. Once the shower came on, he had to force himself to move because all he could think about was her luscious body without clothes on.

Yep. I have lost my damn mind.

The moment he stepped out of the bedroom and into the hallway, his cell phone vibrated. He welcomed the intrusion.

"Yeah," he said, recognizing Mason's number on the screen. Hamilton dropped down on the oversized sofa and stretched his legs out in front of him, crossing them at the ankle.

"You okay? Egypt told me about the shooting."

"Yeah, I'm fine."

"What about Dakota? How's she holding up?"

Had Mason asked a half an hour ago, Hamilton would have said not too good. But considering how she had kissed him moments ago, said otherwise. The way she'd handled herself tonight impressed the hell out of him. Except for the dream she'd had on the drive to the house and the few tears that slipped through, she had held up well. It was the strong chemistry between them that had him worried.

"She's all right, I guess." Hamilton gave him the short version of what took place and how they ended up at the safe house.

After a slight hesitation, Mason said, "I know how you feel about her father. If you being there is going to be a problem, I can send Kenton to relieve you within the next half an hour. Just say the word."

Hamilton dropped his head back on the sofa and closed his eyes. He had extra clothes in his truck to get him through a few days, and he already arranged for his parents to look after Dominic. The smart part of him wanted to say 'yes, get Kenton over here.' Dakota was already testing his willpower. But a larger part of Hamilton, the part of him that feared she might be in danger, couldn't abandon her.

He opened his eyes and lifted his head, only to look right at Dakota. She had changed into an oversize T-shirt and a pair of leggings. Her short hair, which was now curly, was brushed and held back with a headband, and her face had been freshly scrubbed. Hamilton had already thought her beautiful, but her natural beauty was on full display.

"Ham? You still there?" Mason asked on the other end of the phone.

"Yeah, I'm here."

Hamilton's gaze connected with Dakota's. The spark of desire in her eyes ignited a need within him that he wasn't sure how long he'd be able to fight. But then she narrowed her eyes as if to say 'Why are you looking at me like that?' He couldn't stop the smile from slowly spreading across his mouth.

Yep. Definitely a sexy distraction.

"Mase, I'm good. I'll be in touch."

"All right, then. Well, as my pops often says, be good. And if you can't be good, be careful."

"Right," Hamilton said absently, his attention still on Dakota. He ignored Mason who was chuckling on the other end before disconnecting.

"Was that about me?" Dakota asked, her hands on her hips. The T-shirt she wore was a little big, but it did nothing to hide the fact that she wasn't wearing a bra and her nipples were standing at attention.

This woman and her lush body were going to be the death of him. But that didn't stop his gaze from going lower to her toned thighs and shapely legs. He continued his perusal until he reached her pretty bare feet where her toenails were painted a hot pink.

She was a vision from head to toe and somehow, he had to figure out how to rein in his libido. He could easily go with Mason's idea and get one of their other guards to hang out with her until Laz and his team found answers. However, the possessive side of Hamilton couldn't let that happen. He didn't want anyone having her back but him.

His gaze traveled back up her body, stopping at her full breasts. She was definitely more than a handful.

"Hey!" Dakota snapped her fingers, snagging his attention. "Eyes up here, Romeo," she said, pointing at her face.

Hamilton couldn't help but laugh. Her father might be an asshole, but Hamilton was enamored with his daughter. He didn't know her well, but in the short time they'd spent together, he knew she was tough, had a mean right hook, and had a good sense of humor. He liked her. A lot.

"I asked you if that call was about me."

"Sort of. It was Mason checking on us."

"Was he making sure that you hadn't buried me under the house for my father's sins?" she asked and headed to the kitchen.

Again, Hamilton smiled. He had a feeling the time hidden away with her wasn't going to be boring.

He stood, yawned and stretched as Dakota roamed around the kitchen, checking the contents of the cabinets and the pantry. She lifted out a box of cereal but returned it to the shelf. Then she grabbed a bag of potato chips but placed them back in the pantry.

Hamilton strolled over to the long breakfast bar and sat in one of the four high-backed bar stools that separated the kitchen from the small dining area. With the home's open floor plan, he could see the whole house, except the bedrooms and bathrooms, from where he sat.

When Dakota opened the refrigerator, she let out a long whistle. "When you said the house had been stocked with anything we could need, you weren't kidding. I might have to hire the person who was responsible for the grocery shopping. They thought of everything."

"That would be Egypt. She's my and Mason's executive assistant and queen of Supreme Security. She's the most detailed and organized person I've ever met. It probably doesn't hurt that she's also a little OCD."

Dakota nodded. "I met her. Now I know why I liked her instantly. She's everything I'm not," she cracked.

Hamilton studied her. The shower had done her good. She looked more like herself, confident and relaxed. This was how he wanted her to stay. He never wanted to see the fear and sadness he'd witnessed in her eyes earlier.

"I'm starving. I think I'm going to bake some cookies."

"Cookies?"

"Yeah, cookies." Dakota started pulling ingredients from the refrigerator and pantry. "When I have nervous energy, I bake. Besides, I'm not that great of a cook, but I can bake. My specialty is homemade cinnamon rolls."

"So, when you say you're not that great of a cook, does that mean you *can't* cook?"

"It means what I said—I'm not that great. That means I do all right."

"Definitely code for can't." Hamilton pushed away from the counter and rinsed his hands in the sink. It was after ten, and though he was hungry, cookies were the last thing he wanted.

"What do you think you're doing? This kitchen isn't big enough for both of us," Dakota said.

"I'm making us something to eat, and the kitchen is big enough as long as you stay out of my way." Hamilton took the eggs from her and grabbed milk and a pack of bacon out of the refrigerator. "Are you allergic to anything or is there anything you don't eat?"

"*You're* going to cook for me?" She sidled up to him, standing next to the stove. "This whole sequestering thing might not be that bad. I get to stay in a cute house, have a cook, and a gorgeous hunk watching my six. What more could a girl ask for?"

"Watching your six? What do you know about that?" Hamilton pulled pancake mix from the pantry. Breakfast for dinner, or anytime, was always a favorite growing up and right now, he could go for a few flapjacks.

"I know it means you'll be watching my back."

Hamilton just hoped that he could keep his attention on just her back. Right now, her closeness was wreaking havoc on him. The fresh scent surrounding her was a mixture of soap and vanilla. He wanted nothing more than to press his nose to her neck and inhale, but that wouldn't be enough. Besides, he needed to keep his mind on what he was supposed to be doing. Watching her back. Not her backside.

"Since I have your undivided attention, let's discuss a few rules."

She stepped away and grabbed an apple out of the refrigerator. "I know you don't know me well, but I'm not really good with rules."

"The safe room for you is the bathroom in your bedroom," he continued as if she hadn't spoken. "If something goes down, like me sensing danger of any sort, go to that bathroom and lock the door. You are to stay in there until I come and get you."

"Hamilton, I—"

"If someone rings the doorbell for any reason, I want you in that bathroom with the door locked. If there's a breach of the house, of any kind, I want—"

"Me in the bathroom. I got it, Ham," she said, exasperation dripping from her words. "Dang, bossy much?"

"How many pancakes do you want?"

"Five."

He glanced at her with raised brows.

"What? I said I was starving. And I'd like three strips of bacon, two egg whites and a glass of orange juice."

Hamilton chuckled and shook his head. This woman was going to keep him on his toes.

While he prepared their meal, they chatted about her work, upcoming projects, coworkers, and she even told him about the *pain-in-the-ass* director who was over the current project. That reminded Hamilton of the conversation he'd had with his brother that day on the set.

"Why do you think the director is giving you a hard time?" Hamilton brought their plates and serving dishes to the round dining table. Dakota, who was slow to respond, brought over the drinks before sitting at the table.

With the threats her father was getting and now the shooting, Hamilton wanted to know as much about her and her life as possible. He wanted to believe she wasn't the target for the hit at her place, but until they knew for sure, he wasn't taking any chances.

"I'm not sure. I hadn't really cared until the other day."

"What happened the other day?"

Dakota explained how she was forced to do a stunt over and over for no good reason, and how she had gotten into the man's face.

"I think he's had run-ins with my father in the past."

"What does that have to do with you?"

She looked at him pointedly, her left brow lifted as if surprised he even had to ask.

"Typically, those in the entertainment who have issues with my father automatically turn those issues onto me."

Hamilton could maybe see that happening, though he didn't like it. She didn't sound bitter by that observation, just stating a fact. He happened to have been one of those people lumping her in the same category as her father. He might not know her well, but he knew enough to know she was nothing like Wesley Bradford.

"I probably should've said this sooner, but I'm sorry for my behavior and the way I walked out at the agency the other day. Seeing your father brought up some old feelings I thought I had dealt with years ago. There is still some underlying tension between us."

"He tends to have that impact on people. So, why do you hate my father's guts?"

Chapter Twelve

Dakota placed a forkful of pancakes into her mouth, waiting for Hamilton to respond. She could add good cook to the growing list of positive traits. The food was delicious and he had moved around the kitchen effortlessly, making quick work of their meal.

"Tell me, what did my father do to you?" she rephrased her question when he still didn't respond.

"What did your father tell you when you asked, because I'm sure you asked."

"So, you think you know me that well, huh?"

"Mm-hm." He continued eating.

Dakota studied his every move, loving how his long-sleeved henley bunched around huge bicep muscles each time he brought the fork to his tempting mouth. And the way his Adam's apple bobbed when he drank his juice. And how he looked at her with those dark, sexy eyes. And then there were those damn dimples that flashed from time to time.

She released a wistful sigh. She had it bad for this man and having him around was a wonderful distraction, taking her mind off the night's events.

"You're right, I did ask. Like you, he didn't say much. Only mentioned a run-in when you were with Atlanta PD.

Did you arrest him or something? Was it because of one of his wild celebrity parties? They tend to get out of hand."

"Just drop it, Dakota."

"I can't. I don't understand why neither of you won't discuss what happened. Besides, the beef between you two is keeping anything from happening between you and me, and I want to know why."

Hamilton set his fork down and leaned his forearms on the table. She could almost hear the wheels turning in his head as he struggled with whether to tell her. Whatever went down must have been serious. Dakota knew that she could eventually get the truth out of her father, but for some reason, she wanted...no, she *needed* to hear it from Hamilton.

"That's the past. I don't discuss the past," Hamilton said. "So, you can either change the topic and discuss something else; or until we hear from Laz, we can keep our distance from each other. Your call."

Dakota studied him. "Okay, I'll drop it...for now, but when we start dating, and we will, I'm going to ask again."

Hamilton laughed and leaned back. "You are a trip. You know that?"

"So I've been told."

Dakota shifted in her seat and winced, her hip still bothering her.

"Still sore?" Hamilton asked. It was safe to say he didn't miss much.

"A little."

"Maybe you should've taken a hot bath instead of the shower. I'm sure it would have helped."

"I can think of something else that could help." Dakota wiggled her eyebrows at him, and he shook his head, smiling. Taunting him was quickly becoming one of her favorite pastimes.

"I guess the only thing left for us to do is to get to know each other better. What's your favorite movie?" she asked.

"*Animal House*. What's yours?"

"*Love*...wait. *Animal House*? Really?"

He shrugged. "Yeah, it was funny. Reminds me of my college days. What's yours?"

"*Love Jones*. What's your favorite color?"

He stared at her and then drained the last of his juice, setting the empty glass on the table. "Hot pink."

Dakota laughed. She flicked the shoulder of her hot pink T-shirt. "You're welcome to borrow it sometime."

He grinned and those dimples made their appearance again. "I'll keep that in mind, but I'm sure it won't look as good on me as it does on you."

Hmm…flirting. He went back to eating as she pondered her next question.

"What's your favorite sexual position?"

Hamilton choked, coughing around a mouthful of food and patting his chest. "What?" His voice cracked and he reached for a bottle of water.

"You heard me. Your favorite position. Missionary position? Doggie style? Froggy style? What?"

He wiped his mouth, taking his time in responding. "Against the wall."

Dakota's mouth dropped open. "For real? Mine, too!" They burst out laughing. "I knew the moment I spotted you on the movie set that we were perfect for each other."

"I have a question. What made you become a stuntwoman?"

"I've always been adventurous and wanted to do something outside of the box. At first, I wanted to be an actress. Tried that for a couple of years while living in LA, and quickly got bored. Then a casting director, who knew about my martial arts experience, approached me about being the body double for Zoe Saldana. I literally jumped at the opportunity and ten years later, I'm still at it."

Hamilton didn't speak, only watched her intently.

"Lately, I've been thinking of trying something different. Something less dangerous and not so physically draining."

"Like what?"

Dakota shrugged. "Not sure. There aren't many other careers that provide the excitement and adrenaline rush I get from stunt work. I also want to get married and have a family," she said, wanting to get a rise out of him. He didn't bite, and she continued. "Crashing through glass doors and leaping off buildings while pregnant probably wouldn't work."

"Yeah, I could see that being a problem."

"Do you think you could marry someone who risked their life on a daily basis?"

Hamilton placed his elbow on the table and wiped his hand slowly over his mouth. "I think when I meet the right person and fall in love, it won't matter what she does for a living."

"Does that mean you *do* want to get married?"

Hamilton laughed. "Yeah, one day." He told her that he'd been engaged to Dominic's mother, but things hadn't worked out. Dakota sensed there was more to the story, but it seemed to be another topic he didn't want to discuss—yet.

They lobbed questions and responses back and forth for the next half hour, talking and laughing like old friends. It had been a long time since she had enjoyed a man's company as much as she was enjoying his.

"When we get married, how——"

"You know what? I'm done with the questions." Hamilton chuckled. "Maybe you should go to bed—alone— and I'll clean up the kitchen." He stood and started clearing the table, and Dakota joined him.

"I don't think I'm ready to close my eyes. I'll take care of the kitchen. I might not be a good cook, but I'm a beast at cleaning."

"Want something to drink?" Hamilton asked.

"Only if it's stronger than orange juice."

"How about brandy?" He pulled a small bottle from the top shelf of the pantry and poured the dark liquid into a glass for her and made himself a cup of coffee. While she worked in the kitchen, Hamilton retrieved the television remote from the living room. She glanced up from rinsing dishes and loading the dishwasher periodically as he flipped through channels.

A photo of Sonny appeared on the screen and Dakota gasped. Hamilton stood and turned up the volume as he moved closer to her.

According to authorities, a man was killed during a drive-by shooting on Peachtree St. Sonny Jackson, age 34, known in the neighborhood as a street captain with the 4-1 gang. A woman was also killed. Her identity has not yet been released. Authorities are viewing these actions as a murder-for-hire with Mr. Jackson as the target. We'll bring you more information as it becomes available.

"Oh. My. God." Dakota's hands shook. She didn't realize she was still holding a ceramic bowl until Hamilton removed it from her hands and placed it in the sink. "I don't understand. There was no one else in the hallway but Sonny and me. Who—"

"Calm down. Let me call Laz and find out what's going on. Come on and have a seat."

She didn't move, she couldn't move. Her mind raced a mile a minute. Had there been someone else there she hadn't seen? Or did the media think she was dead?

Hamilton wrapped his arm around her waist and guided her away from the sink and over to the sofa. Once she was seated, he handed her the glass of brandy she had been nursing and then went back to the dining area where he'd left his phone.

"Laz, what the hell's going on, man?" he asked seconds later. "We just saw the news report."

Dakota set her glass on the table and watched as Hamilton paced the room. She couldn't hear what Laz was saying on the other end of the call, but by the scowl on Hamilton's face, it wasn't good. A short while later, he pocketed the phone and grabbed the bottle of brandy.

"So?" she asked, her pulse pounding loudly in her ears. Hamilton added more of the dark liquid to her glass.

"You and Sonny were the only ones in the hallway, but according to one of Laz's CIs, they—"

"CI?" Dakota questioned.

"Confidential informant. Word on the street is that the hit was definitely for Sonny. He'd stolen some money from the crew and...well, you weren't the target."

"But why did the reporter say two people were killed?"

"Laz leaked that to a reporter. They still haven't found the car, but his CI has been running his mouth about Sonny having company when he got smoked. And if that's the word on the street, Laz wanted to make sure that those involved, not think that there was someone out there who could ID them."

Dakota shook her head. "That doesn't make sense. Someone's going to know that there was only one dead body on the scene."

Hamilton cracked a slight smile. "You don't know Laz. He's one of the best detectives on the force, and he has a lot of friends in high *and* low places. If anyone can make a dead body appear out of thin air, it's him."

Dakota stood and paced in front of the coffee table. "I don't like it. I—I just don't want this to come back on me in any way. What if someone saw me? What if someone figures out that I was in the hallway with Sonny at the time of the shooting?"

She gasped and her heart dropped at another thought, and her hand flew to her chest.

"Hamilton, there are cameras in the hallways."

"When the cops reviewed the footage, all they saw was blackness. Seems the cameras weren't working during that time."

Dakota stared at him, trying to read into what he wasn't saying with the nonchalant way he spoke to her. That couldn't be true. Management took security very seriously. She found it hard to believe that the cameras suddenly stopped working.

Hamilton stood. "Dakota, we all were very careful with how we handled the situation after the shooting. You're safe. Laz made sure that they questioned everyone on the first floor who was home. If anyone saw them going into your apartment, they wouldn't have thought anything of it. They would have assumed that you were being questioned just like everyone else. I assure you, Laz hasn't and won't include your name in any of his reports."

"But..." Dakota couldn't wrap her brain around that. Would he lie on an official report?

She resumed her nervous pacing. Would it be so bad if it was made to look as if she hadn't been in the hallway? God, she hoped all of this wouldn't come back to bite them in the ass. So far Hamilton hadn't steered her wrong, and with Laz's swag, no doubt he was a badass. She just didn't like the idea of being a part of any deception, especially where the law was concerned.

"Try to get some rest," Hamilton said. He kept his distance, but the concern in his eyes couldn't be missed. They had been having a great evening and despite the events at the apartment, she'd been able to laugh and forget, if only for a little while. Now, he was back to being professional and sounding all businesslike, and she was too exhausted to argue that fact.

"I need to call Ty," she said. "If she hears about what happened at the apartment, I don't want her to think that the body...I don't want her to think it was me." Dakota swallowed and stared at Hamilton. She wanted so bad for him to pull her into his arms and make her feel like this was all going to work out, but he didn't. Instead, he moved to the kitchen and reached into the pantry for something.

"Here's the thing." His voice was muffled until he stepped out of the pantry with a phone. "You can use this burner phone, but you can't give your roommate any details about you and Sonny being in the hallway."

Dakota frowned at him. "Why not?"

"As far as anyone is concerned, you weren't there. You were in your apartment and heard something but didn't know what happened until the cops knocked on your door."

"You want me to lie?"

"I want you to not volunteer any information and evade any questions that might put you at the scene."

"Hamilton...I—I can't."

Now he stood in front of her, the burner phone in one hand, and his other cupping her chin. They were only inches apart.

"My number-one goal right now is to keep you safe. I can't do that without your cooperation. Remember, whoever did the shooting is still out there. Until they are caught, we're going to take every precaution."

She pushed down the conflicting emotions building in her chest. Why'd he have to remind her? Would she ever be able to go back to her normal life?

As if reading her mind, he said, "You're going to get through this and I'll be with you for as long as necessary to ensure your safety."

She nodded and accepted the cell phone.

"Go ahead and make your call. I'll give you some privacy while you talk to your friend."

Dakota watched him walk to the back of the house before she called Tymico.

"Hello?"

"Ty, it's me."

"Dakota! Oh my God. Where are you?"

"Ty—"

"I heard there was a shooting at the complex. Two people are dead. Sonny was one of them," she said, her words flying through the telephone line faster than Dakota could think. She couldn't get a word in.

"I've been calling you ever since I heard."

"How—"

"I'm not going to lie. I thought it was you who they found with Sonny. You know how he's always cornering you in the hallway. I was afraid that—"

"Ty," Dakota interrupted, but her friend kept talking. "Ty!"

"What? Why are you yelling?"

"Because you won't let me get a word in."

"Oh, sorry. Are you okay?"

"I'm fine. I just wanted to call in case you heard about the shooting. How did you find out anyway?"

"Girl, Sabrina called a couple of hours ago," she said of their friend who lived on the second floor. "She stopped by our apartment but didn't get an answer. That's when I started calling you."

"Oh. Well, if you talk to her, tell her I'm fine."

"You don't sound fine. Are you sure you're okay? Do you want me to fly home? And why haven't you been answering your phone?"

"I'm with Hamilton."

"Who? Hamil... Wait. What?" she screamed, excitement ringing in her voice. "Are you kidding me? I've been worried sick about you and you're off on a romantic rendezvous." Ty paused regaining her composure. "Tell me every detail. How? When? Last I heard, you were waiting for him to bring you your jacket. What happened when... You know what? Just tell me everything and don't leave out a single detail!"

"Ty," Dakota dragged out her friend's nickname. "I'm so tired, I can barely think straight. Can we talk tomorrow? I only called tonight because..." She wasn't sure what to say but figured it would be best to stay as close to the truth as possible. "I realized I had left my phone at the apartment and I didn't want you worrying. I just want to go to bed."

Her friend laughed. "Yeah, I bet you do. If that guy is as hot as you described, I'm surprised you even thought to call me."

Dakota said nothing. She wished the night had been as juicy as her friend assumed, but then she recalled the kiss.

Now that was something to talk about. Throughout the evening, Dakota was more convinced than ever that she and Hamilton were a good fit.

"Dee, your dad heard about the shooting. When he couldn't reach you, he called me to see if we were okay. You should call him."

Dakota sighed, exhaustion settling in deeper. She didn't want to talk to him, knowing he'd have even more questions than Tymico. He would also insist on her moving in with him at the big house, the large estate he owned in Sandy Springs that she grew up in. The last place she wanted to be.

Once she finished talking to Tymico, Dakota slammed back the remaining drops of brandy lingering in her glass, then called her father. She braced herself for the questions that were bound to come. *Here goes.*

"Hello?"

"Hi, Dad."

"Dee Dee! Where the hell are you?"

Chapter Thirteen

The next morning, Dakota slowly opened her eyes but didn't move her head which pounded like a jackhammer hard at work inside her skull. She couldn't remember climbing into bed, but she had tossed and turned for most of the night, unable to shut down her brain. At least she didn't dream about Sonny, but thoughts of him, the detectives, and Hamilton wouldn't let her rest.

Dakota moved her head slightly toward the window, a sliver of sunlight filtered through the side of the closed blinds. It was morning...or maybe it was afternoon. She didn't much care. All she wanted was to go back to sleep, but her bladder screamed for her to get up.

Instead, she closed her eyes and played the conversation with her father the night before over and over in her mind. He'd been livid that she hadn't thought enough of him to call and let him know she was okay. She gave him the same phony story she told Tymico, leaving out the part about Hamilton. Saying that she was hanging out with a friend didn't go over any better. He wanted her under his roof where, according to him, she'd be safe.

All thoughts of her father and sleep slipped away when Dakota inhaled. The intoxicating scent of strong coffee swirled around her, and then she heard a sound near the door. Slowly, she glanced that way.

Hamilton.

He stood, leaning against the doorjamb, holding a steaming cup of coffee. God, she could kiss him. Not because he looked downright sexy in the white T-shirt that stretched across his wide muscular chest and jeans that revealed thick thighs. No, it was the coffee that really had her attention. How'd he know she never started her day without at least one, two, or four cups of coffee?

"You are truly a sight for tired eyes." She sat up slowly, wincing at the pain the simple act evoked. Popping a few ibuprofens and soaking in a warm, steamy bath rose to the top of her priority list; right after she drank her coffee.

A sexy smile graced his lips and he strolled toward her, his dimples twinkling. He handed her the cup and sat on the edge of the bed. "Rough night?"

Dakota didn't speak until after a few sips of strong brew. "How'd you know I take my coffee black?"

He shrugged. "According to you, we're perfect for each other. Since I like my coffee strong and black, I assumed you did, too."

She grinned at him over the rim of the mug. "You assumed right, Mr. Crosby."

"How'd you sleep? Or did you sleep?"

"A little, but what I really could use is something for this pounding headache."

Hamilton nodded toward the table next to the bed, and she spotted a bottle of water and ibuprofen. "Considering how much you drank after speaking to your father, I figured you'd probably need those this morning."

"I can't believe you're not married. You are truly a godsend. I don't know if I could've gotten through last night without you. Thank you."

"No problem. Glad I was there."

"We didn't discuss this yesterday, but how do you get paid for the services you've providing me?"

He leaned his arms back, propping himself up with his palms flat on the bed. Dakota started to move her legs, but she liked having him close. She had stayed up with him, falling asleep on the sofa. Since she couldn't remember climbing into bed, she assumed he had carried her.

"This situation is a little unusual. As of right now, there's no charge."

"You're doing this pro bono?"

"Something like that. No need to worry about how I'll be paid. Hopefully, we'll get an all-clear from Laz today and you'll be able to go back to your life."

Dakota didn't miss the way his appreciative gaze was taking her in. She could only imagine how awful she must look, but the desire radiating in his eyes said otherwise. Then again, he had already seen her at her worst, covered in blood. This morning was probably an improvement. "Any new developments?"

"Nothing new, but I'm glad you weren't the target. Now, we need to make sure that once you leave here, it'll be safe for you to return home." He stood. "Are you hungry?"

"A little, but I think I'm going to lay here a while longer. You're welcome to join me." She patted the other side of the bed and tried to keep her voice serious, but her lips twitched, fighting a smile.

Hamilton laughed. "You don't quit, do you?"

"Nope. Not when I really want something."

He released a long breath. "It's tempting, Dakota. Damn tempting, but I need to stay focused, alert while we're here. That'll be hard to do if you...if we...are in a compromising position."

"Or *positions*," she added, and he shook his head grinning.

"Unfortunately, I have to pass. Try to get some more sleep. You had a long day yesterday."

"I could sleep better if you're lying beside me," she said, giving it one more shot as he moved closer to the door. He chuckled again but didn't stop. "Oh well, I tried."

*

The moment Hamilton stepped out of Dakota's room, he released a breath he hadn't realized he'd been holding. Even when she wasn't feeling her best, she was still one of the most desirable women he'd ever met. He loved her fire, her sense of humor, and her resiliency. She was everything he hadn't known he wanted.

Too bad the timing is all wrong.

He pushed away from the wall and headed to the bedroom he'd slept in—or at least tried to sleep in. Staying up most of the night, keeping an eye on her just in case she had another bad dream, denied him much needed rest. Normally, with only four hours of sleep, he was good. But right now, he could use a little shut-eye.

Sitting on his bed, he dropped back and stared at the ceiling, his mind on Dakota's offer. Though he had almost married Jackie, a needy, insecure woman, Hamilton had always been attracted to badass, adventurous women who weren't afraid to go after what they desired. Dakota had those qualities in spades.

But he couldn't think of her without thinking about Wesley and remembering the shit he endured because of her father. Nor could he forget about Jackie's betrayal during the ordeal with Wesley. Between those two, it was a wonder he wanted anything to do with any woman.

And then along came Dakota. He wanted her. God, he wanted her.

His dick throbbed with need, and he slid his hand to his erection that pressed against his zipper. Despite his resistance to Dakota's invitations, Hamilton didn't know how much longer he could go without having her. Their attraction was too strong to keep ignoring.

When this situation is over and she's safe, no more holding back.

*

Dakota stumbled out of bed, yawned and ran her hands through her hair. She couldn't believe she had fallen back to sleep and had slept for three hours. Still, she didn't feel completely rested, but hunger pains had awakened her.

She headed to the bathroom to freshen up, then slipped into a T-shirt and a pair of shorts. She debated on tidying the bed or going in search of food and coffee.

Definitely coffee.

The house was quiet, and she wondered what Hamilton was up to. Moseying down the short hallway, Dakota slowed when she reached his bedroom door, but then stopped suddenly. An intense pool of warmth ricocheted inside of her and it took all she had to remain silent.

Stepping back a little as to not be seen, she took the opportunity to get a good look at Hamilton's profile as he stared down at the cell phone in his hand. His body was amazing in clothes. His muscles evident with every move he made. But seeing him without a shirt on took her breath away.

Her hands itched to touch his skin, run her fingers *all* over his sculpted body. His biceps bulged as he typed something into his phone. Then he tossed the device onto the bed and snatched up the T-shirt.

Dakota didn't know if she made a sound or if he sensed her near the door, but his gaze met hers. He turned fully toward her, his shirt still in his hands and her heart slammed against her chest.

Hot damn.

The man's body was absolute perfection.

"Hey, I didn't know you were awake. Everything okay?" he asked.

Hell no, everything wasn't okay!

She was in lust with a man whose professionalism and issues with her father kept him away from her, leaving her sexually frustrated at every turn. Now she was only allowed to look at God's best work—this man's incredible body.

No, she was not okay.

Her mind spun at the site of his wide shoulders that tapered down to a narrow waist. Flat abs hosted a wisp of hair that started just below his navel and disappeared behind the low waistband of his unbuttoned jeans.

Dakota felt like a damn pervert for imagining all the ways she could love on that body, and the gifts she could discover behind the zipper of his pants.

Her gaze went back up to the impressive ink, a tribal tattoo. Parts of it had peeked out above his button-down shirt the day before, making her curious, but now she had the pleasure of seeing the design. The tat started along the right side of his torso and trailed up his chest and wrapped around his right shoulder and bicep. The sight only made him that much more intriguing.

Just one touch. Just one little touch. Or...maybe a lick.

Clearly, she needed to get laid. She had never obsessed over a man like this before.

"Dakota?"

Hearing her name snapped her out of the trance and Dakota brought her attention up to his handsome face. She ran her sweaty palms down the sides of her shorts, suddenly wanting to strip out of her clothes. She had never thrown herself at a man, but there was something about Hamilton that made her stupid...and horny as hell.

"Dakota?" He moved forward and she took a step back. She wanted to respect his feelings and professional morals, but...

"Um...damn, Hamilton. Why the hell do you walk around with fucking clothes on?" she yelled.

"What?" he asked, confusion in his tone.

She turned and stomped away from the door, ignoring him when he called her name. He was right yesterday when he said they might have to keep their distance while at the house. Anything else was just torture. He must've had willpower of steel.

"No one who looks like you should cover up all of that...that perfection! Urgh!" she growled and stormed into her bedroom, trying to slam the door behind her, but he caught it before it closed.

"You care to tell me what's wrong with you?" he asked and leaned against the doorjamb, shirtless.

"What's wrong with me? You're what's wrong with me! "She poked his chest with her finger, feeling as if she was jabbing a brick wall. "I'm weak, all right. I'll admit it. I'm so frickin' weak and turned on right now, I'm about ready to jump you."

The corner of his lips tilted into a sexy grin, and her body tingled as warmth spread through her. But when he pushed away from the door jamb, every sexual nerve in her body went on high alert.

"I suggest you not come any closer because I can't be responsible for what I might do to you," she said. He probably thought she was kidding, but now he was playing with fire whether he knew it or not.

"That's right. You have a mean right hook and from what I hear, you have the ability to kill a man with your bare hands and feet."

She gave an unladylike snort. "Killing you is the last thing I have in mind. What I'd rather do is—"

"Just stop talking." Hamilton tugged on the tail of her T-shirt and pulled her closer. Then he shocked her when he lifted the garment over her head and tossed it to the floor.

For the first time since meeting him, Dakota stood speechless. Their gazes collided and she shivered when the back of his chilly fingers grazed her bare breast. Her senses were on high alert as he dragged his large hand slowly down her side, dipping at her waist before sliding over the curve of her hip. All the while their gazes never wavered from each other.

She had a feeling anything she experienced with other men in the past wouldn't compare to whatever happened between her and Hamilton. The thought thrilled her to the tip of her toes, sending a wave of heat pulsing through her veins.

"You talk about my body…" He unfastened her shorts and they slid down her legs and puddled around her ankles before she kicked them off. The tiny pair of lace panties went next. "I've been dreaming about yours and that was before I saw all of...all of this." He waved his hand up and down at her body the way she'd done to him moments ago.

"Well, um...I guess we're on the same page. So, what are you going to do about it? And um...what about your rules?"

"Fuck my rules."

Chapter Fourteen

Before Dakota could blink, she was crushed against Hamilton, his mouth devouring hers. For a man to have exhibited such control moments ago, he wasn't holding back now. Her body responded instantly, aroused by the way he kissed her, the way his hands boldly explored every dip and valley of her curves. But when he placed fiery kisses along the length of her neck, lingering behind her ear while his large hands settled on her breasts, she practically leaped out of her skin.

Already he had ignited her erogenous zones and she whimpered with each kiss, every nip, and lick as his mouth worked its way down her body. When he lightly bit her nipple, Dakota squeaked and almost lost it. His tongue twirled around the hardened peak, sending a wave of heat pulsing to the center of her core. Her knees weakened, but she refused to lose control.

"Okay, okay, wait." She pushed lightly against his shoulders.

"Wait?" Hamilton said, his voice thick with desire, and his chest heaving up and down.

"Yes. No. I mean...I want to see you. All of you." Her breaths came fast and unsteady as she brushed her hand down the center of his chest and stopped at the waistband. "Take 'em off."

His gaze never leaving hers, Hamilton retrieved a condom from his wallet, setting it on top of the tall chest next to them. A rush of excitement, like Dakota got when skydiving, coursed through her body as he unzipped his jeans and let them ease down his muscular thighs.

She had to touch him.

Hamilton sucked in a breath when her hands made contact with his torso. Dakota worked her way up his abs, and let her fingers linger near the bold tattoo. He flinched when the tip of her finger grazed his nipple and she smiled. Hmm...sensitive.

Her gaze went lower. Boxer briefs. Nice. Sexy.

Looking at him, there was no way he could hide his desire for her, not that he was trying. The bulge behind his shorts was impressive and she itched to see all of him.

Hamilton cupped the back of her head with one hand, bringing her lips to his as he struggled to kick off his pants. She loved how he could be so tender one minute and then a beast the next. The pressure of his lips increased against her mouth with a hunger that defied any type of control. Their tongues dueled, exploring the inner recesses of each other's mouths.

Dakota wanted more. She needed to feel him, touch all of him. She slipped her hands inside the waistband of his shorts and pushed them down as far as her arms would allow. Her insides churned and liquid heat pooled at her core when she wrapped her hand around his shaft.

Goodness. He was big...and thick...and long. Her hand slid smoothly up and down his length, squeezing, tugging, and loving the deep masculine sounds she elicited from him. When she ran the pad of her thumb over the tip and applied a little pressure, a growl rumbled from his chest and he ripped his mouth from hers, cursing.

"Don't move." Breathing hard, Hamilton snatched up the foil packet and ripped it open before quickly sheathing himself. Dakota liked seeing him like this. Hurried, undisciplined, and basically not himself. Not the man who'd been unshakeable, her rock, for almost twenty-four hours.

Dakota gasped when he lifted her off the floor, but her legs went automatically around his waist. Her bare back touched the wall and Hamilton lowered her slightly, lining her up with his erection. A shock wave of desire rocked her to the core when the head of his shaft teased at her opening.

"D—Don't play with me, Ham. Please." She wasn't above begging for what she wanted and barely got the words out as her pulse raced. The apex between her thighs throbbed with need and she moved against him, needing him inside of her. "Quit pl—"

Dakota's mouth dropped open when he slid between her slick folds, and she released a whimper as she adjusted to his size. Her moans pierced the air before his lips found hers again, kissing her with a need that rivaled hers as they moved together.

Hamilton stared into her eyes and thoughts of everything else flew from her mind as he thrust into her, but then slid out excruciatingly slow before plowing into her again. He did that several times, rocking his hips and pushing her closer to the brink of an orgasm, pleasure building within her.

Dakota didn't want this to be over before they got started good, but as his pace increased, that's exactly what was about to happen. She tightened her legs around him, slowing his moves and then started rotating her hips. The louder his ragged breathing got, the faster she moved until they were both frenzied, her release inching closer to the edge.

Hamilton tightened his hold on her thighs and opened them wider. His thrusts were harder, and he went deeper, and Dakota's eyes slammed shut and her nails dug into his upper arms as she tried to hold on. She lost it. Her screams filled the quietness of the room as her orgasm came fast and hard, stripping her of all control.

Even when she collapsed against him, Hamilton didn't stop. He kept driving into her until he soon followed, groaning his release and falling against her.

Pinning Dakota to the wall, he panted loudly, his mouth near her ear as his forehead pressed against the wall. She dropped her head back, struggling to get air into her lungs as he maintained a death-grip hold on her.

"That was amazing," she huffed out, holding his handsome face between her hands and kissing his lips. Then she laid her head on his sweat-slicked shoulder because she didn't have the energy to do much else.

"Yeah, it was," he wheezed. They stood that way, with her back against the wall and his manhood still buried deep inside of her until he eventually pulled out. "Hold on."

She did as he asked and wrapped her arms tightly around his neck, still unable to lift her head from his shoulder. He pushed his briefs the rest of the way down his legs and then left them in a puddle on the floor while he carried her to the bed. Dakota curled onto her side the moment her body touched the sheets and struggled to keep her eyes open. Every muscle felt limp.

She watched through barely opened lids as Hamilton made his way to the bathroom. That was when she noticed the ankle holster. A laugh bubbled inside of her. It was no wonder he struggled to get free of his pants and underwear. They'd probably gotten hung up on the pistol handle.

What a badass, she thought as her eyes drifted shut. In her mind, she replayed what they'd just done, feeling deliciously satisfied and looking forward to when they'd do it again.

Dakota dozed off. When she opened her eyes, Hamilton, clad in his briefs, covered her with a sheet. He set his gun and holster on the bedside table, and she scooted over to make room for his large frame.

He said nothing when he settled onto the bed and pulled her close, her head resting on his chest. Dakota wondered what changed his mind. He'd been thwarting her advances and then all of sudden, he was inside of her. She understood him wanting to remain focused on guarding her, but she had no regrets. However, she could almost hear the wheels in his head turning.

She tilted her head back to look at him and traced his perfectly groomed goatee with her finger. "Do you want to talk about it?"

"Nope."

"Do you want to do it again?"

"Hell, yeah," he mumbled.

She lifted her head with renewed energy and grinned. "Well, what are you waiting for?"

A hint of a smile played around his mouth. "What am I going to do with you?" His words were spoken so low, Dakota wasn't sure if he was asking her or talking to himself. Or maybe it was a rhetorical question.

"I have some ideas."

"I'm sure you do, but save them." Hamilton turned onto his side facing her, his hand resting on her hip. "What just happened...can't happen again while we're here."

"But once we leave..."

"We'll see."

Dakota scurried out of his hold and sat up, letting the sheet drop to her waist. "Not good enough. There's something between us and I think we should see where it goes."

Hamilton flopped onto his back, his frustration with her evident. He placed his forearm over his eyes as if that would stop her from saying what was on her mind. But his body distracted her. She couldn't help herself. She couldn't stop her hand from going to his six-pack, tracing the muscular ridges of his upper body.

Yep, perfection.

"I know I come on a little strong," she said, "but when I want something, I go after it. With that said though, for now on, I'll follow your lead. Just know that I'm *very* impatient. I won't wait around forever."

That got his attention and he lifted his arm slightly and stared at her.

Okay, maybe she would wait for him. The man was so damn irresistible, especially when that intense gaze nailed her in place. When it came to men, she had chosen wrong too many times to count, but Dakota had a good feeling about Hamilton. She already knew he was different, special. All she had to do was show him that she was, too, and that they should build upon their attraction to each other.

It wasn't until her stomach rumbled did they break eye contact.

"I don't know about you, but I've worked up an appetite." Dakota straddled him with the intention of climbing over him to get out the bed. But she made sure to grind against his semi-erect package, laughing at the way he growled. Before he could hold her in place, she slipped from his grasp. Then she grabbed some underwear and sweats and headed to the bathroom.

He'd be a fool to let her get away, and Dakota already knew he was no fool.

Chapter Fifteen

Hamilton thought he would regret breaking his rule about sleeping with a client, but if anything, he wanted Dakota all over again. The fact that he wasn't technically working for her gave him some peace, but there was still that little nagging something that had him questioning his decision.

Sitting at the breakfast bar, he studied her moving around the kitchen, preparing them both a sandwich. Her loose-fitting sweats did nothing to hide the tight body he knew was hidden beneath the clothing. He was so screwed. What the hell was he going to do about her? She intrigued him beyond understanding, and once this mess was over, he couldn't see himself walking away.

"Do you want tomatoes?" Dakota asked over her shoulder but then turned to him fully. "You look tired. Maybe you should take a nap."

He almost laughed out loud as she regarded him seriously. Hell yeah, he was tired. He had followed her into the bathroom after her comment about not waiting around, and they'd had sex in the shower. Then another quickie in the bed. Not only was he exhausted, but he clearly needed his head examined. His common sense checked out when it came to her.

"No tomatoes and I'm fine."

She finished the sandwich and placed it, along with potato chips, in front of him.

"If you're concerned that I'll leave the house while you're asleep, I promise to be right here…or lying next to you when you wake up."

"You're too much," he said under his breath, trying to keep from laughing, knowing it would only encourage her to keep going. He had never been a big talker, especially after sex, but she insisted on carrying on a conversation whether he responded or not.

"I'm just sayin'. I know I probably wore you out this afternoon. I'll understand if you need to recharge." Her commentary continued as they ate. "We're good together. As I knew we would be."

Finally, something he could agree with. In the short amount of time he'd known her, he found that they were compatible, especially when it came to sex.

When she finally stopped talking, he glanced at her, surprised to find her staring down at her plate.

Hamilton wiped his mouth. "What's wrong?" He couldn't believe he was thinking this, but he liked it better when she was running off at the mouth. At least then he knew what was on her mind. When she still didn't speak, he placed his hand on her back and shook her a little. "Dakota?"

"I—I just remembered."

"Remembered what?"

"Today would've been my mother's fifty-sixth birthday. The day is almost over and I—I hadn't thought about it. I forgot."

Hamilton rubbed her back, unsure of what to say. Instead of saying anything, he stood and pulled her into his arms. "But you didn't forget," he said against her hair. "Is there anything special you usually do on her birthday?"

She allowed him to comfort her for a moment before stepping out of his hold, and they both reclaimed their seats.

"Nothing specific. She was cremated, so I don't do the whole flowers and grave thing. My father once told me she wouldn't want that anyway. He said she would want us to remember her as vibrant and full of life. Not buried in the ground."

Hamilton knew Wesley had been married and had lost his wife many years ago, but he couldn't for the life of him remember anything about a daughter. "How old were you when she died?"

"Five. I don't remember much about her. Only little things like how good she smelled and that she would always take me to amusement parks and fairs." She smiled, clearly remembering a happier time. "Her name was Katrina. My father says that I have her eyes, her fire, and stubbornness." She laughed and Hamilton smiled. He could picture an older version of Dakota.

They sat in silence and he thought about his parents. He couldn't imagine losing either of them, especially his mother. Being married to a cop and raising three boys, she was undeniably the rock of their family.

"How did your mom die?" he asked, after debating on whether to go there with his questions.

"Car accident. It was raining and she lost control of the car. From what I'm told, the vehicle spun out and hit a light pole."

"I'm so sorry, Dakota." Hamilton pulled her close and placed a kiss on her temple. "I hate your family had to go through something like that."

"I was in the back seat," she added quietly.

Surprise kept Hamilton from moving, waiting for her to continue.

"I remember her crying while she was driving."

"Were you hurt?"

She shook her head. "Only a few cuts and bruises. I guess I was invincible even back then." She tried to smile, but it faded on her lips. "My father blamed himself for years for her death, saying she had taken off in the car after they'd argued. He had just started his talent agency, putting all his time and money into the business. They argued about him working too much, but I also remember them kissing and hugging a lot whenever they were together."

This time she really did smile, her honey-brown eyes glittering with unshed tears.

"My father is many things, most not good, but I think he truly loved her. He took her death hard, not because he felt responsible, but he also said that he would never love another like he loved her. After that, I rarely saw him. He poured himself into his work. My grandmother—his mother—pretty much raised me." Dakota stood suddenly and gathered their empty plates. "Okay, that's enough. I'm sorry for casting a shadow on our amazing day."

"Not a problem. I'm glad you told me." The information didn't change his feelings about Wesley, but Hamilton had even more respect for Dakota and her resilience. Their childhood had been very different, with him having both of his parents and in a loving relationship. They might've had minor disagreements on occasion, but nothing too serious.

"You're a good listener," Dakota said.

"Thanks. It's—" They both froze when they heard a rustling sound outside the kitchen window. "Get to the bathroom." Adrenaline pulsed through Hamilton's veins as he pulled the pistol from his ankle holster. "Now!" he said when Dakota didn't move.

"Okaaay." She hurried off.

Once he was sure she was in the bathroom, he headed to the back hallway. It was almost seven o'clock in the evening; with dusk slowly approaching, he'd be able to see anyone lurking around.

He reached the back door that sported a small curtain-covered window. Slightly nudging the material aside with the tip of his gun, he peeked out. The footsteps he heard moments ago sounded like they were heading to the backyard, but he couldn't see much through the window.

He eased the door open and stepped out onto the concrete stoop, which was when he spotted movement on the side of the house. Staying in the shadows, he moved silently along the backside of the house and stopped when the tall figure came into view.

"What the hell, man? You tryin' to get yourself killed?" he growled quietly, lowering his weapon.

"I could ask you the same damn thing," Kenton snapped, slipping the gun he had in his hand to the back waistband of his jeans and covering it with the tail of the shirt. "Why the heck haven't you been answering your phone? Mase has been calling you for the past hour."

"Shit." His phone was on the bathroom counter in the bedroom. Whenever anyone from the office called while a specialist was on duty and they couldn't be reached, someone on the team was sent out to investigate.

Kenton just stared at Hamilton. At first, there was concern in his eyes until a stupid grin spread across his face.

"Mase wanted me to make sure the woman you're guarding hadn't kicked your ass. His words, not mine. But clearly, she's done something to you. This has to be a first. You never fall off the grid. You okay?"

"Yeah, fine." Hamilton turned on his heels and headed for the back door.

I'm never going to live this down.

This was why he had rules. He prided himself on being on top of everything, which meant no mistakes. It also meant no one had ever been killed on his watch, which is exactly what could've happened while he was messing around with Dakota.

"Mason speaks highly of this woman." Kenton followed behind him. "I hear she's a hottie and a stuntwoman. I can't wait to meet her."

Hamilton pulled up short, almost causing Kenton to bump into him. "Keep talking and you're going to find yourself with every shitty assignment that comes through the doors of Supreme Security."

Kenton burst out laughing. "Oh, so it's like that, huh? Now I really have to meet her." He moved around Hamilton and sauntered into the house.

When Hamilton walked in, he didn't find Dakota in the bathroom. Instead, she was standing in the kitchen, leaning against one of the counters, arms folded across her chest. He glared at her.

"What did I tell you about the rules?"

"You said, *fuck* my rules."

Hamilton cursed under his breath, running his hand over his head to keep from reaching for her throat. He was going to kill her. Before this was all over, he was sure he was going to end up strangling this woman or taping up her smart mouth.

"Hi, I'm Dakota," she said to Kenton, who was grinning like he held the world's deepest secret. "You must be our prowler?"

"Kenton Bailey. Pleasure to meet you," he said, chuckling. "Not a prowler, but I did stop by to make sure you guys were okay."

"I thought I recognized you. I saw you talking to Ham that day I was at Supreme."

"*Ham,*" Kenton said in a mocking tone when he turned to Hamilton, probably surprised she was using his nickname. "Why didn't you introduce me to Dakota then? I probably could have ended up with this detail."

"Man, shut up." Hamilton left the room and went in search of his cell phone. He knew early on that Dakota would be a distraction he couldn't afford, and he'd been right. He hadn't even thought about the device and now wondered if he had missed any other calls.

He snatched up the phone and stepped back into the bedroom as he scrolled through his missed calls.

"I like her."

"Good. Now stay the hell away from her," he said to Kenton without looking up from the phone.

"It's like that, huh?"

On that, Hamilton glanced up. "Yeah, it is." He wasn't exactly sure what he was saying, but a possessiveness he hadn't experienced in a long time descended upon him. He didn't want any other man near her. Not even one of his guys.

"Gotcha. I'm going to say bye to Dakota and then head out. I'll be sure to spread the word around the office that she's off-limits." Kenton walked out of the room, laughing. Hamilton already knew he was going to be sorry for missing Mason's call, and even more so now that he had suggested that Dakota meant something to him.

A short while later, when he strolled into the kitchen, his phone vibrated in his hand and Laz's name popped up on the screen.

"Hello," he answered, and his gaze went immediately to Dakota who was watching him, her gorgeous eyes suddenly full of worry. He wondered if she sensed this was about her, or if she saw something on his face that might've clued her in.

"The suspects are in custody, and we're positive Sonny was the target."

Hamilton sighed with relief. "Good to hear."

"One of the dumbasses in the car bragged about the hit on social media." Laz explained how they had tracked down the two guys who were in the car and had just picked up the shooter.

"Okay. Does that mean it's safe for Dakota to return home?"

"If you're asking me if she's in any danger, no, I don't think so. I reached out to a couple of my CIs. So far, her name hasn't come up as a possible loose end, and we've kept her name quiet as far as the media. We believe we have everyone involved."

"That's good." They hadn't watched television since hearing the news report regarding the shooting.

"Something else you might be interested in knowing."

"What's that?"

"Wesley Bradford's vehicle was run off the road this morning in my jurisdiction. He's definitely convinced someone is after him, says he's received another threat last night."

When Wesley showed up at Supreme, Hamilton had no doubt the guy thought someone was after him. He had too much ego to seek help unless he really had to.

"He's hired personal security from your competitors, but I have a feeling they're not going to last long. The man is an asshole. He almost got arrested for disorderly conduct while filing his report. Told the desk sergeant he was a paper-pushing loser, among other things."

Hamilton didn't give a damn about Wesley. All he cared about...

"Before you ask, the threatening message included nothing about Dakota. Unless you'd prefer to keep her all to yourself, I think you can let her go home."

Hamilton didn't miss the amusement in his friend's voice. Though as tempting as it was to keep her to himself, he wasn't sure if that was a good idea. He hated Wesley, but he really liked spending time with Dakota. Unfortunately, he didn't know if he could separate the two.

"Thanks for the suggestion. I'll fill Dakota in."

Laz chuckled. "Ham, she seems like a nice lady. If you like her, and I know you do, don't let the bad blood between you and her old man get in the way. Besides, she's very easy on the eyes."

Laz disconnected the call before giving Hamilton a chance to respond.

"I can leave?" Dakota asked.

Hamilton relayed all that Laz had told him, except for the part of him keeping Dakota to himself. Fidgeting with the sleeve of her sweatshirt, he watched as she moved away from him.

"I'll give my father a call later, or maybe I'll stop by his office tomorrow to find out what's up with him. But...I'm glad I wasn't the target and that no one knows I was there, but I don't think I can stay at my apartment. It would be a little too weird."

She had mentioned that her and Tymico's lease was up in a couple of weeks.

"Can you move into your new place sooner? Or is there someone else who can put you up for a few days?" Hamilton asked. He started to suggest her staying with her father but changed his mind.

"I'm not sure if I can move into the new place, but I think I'll stay at a hotel while Ty and I figure out our next steps."

"Remember what we talked about. No one can know that you were in that lobby at the time of the shooting."

She nodded. "I know. I won't say anything. Would you mind taking me to my place so that I can pack up some of my clothes and get my car?"

"I don't mind at all. How about we leave in twenty minutes?"

"That's fine." She started toward the room she'd been using but turned back to him.

"I don't know what happened between you and my father, but I'm not him, Hamilton. What went on between you two has nothing to do with me."

"I know."

She moved closer and he stood stock-still. All he wanted to do was pull her into his arms and taste her sweet lips one more time before they left. But he restrained, knowing he wouldn't be able to stop at just one kiss.

"I like you," she said, as her hands did a slow crawl up his arms. "There's something between us, and I know you feel it, too. Since I'm not in danger and I don't need a bodyguard, you and I should explore this attraction between us."

"I—"

"Don't say no."

He hadn't planned to say no. "How about we meet up for a drink Friday night?"

126

Chapter Sixteen

Dakota stood outside the door of Bradford's Talent Agency, her father's office, debating on whether to go in. After Hamilton dropped her off at the hotel the night before, she had called her dad, hoping he'd mention the incident from the other day. He hadn't, only making her more concerned about his well-being.

They might not get along, but they were the only family each of them had, and it was time they worked on rebuilding their relationship.

Pushing open the thick wooden door to the office, Dakota stepped in and the first person she saw was Wesley's long-time secretary. "Hey, stranger," Dakota greeted.

Lynn beamed. "Oh, my goodness." The grandmotherly woman with her gray hair in a tight bun at the back of her head, and stylishly dressed strutted around the desk. She pulled Dakota into a loving hug. "Where have you been? I haven't seen you in months."

"Oh, I've been around. I've missed you," Dakota said, returning the woman's hug.

"Are you still spending most of your time on the west coast? Your dad mentioned you had a few assignments out there."

"Nope, I've been here for over a month. Just busy with a new project." They caught up for a few minutes with Lynn filling Dakota in on the staff changes and the number of new clients Wesley had acquired. He went through more staff members than most people went through toothbrushes. Though he paid well, he wasn't the easiest person to work for.

"Did Wes know you were coming?" Lynn reclaimed her seat behind the desk.

"No, it's a surprise. I figured I'd swing by on my way to work and invite him to dinner later." Dakota glanced at the numerous photos of her father's clients. Mixed in among the familiar were several new faces.

"That's lovely, dear. He's been working so much. It would be good for him to do something fun. I know how much he misses you."

She missed him too, but no matter how they tried, they just didn't get along, especially lately. That's why she kept her distance, only talking to and seeing him on occasion. Hopefully, they could change that negative dynamic.

"He's meeting with someone right now but let me call him. He'll probably be glad for the interrup—"

"Wes, you owe me!" A woman's voice carried to the outer office. Dakota could only hear every couple of words, but whatever they were discussing was getting more heated.

"Who's in there?" she asked Lynn.

"Zondra Monroe."

Dakota rolled her eyes. Her nemesis. They'd started in the business around the same time and were often up for the same roles early on. That was when Wesley was Dakota's agent, making her the victor each time.

The door swung open and Zondra stormed out, her long hair whipping around her face.

"And don't come back until you get some talent!" Wesley yelled.

"Screw you! I can do better than you anyway!" Zondra screamed back and stumbled when she saw Dakota.

Grabbing hold of the wall, she righted herself and acted as if nothing happened.

"Hello, Zondra." Dakota struggled to keep a straight face.

Instead of responding, Zondra gave Dakota the finger and blasted out the door.

Lynn gasped. "I *cannot* believe a grown woman behaves like that. Each time she comes in here, they go at it like alley cats. Why does she keep coming back?"

That's a good question, and what was Zondra talking about when she said he owed her?

Instead of voicing her thoughts to Lynn, Dakota said, "She probably wants the big bucks my dad demands for his clients." Dakota strolled toward her father's office and stopped in the doorway. "Hey, Dad. I see you're still making enemies."

Wesley startled. "Dee Dee, I didn't know you were here." He reached for something, and Dakota spotted the nine-millimeter on his desk.

Shocked, she hurried and closed the door. "A gun? Really?" He quickly shoved it into the desk drawer before standing. "Do you have a permit for that? Do you even know how to use a gun?"

"Yes, to both questions." Wesley hugged her, and Dakota wrapped her arms around him. "What are you doing here?" he asked when they separated, and he returned to his seat.

Ignoring his question, Dakota dropped down into the chair in front of the desk. "What did Zondra want? She left out of here pretty steamed."

He waved off the comment with a flick of his hand. "Don't mind her. That girl has issues. I will never represent her. She's too hard to work with."

Dakota laughed. "Hard to work with? I'd think that would make you two a perfect fit. Do you think she's behind the threats? Is that why you had the gun out?"

"Like I told you the other day, I don't know who's sending me those letters. Which is why I don't want you running around town without a bodyguard. Hearing about that shooting at your building scared me to death. What if it had been you? If someone goes after you because of me, Dee Dee, I'd never forgive myself."

Flashbacks of the shooting pierced Dakota's mind. She no longer felt paralyzed by the memories, but only hours ago, she had to force herself to leave the hotel. Even then, she kept looking over her shoulder, scared someone would catch her off guard.

"I've been so worried about you," her father continued. "I know you think you can take care of yourself, but it wouldn't hurt to have security, just in case."

"I already told you. There's only one way I'll agree to have someone follow me around."

Wesley shot out of his chair. "Don't start that mess. I don't want you anywhere near that man!" he spat and turned to the window behind his desk. He stood rigid for a moment as if expecting her to argue. When she didn't, he released a drawn-out sigh.

Dakota shook her head, deciding not to go there about Hamilton. "Dad, what happened to your security detail?"

Her father didn't respond but then turned to her with narrowed eyes. "How do you know I hired security?"

Crap! Laz had told Hamilton, and Hamilton had mentioned it to her, but it wasn't common knowledge. "I—I assumed since you stormed out of Supreme Security last week you would've found another company."

He hesitated before saying, "I did, but it didn't work out."

"When are you going to stop alienating everyone you meet?"

"Why do you assume it was me who was the problem?" he asked indignantly, as if pissing people off wasn't his M.O.

"Because I know you. It's what you do." She walked over to him. He seemed to have aged ten years since she'd seen him days ago. This situation was really weighing on him. "Dad, you know how you worry about me? Well, I worry about you, too. That's why I came by, to make sure you're doing okay."

"You don't have to worry about me, sweetheart. I carry protection and instead of a full-time bodyguard, I have a driver who has a military background." Wesley placed his arm around her shoulder and kissed her on the forehead. "He'll serve as security when I'm out in public or traveling. And now I want to make sure you're taken care of. You should seriously consider getting—"

"How about dinner tonight? My treat," Dakota interrupted, not wanting to argue. She pulled out of his hold. Now that she had spent time with Hamilton and saw how his team had come through for her, there was no way she would consider another agency outside of Supreme.

Wesley smiled for the first time since she had arrived. "I can't remember the last time you and I had dinner together. I would love that, but you don't have to treat. It'll be nice to spend time with you."

"It'll be good to hang out with you, too," she said. "I have to work this afternoon, but I can pick you up around—"

"There is no way in hell I'm letting you drive me anywhere."

"Wh—"

"Dee Dee, you drive like a damn maniac." He chuckled. "No. I'll have my driver pick you up."

"Fine, but where's the fun in that?" Dakota joked but then turned serious. "Did you remember Mom's birthday?"

"Of course." He turned back to the window. "Not a day goes by that I don't think about your mother. I still miss her and wish I could go back all those years ago and do things differently."

Dakota stood next to him, wishing she could have had more time with her. Her father used to talk about her often. Sharing stories of how they met and recalling funny tales of her mother's shenanigans around the house. He often said

Dakota reminded him of her, not just in looks, but also their personalities and need for adventure.

"She would've been pissed on how I've been living my life," her father said, interrupting Dakota's thoughts. "But she would've been so proud of the woman you've become."

Dakota smiled at the thought, and they both turned at the knock on Wesley's door before it swung open.

"Hey, why didn't anyone tell me we were having a family meeting?" Tymico joked as she walked in carrying a large white paper bag with grease stains.

"Hey, you. What are you doing here?" Dakota moved across the room, giving her friend a quick hug. "I thought you were still out of town."

"I returned a little while ago, and thought I'd bring Wesley lunch."

Dakota frowned, but before she could question that, Wesley approached, gathering them both into a hug.

"I feel like the luckiest man alive." He kissed them both on their cheeks. "My two favorite girls came to see me at the same time. That hasn't happened in years."

"I was concerned when you called me the other day looking for Dakota," Tymico said, setting the bag of food on the round conference table. "Since you didn't sound like yourself, I decided then that when I got back in town, I'd stop by and visit you."

"If only my daughter could be that thoughtful." Wesley quirked a brow at Dakota.

Tymico unpacked the bag, the pungent scent of garlic and other spices filling the space. "Dee, why haven't you been answering your phone? I've been calling you. I was going to see if you wanted to come here with me, but I guess we had the same idea."

"Oh, I forgot my cell at home." Dakota hadn't thought to grab her phone when she returned the night before to pack enough clothes for a few days. She wouldn't have one at all if Hamilton hadn't given her the burner phone she had used while at the safe house.

"I hope you guys are hungry. I stopped by that little bistro up the street. There should be enough for all of us."

"It smells delicious, but I can't stay. I need to get to work," Dakota said, distracted at how her father pulled out a chair for Tymico to sit at the table. Her friend smiled up at him as if he were an Egyptian prince. Now that Dakota thought about it, her dad totally lit up when her best friend walked in. Now they seemed really comfortable as if they ate together all the time.

"You sure you don't want some of this, Dee Dee? There's a lot of food here." Wesley bit into a steak sandwich.

"I'm sure, but you guys enjoy lunch." Dakota headed to the door. "Ty, I'll talk to you later, and Dad, I'm looking forward to dinner tonight."

As Dakota left, she overheard her father invite Tymico to dinner with them. Dakota should've been glad about the possibility of the three of them dining together. But instead, she walked out feeling conflicted about her friend's familiarity with Wesley.

She's treating my father better than I do. I have to do better if I want our father-daughter relationship to go back to what it used to be.

Chapter Seventeen

Dakota handed her car key to the valet standing in front of Club Masquerade, the club Mason's family owned. She gave her name to security who monitored the entrance and waited as he checked the VIP list. Friday night hadn't come fast enough. She'd been thinking about Hamilton all week and couldn't wait to see him again.

"Welcome, Ms. Sherrod. We've been expecting you," he said and spoke into a mouthpiece attached to his black suit jacket. "Ham, your guest is here."

The security guard gave a slight nod and smiled at Dakota as he held the door open for her.

It pays to know people, Dakota thought. The few times she had stopped by the club, she'd been one of those who had to stand in line outside hoping to be allowed in.

Entering the enormous space, she squinted until her eyes slowly adjusted to the dim lighting. "Excuse me. Sorry," she said as she weaved around people hovering near the entrance. As she blended into the crowd, music blared through the speakers and right away Dakota's head bobbed and her body rocked to Beyoncé's latest hit.

This is what she needed tonight. After a busy work week, having a drink or two, letting loose and soaking up the energy surrounding her was in order. Seems that was the case for many others. The place was packed with people talking loudly, laughing with friends and having a good time.

All right, Hamilton. Where are you?

She lifted up on tip-toes and stretched her neck searching for him, wondering how he'd find her or how she'd see him in the large crowd. They hadn't talked in a few days. Not since the first night after leaving the safe house. He had called then to check on her and to confirm their plans to have a drink. It had taken all her self-control not to call him during the week, especially at nighttime.

Dakota shifted to her left and a sweet thrill skittered up her spine when she spotted him in the distance. His tall powerful frame stood in the middle of the staircase that led to the VIP section and he glanced around, searching for her. Tonight, he wore a dark suit that molded over his muscular body, emphasizing his wide shoulders and thick biceps while highlighting his commanding presence. The man looked absolutely delicious.

"Dance with me," a deep voice said from behind her.

Dakota turned, stunned to see a familiar face. "Lester?" Normally she only saw him when he parked his food truck outside of the movie set, but today he actually looked human. Gone was the greasy hair, and the nose and lip ring he sported proudly. He had even shaved, getting rid of the raggedy scruff on his face. "You clean up well," she finally said.

"Thanks." He grinned, apparently thinking her compliment gave him permission to touch her. He wrapped his arm around her waist and leaned in close. She was reminded of what Hamilton had said about Lester, claiming they were an item. She hadn't stopped by the food truck in days and hadn't had a chance to address that declaration.

"Funny running into you here. Dance with me."

Dakota eased out of his hold. "I can't, but I'm glad I ran into you," she said loudly over the music. "You need to stop telling people we're dating and getting married."

He lowered his head within inches of hers, alcohol tainting his breath. "It's only a matter of time, sweetheart."

Dakota chuckled at his arrogance. "That's never gonna happen. So you might as well move on. I'll see you around."

"Come on, Dakota," he pleaded. "Just one dance. Give me a chance to get to know—"

"Find someone else, man."

Dakota recognized Hamilton's voice, and even if he hadn't spoken, with the sudden heat that shot up her back she would've known he was close.

"Man, I saw her first," Lester said, sounding like a three-year-old and then grabbed her arm with force, surprising the hell out of her.

"Lester, I suggest you—"

"Let her go or lose a hand." The lethal rumble of Hamilton's tone left no doubt about his intentions. That's when Dakota saw a couple of monster-sized security guards coming from two different directions and heading toward them.

Dakota tried easing out of his hold, hoping to thwart the tension building between the two men, but Lester gripped her arm a little tighter.

"Let. Her. Go," Hamilton said in a deadly calm voice.

"Or what?" Lester taunted. "You think y—"

With lightning speed, Hamilton snatched the guy up by the front of his shirt. "Let's go."

"Get off me!" Lester jerked, but Hamilton didn't loosen his grip and started to drag the guy away. He hadn't taken two steps before his men were by his side.

"Get him out of here. Make sure he never returns."

"Let me go! You're not getting away with this!" Lester yelled until he was out of earshot.

Hamilton turned back to Dakota and cupped her cheek with such gentleness, it was as if the last five minutes hadn't happened. "You okay?"

"I'm fine, but you know I could've handled him, right?"

"Right. I forgot you can take care of yourself," he said, staring at her lips, but didn't make a move to kiss her.

Dakota slipped her hands beneath his jacket, loving the way his muscles contracted beneath her touch. "That doesn't mean I don't want you coming to my rescue. And was that jealousy I sensed? Surely, you're not the jealous type, Mr. Crosby," she teased.

Without smiling, Hamilton leaned in close enough for them to kiss. "Actually, I am. So, remember that." The huskiness of his voice washed over her like an intimate caress, and then he covered her mouth with his. The greediness of the kiss wiped away any more questions and everything and everybody around them faded away. It became abundantly clear he was staking his claim.

Knees weakening, Dakota fisted his shirt and held on to him until someone bumped into them, jarring them out of their lip-lock.

"Mmm, I like the way you say hello," she said, dazed, her eyes slow to open and when they did, he was staring down at her.

He placed another quick kiss on her lips and tapped his ear. "Yeah, I have her. Thanks," Hamilton said through a concealed mouthpiece, as he gave additional instructions to whoever he was speaking to.

"Sorry about that. Let's head upstairs." He wrapped his arm around her, his hand resting on her hip as he shouldered them through the crowd. Dakota liked this domineering side of him.

He guided her deeper into the throng of people. Seemed everyone knew him, greeting him like an old friend. He didn't stop to talk. He and Dakota skirted around a few belly bar tables and past a spectacular circular glass bar. It was clearly the focal point of the first floor with the way it was illuminated, sparkling like something out of a futuristic movie.

They headed upstairs and along the way to a secluded corner of the large VIP section, Dakota stopped. "This is impressive," she said to Hamilton as they peered over the railing that overlooked the lower level. That vantage point gave her an imposing view of the club.

"Yeah, a lot of work went into this place, and it turned out perfectly. Mason's sister spearheaded the renovations and the designers captured the essence of what she, Mason, and his brother wanted."

They started moving again and once they were settled on a long black velvet sofa, a server came to take their drink order.

"So, did you know the guy downstairs?" Hamilton asked, resting his arm on the back of the sofa, creating an intimacy between them.

"Actually, that was Lester. He owns the food truck that—"

"Wait, the guy with the picture of you?"

She nodded. "Yep, that would be the one. I made it clear, before you tossed him out, that there is and will never be anything between him and me."

"Good."

"Why is that good?"

"Because I don't like the competition."

Dakota laughed, giddiness swirling inside of her at what he was implying. "Trust me, you don't have to worry about Lester," she said just as the server returned with their drinks.

"Here's to getting to know each other better," Hamilton said and they tap their glasses before she sipped her martini and he took a long drag from his beer bottle. "It's good seeing you again."

Dakota set her drink on the glass table in front of them. "You too." She almost said more about how much she had missed him, but didn't, wanting to follow his lead tonight and not come on too strong.

Besides, the way he looked at her with those dark, soulful eyes roused the butterflies fluttering inside her stomach. She was determined to play it cool and not let on that being in his presence did wicked things to her body.

"How have you been? I mean since the shooting. Have you returned to the apartment?"

Dakota sighed. She hadn't had a good night's sleep since the night before the shooting. Even in the comforts of a five-star hotel, she hadn't been able to close her eyes without seeing Sonny's face when he got shot.

"Your silence speaks volumes," Hamilton said. His hand caressed the back of her neck sending tingles through her body. Then he placed a lingering kiss on her lips and Dakota's insides melted just a little bit more. "Tell me what's going on."

"I normally can compartmentalize everything in my mind." She tapped her finger against her right temple. "But this, this shook me. You would think that with all the stunts I do, I could just treat the shooting as another stunt, but..."

"But it's not. Your stunts are usually choreographed. What you went through the other night was very real. When I was a cop, facing danger was a daily occurrence. After each obscene situation, you think—it can't get any weirder than this. And then you hit the streets again and bam, the day's drama is as jacked up as the one before. You just pray that you can keep it together and not succumb to the craziness in the world."

Dakota shook her head. "I can only imagine. What made you become a cop knowing how dangerous it can be?"

"My dad. He was a police officer for over twenty-five years. As a kid, I thought he looked cool in his uniform. Then he made detective and was a total badass." Hamilton chuckled, love and respect radiating from his eyes. "He never glamorized the job, but in my head—he was *the man*. Of course, I wanted to be just like him. Now that he's retired, he spends most of his time in his garden."

Dakota wished she felt the same about her dad. Sure, she loved him, but she had lost respect for him years ago, hating the way he threw his weight around. It was admirable that he negotiated lucrative contracts for his clients, but he often used intimidation or other seedy ways to get what he wanted.

The other night she'd hoped they'd be able to start fresh and spend some quality time together. Granted, the evening was nice, but it hadn't been what Dakota had planned since Tymico joined them. Her dad and her best friend carried on like old buddies while Dakota felt like an interloper, crashing their dinner. But still, it was a start.

Dakota and Hamilton talked and laughed like they had at the safe house, confirming they had a connection. The more time she spent with him, the more she wanted to get to know him.

Dakota lifted her martini glass to her lip just as a man and a woman, around her age, caught her attention. They were walking hand-in-hand toward the stairs, laughing at something the man said. What really stood out was how the woman smiled at the guy. The love radiating in her eyes could light up the darkest sky, and it wasn't much different in the man's gaze.

A wave of jealousy stabbed Dakota in the chest. That's what she wanted. She wanted a man who looked at her as if she was his gift from God. She also wanted to be so much in love that others could feel the passion seeping through her pores like this couple. There was no doubt how much they loved each other.

When would it be her time, Dakota thought. When would she find a man of her own, get married and have a family? She was so ready for the next chapter in her life but feared she was destined to be alone.

And what about kids? She was thirty-five. If she didn't get started soon, she'd have to have twins in order to have at least two before she turned forty.

A weird sensation fluttered in her stomach when she glanced at Hamilton and found him studying her. God, she hoped he couldn't read minds. Then again, if he could, maybe he'd know she was interested in more than just a friendship. She had no doubt he'd be a wonderful husband and an amazing daddy.

*

Hamilton wondered what Dakota was thinking. One minute she was chatting and laughing it up with him, the next, she had zoned out. Maybe she was tired. She'd so much as said that she hadn't been sleeping well.

"You feeling okay?" he asked, gently massaging her neck.

"Yeah, I'm fine. Just thinking."

"About that couple who just left?"

"Wow, clearly you don't miss much. What did you notice about them?"

"That they were mid-thirties. The guy was approximately six feet tall, two hundred and ten pounds. The woman was about four inches shorter than him, wearing three-inch-heels, and couldn't have been more than a hundred and twenty pounds soak and wet."

Dakota laughed. "Man, I should try to catch up with them to see how close your estimations are. Did you notice how they gazed into each other's eyes? That they were holding hands?"

"I did. I also noticed that they looked very much in love, and she didn't slap him when he patted her on the ass."

Dakota burst out laughing, the sound like a sweet melody to Hamilton's ears.

"Okay, I missed that part. I guess you know how to spot loving couples."

He should. Between his parents, brothers, and lately his friends, he was surrounded by happy couples. One day he'd be in that group.

Hamilton's gaze followed Dakota's moves when she crossed a long jean-clad leg over the other. She swung her foot, encased in a pair of sky-high red heels, back and forth.

Earlier, when she had removed her denim jacket, his tongue almost lodged in his throat. She wore a white fitted shirt and had the top two buttons undone, showing off smooth caramel skin and perky breasts. The garment molded over her curves in all the right places to tempt a man.

"So, Egypt told me that you need a good woman," Dakota said, breaking the silence and surprising the heck out of Hamilton. She picked up her drink, a sly grin on her ruby-red lips.

"According to my mother and sister-in-law, I needed one years ago."

"What are you waiting for? I'm sure there are plenty out there who would leap at the opportunity to be yours."

"Maybe, but I'm waiting for the right one."

"You're a nice, great-looking guy. Are you telling me the right one hasn't come along?"

"I guess i could ask you the same thing. What are you waiting for?"

She took a delicate sip of her drink and set the glass on the table. "I'm waiting for you."

Hamilton laughed. Something he did more of whenever she was around. "In that case, we should probably get together again."

Dakota leaned into him and brushed her lips over his. "I'd like that."

Chapter Eighteen

Dakota sat in the back seat as the Uber driver maneuvered through the streets of Atlanta. The past few weeks had been a blur, but they'd been some of the happiest weeks of her life. She and Hamilton had been officially dating for almost a month and it was as if they'd known each other forever. Falling for someone so fast normally would've given her pause, but that wasn't the case. The man was everything she'd hope he'd be.

The driver pulled into the strip mall's parking lot.

"If you could pull up in front of that bakery, that would be great."

Dakota gathered her oversized bag and thanked the driver before getting out of the vehicle. She was meeting Tymico, who she hadn't seen in almost two weeks and had only talked to her once during that time. They had a lot of catching up to do, which was why she suggested the outing, and according to Tymico, Dakota would finally get to meet her boyfriend, Brad.

Pulling open the glass door of the establishment, she walked in and removed her sunglasses, waiting for her eyes to adjust. The smell of fresh bread and strong coffee enticed her as she searched for Tymico, wondering if her friend had arrived yet.

Ah, there she is.

"Hey, girl. I hope you haven't been waiting long," Dakota said, hugging her friend.

"Nope. I got here maybe five minutes ago and figured I'd grab this table before someone else snatched it up."

"This is perfect, but where is Brad?"

"Oh, he should be here in a few minutes. We drove separately because I was coming from getting my nails done. Since I'm starving, I hope you don't mind if I go first."

"No problem." Dakota sat in the chair that faced the door, wanting to be able to see Hamilton when he arrived. She was looking forward to introducing him to Tymico, almost as much as she was anticipating meeting Brad for the first time.

A short while later, Tymico returned to the table with a ham and egg sandwich, a bowl of fruit and a large cup of coffee. "Okay, your turn."

While waiting her turn in line, Dakota scanned the items in the glass display case, debating on whether to get a cinnamon roll or a chocolate croissant. Getting full off of junk food wouldn't be a good idea since Hamilton was picking her up from the bakery soon. They had dinner plans and then were attending a movie premiere and afterparty later that night.

"What can I get you?"

"May I have a cinnamon roll and a medium black coffee?"

"Coming right up."

When Dakota returned to the table with her items, Tymico had almost finished off her sandwich. "Don't judge me. I was starving," she said, and they immediately started talking at once, catching up on their work lives as well as their love lives. "So it sounds like you and Hamilton are getting pretty serious."

"I'm crazy about him." A joy Dakota felt to her core blossomed whenever she thought about her man and how close they had become. At first, she was just enjoying the chase and being chased, but now that they spent practically every day together, she could actually imagine a life with him. "He gets me, Ty. It's like we've known each other forever. Like we were made for one another. I can't explain it any better than that."

"I'm so happy for you, Dee. I wish you the best. Who knows, maybe we'll be planning a wedding soon."

Dakota was cautiously optimistic that what they felt for each other would only grow stronger with time. But, Hamilton wasn't the easiest person to read. He made it no secret that he cared deeply for her, but he was slow to talk about a future together.

"We'll see. Things are still new between us," she said. "Okay, enough about me. Let's talk about you." Tymico had been traveling more than usual, saying she was trying to make extra money. She hadn't found a place yet, even though they had both moved out of their previous apartment.

The fact that her friend had been staying with her new boyfriend whenever she wasn't flying was bothering Dakota. It really wasn't any of her business, but she didn't want to see Tymico hurt again, and something wasn't right. She was being too secretive about this guy.

"How did the house hunting go? Did you see anything you liked?" Dakota asked, sipping her coffee.

"Actually, I did in Midtown, but Brad wasn't feeling the neighborhood."

"Oh, he went looking with you?"

"No. I told him about some of the places and he gave his opinion. He said it was no hurry for me to find a place, and that I can stay with him for as long as I want. He travels almost as much as I do. So the living arrangement works."

"Is that what you want? To live with him."

"I'm not sure. I guess I'm not in a real hurry to narrow down an apartment or even a house since there's no rush."

"Well, I know we both agreed that it was time for us to get our own places, but you know you're always welcome to stay with me. Just consider my second bedroom yours whenever you're in town."

"Aw, thanks, sis. I appreciate that. But now that you have a man, I don't want to cramp your style. He's not going to want me hanging around all the time."

Dakota waved her off. "Oh, please. Hamilton's not like that. You'll see. I'm glad you're going to finally get to meet him. And speaking of meeting people, what time is Brad going to get here? I hope he shows up before I have to leave."

"Actually, he should've been here already." She dug through her purse and pulled out her cell phone. Disappointment flashed across her friend's face. "He's not going to be able to make it."

"I'm sorry, Ty."

"Don't be. This isn't the first time he's canceled on me, but I'm sure he has a good reason. He's a busy man."

"What does he do for a..." Dakota started to ask, but Hamilton entered the bakery, and whatever she was about to say flew from her mind. Like usual, whenever he was around, a thrill shot through her like fireworks on the Fourth of July. She didn't know if she would ever get used to that feeling of exhilaration that sparked inside her stomach at just the sight of him.

Before she could wave, he headed in their direction.

"Well, I see you didn't exaggerate," Tymico whispered. "That is one fine brotha."

Dakota laughed. "I told you."

"Hey, baby," Hamilton said when he reached the table and gave her a quick kiss.

"Hey, yourself," Dakota said, feeling the giddiness that came with being in a new relationship. "This is my best friend, Tymico. Ty, this is Hamilton."

"Nice to meet you," they said in unison and laughed.

"Ready?" Hamilton asked Dakota.

She turned to Tymico, hating to leave her alone, and feeling awful that Brad stood her up. Whenever Dakota did meet the guy, she was certainly going to remind him of the treasure he had in Tymico. She was one of the sweetest people and deserved to be treated as such.

"Ty, I don't want to leave you here by yourself."

"Oh, girl, please." She waved off Dakota's comment. "I need to get out of here myself. So you guys go and have a good time tonight. I can't wait to hear about the party."

They said their goodbyes and Dakota walked out of the bakery with Hamilton.

"Did you finally get to meet her boyfriend?" he asked. Dakota had shared her concerns about Brad with him and had mentioned that she would finally get to meet him.

"No. The bum didn't show up. I don't even know this guy and already I don't like him."

Hamilton chuckled. "Aren't you being a little hard on the man? Maybe something came up."

"According to Ty, this isn't the first time he's canceled. Besides, I have a bad feeling about him. She only talks about him when I bring up his name, and she hasn't introduced us even though they've been dating a while. I just have a bad feeling about her relationship."

Hamilton guided Dakota through the parking lot until they reached his metallic red Lexus LC.

"Hmm, I see we're riding in style tonight. One day you're going to have to let me take this baby for a spin."

"Anytime," he said and opened the car door for her.

"Hamilton."

Dakota and Hamilton turned as a stylishly dressed woman with long, wavy hair, weaved around a car and approached them.

"You know her?" Dakota asked, realizing it was a dumb question since the woman called him by name.

"Yeah, Dominic's mother."

The words were spoken so cavalier, Dakota wasn't sure if she'd heard right. Before she could question him, the woman was in front of them.

"I'm glad I ran into you. We need to talk," she said.

"Dakota this is Jackie. Jackie, this is Dakota."

Dakota nodded. "Nice to meet you."

Jackie looked her up and down before saying, "Same here. Dominic speaks about you often." Then she turned to Hamilton. "I need to talk to you."

"As you can see, Dakota and I are getting ready to leave. Unless this has something to do with Dominic, I'll call you later when—"

"Now, Ham."

Hamilton straightened. Irritation radiated in his eyes and when he started to protest, Dakota jumped in.

"Go ahead. I'll wait in the car," she said.

He looked as if he still didn't want to have words with his ex, but instead of saying so, he moved to the front of the vehicle and onto the sidewalk.

Dakota stared out the front window, checking Jackie out with more interest now. The woman wasn't what she had expected, not that Hamilton said much about her. But for some reason, Dakota imagined a more docile, shy, homely-looking person. Or maybe that's just what she had wanted her to be. Not the pretty, pulled-together, confident woman in front of her.

Either way, right now Jackie looked as if she wanted to strangle Hamilton, while he appeared disinterested. All Dakota needed was a bowl of popcorn because this had all the signs of being a dramatic performance.

*

Hamilton folded his arms across his chest and glared at his son's mother. "Jackie, I don't see what couldn't wait."

"How could you, Ham?" she spat, looking as if she was about to spit fire.

"How could I what?"

"Don't play dumb. You know what. I can't believe you had Braeden arrested."

Hamilton's brows shot up in surprise. He hadn't known what she was accusing him of, but he hadn't expected that. "I have no idea what you're talking about. I didn't have him arrested."

"Quit lying!"

Barely holding onto his annoyance, he clamped his mouth shut in time to cut off the harsh words dangling from his tongue. Jackie was good at getting him riled up, but he wasn't about to let that happen now. Not in public, and more importantly, not in front of Dakota.

"Despite what you think of me, I have *never* lied to you. Never," he said in a deadly calm voice that had her shrinking back. "Not even when you thought I cheated on you. I didn't lie then, and I have no reason to lie to you now."

She studied him for the longest time before releasing a long, drawn-out sigh. Now her gaze was everywhere but on him and he waited for her to accuse him of not forgiving her for something that happened years ago. Like he explained to her then, he forgave her. He just would never forget that time in their lives for as long as he lived.

"Why was Braeden arrested?" he asked, now curious. He might have done a background check on the guy and found that he had a ton of unpaid parking tickets, but he hadn't ratted him out. Yet.

"Something about unpaid parking tickets and driving without a license."

"So, there was a warrant out for his arrest because of *him* being irresponsible. Why'd you automatically think I had something to do with his issues?"

"Because of the timing. He said that you prob—"

"Ah, there you go again believing something someone said about me without giving me the benefit of the doubt."

"It wasn't like that, Hamilton."

"Sure it was. That's how it's always been with you, Jackie. I can name at least three instances where the same thing happened. Someone spouts off some shit, ropes me into it, and you run with the information, believing the worse."

"It wasn't... I'm sorry if—"

"Save it. It doesn't matter. I've come to expect nothing less from you. And how did you know where to find me right now?"

She frowned at him. "If you think I've been following you, you're wrong. I was leaving Whole Foods," she pointed to the grocery store across the parking lot, "and saw you walk out of the bakery."

Hamilton didn't really think she'd been following him, but he thought it odd that she happened to run into him at that moment.

"I thought you said you weren't dating the stuntwoman," she said quietly.

"At the time I told you that, I wasn't," he said, having no intention of talking to her about Dakota.

Jackie nodded, her anger from moments ago subsided. "Dom likes her. Says she's really nice to him."

"She is. She's a very nice lady." Which was putting it mildly. Hamilton had never been so taken with a woman in all of his life, not even when he and Jackie were together. Back then, he loved his ex when he'd asked her to marry him, but he now knew that it had more to do with her being pregnant with Dominic than it did love.

But what he already felt for Dakota, considering only knowing her a short time, was stronger than he'd ever felt for any woman.

"Well, I wish you well," Jackie said, sounding as if she really meant it.

"Thanks." Hamilton glanced at the car, knowing he needed to get going. "Where's Dom?"

"Birthday party at Jake's house," she said, referring to one of Dominic's best friends. "I'm on my way to pick him up in a few minutes but decided to stop at the store first."

"All right, well, I have to get going. If you want, I can see what I can find out about Braeden's situ—"

"Thanks, but it doesn't matter. We broke up. I was just mad at you because... It doesn't matter. I'll see you around."

She walked away and Hamilton shook his head as he climbed into his car.

"Everything okay?" Dakota asked, fastening her seatbelt.

"Yep. She just wanted to blame me for getting her boyfriend arrested."

Dakota frowned. "What?"

As Hamilton left the parking lot, he filled her in on the conversation he'd had weeks ago with Jackie regarding Braeden. Her accusations bugged him, but if Hamilton were honest, he couldn't blame her in this situation. When it came to Dominic, there wasn't much he wouldn't do to ensure his happiness or his safety. Including making a call to some of his friends at Atlanta PD.

"Though I've wondered, I never asked—who broke off the engagement, you or Jackie?"

"I did. We had trust issues. Well, she had trust issues. Among other things, she accused me of cheating on her."

"Did you?"

"No. I'm a one-woman man, Dakota. I've never cheated on a woman, and I never will," he said with conviction. He was crazy about her, and he wanted it clear that he would never cheat on her.

She rubbed her hand up and down his thigh. "Relax. I believe you. You haven't given me any indication that you're that type of man. Did Jackie have a reason for her distrust?"

Hamilton shook his head. "Not because of anything I did. I can only assume that it has to do with her family. Her mother and sisters are unmarried, and in my opinion, hate men." That last part was an unfair assumption, but that's the way it had seemed. "According to Jackie, they experienced their share of men cheating and pushed their issues onto her. She was always questioning me, checking up on me, fearing that I would step out on her. And I did everything I could to assure her that I wasn't that guy. That she never had to worry about me cheating or disrespecting her."

"Sounds like a sore subject between you two."

Hamilton shrugged. "Doesn't matter now. Except for Dominic, there's nothing between us."

One day he'd tell Dakota about the incident that sealed his decision to break off his engagement. The same situation that involved her father.

Chapter Nineteen

"I'm gonna run to the lady's room, and no, I don't need you to go with me," Dakota said, and Hamilton laughed.

"Okay, hurry back." They kissed before she left his side and he watched as she glided away looking as tasty from the back as she did from the front. He'd admit to keeping her close to his side for most of the night, but who could blame him? Everything about the woman drew attention. From her vibrant personality to the skin-tight dress she was wearing, he couldn't help but be possessive, especially since the sight of her killer long legs could cause a traffic jam.

They were at the afterparty, hosted by one of the A-list actors who had starred in the movie premiere they'd viewed earlier. The gathering was well attended by not only those who were a part of the project but many from the entertainment industry. It really wasn't Hamilton's scene, but he was glad to be there with Dakota.

He ambled over to one of the bars that had been set up in the ballroom.

"What can I get you?" the bartender asked, setting a drink napkin on the bar in front of Hamilton.

"A cranberry and orange juice would be great."

"Coming right up."

Hamilton glanced around at the crowd, feeling proud of the way his guys were handling themselves. Supreme had been hired to oversee the security at the premiere as well as at the party. Considering the square footage of the mansion and the number of people in attendance, Hamilton was glad they opted to add a few extra security guards. His men had been busy. The later the party flowed into the evening, the more the drinking increased, forcing his security team to escort numerous intoxicated guests from the estate. For the most part, all was going well. But Hamilton knew a room full of egos connecting with an open bar was rarely a good combination.

The bartender set Hamilton's juice on the napkin.

"Thanks." He took a few sips before spotting Dakota talking to a guy he'd seen earlier. Sebastian Jeter. He thought it had been his imagination, but over the last couple of hours, each time Hamilton looked up, the guy was eyeing him and Dakota. Now Sebastian had cornered her. Well, maybe he hadn't actually cornered her, but that's how Hamilton saw it. After hugging each other, the guy regarded Dakota as if he wanted to eat her up.

A twinge of jealousy pierced Hamilton in the chest, but he stayed where he was, watching from a distance as the two chatted.

"They secretly have a thing for each other," a sultry low voice said from Hamilton's right. He glanced at the woman, recognizing her from the movie they had watched earlier. She'd been in the industry for a while, but he couldn't recall offhand what else she'd been in. Nice looking with mocha skin, long curly hair, and a friendly smile, but the coldness in her dark eyes was an immediate turnoff.

"Personally, I think Dakota has been playing hard to get with Sebastian. Making him jump through hoops and stringing him along." The woman looked Hamilton up and down. "A good-looking man like you shouldn't settle for someone like her. You can do better."

"Is that right?"

"For sure. I'm Zondra Monroe." She extended her hand and Hamilton hesitated before shaking it. "And you are?"

"Dakota's date, but I guess you already know that."

She quirked a surprised brow before a sneer spread across her lips. "I assumed. But in this business, it doesn't really matter. Entertainers usually share more than just a stage or a screen."

"Well, I'm not in the business, and I sure as hell don't share."

Hamilton's attention went back to Dakota and ignored the woman's seductive laugh. He studied Sebastian, an actor whose stardom was quickly rising in the ranks if the number of films he'd been in recently was any indication. He might've been good at acting, but Hamilton didn't like how touchy-feely he was. The man couldn't seem to keep his hands off of Dakota. First the hand on her lower back which had gotten a little too close to her ass before she eased out of his hold. Now, he touched her arm, rubbing it while saying something to her and smiling.

The tension that suddenly dug into Hamilton's shoulders loosened when a tall blonde strolled over to Sebastian and he put his arm around the woman's waist.

"Don't relax too much, handsome. That's only his *so-called* girlfriend, but he goes through women faster than mail carriers go through mail. Trust me. Sebastian wants Dakota."

"And you know this how?" Hamilton couldn't believe he was having this conversation, but curiosity got the best of him.

"Sebastian and I talk often. So, when Dakota gets tired of you and moves on to him, look me up."

Hamilton finished off his drink and set the empty glass on the bar. "What's your problem with Dakota?"

Zondra glanced down at the dark liquid in her glass, studying the drink as if it held answers. "Dakota and I started in the business around the same time, and we've worked on a number of projects together. At one point, we might've even been considered friends."

"I assume that's changed."

"Yeah. The tramp lured my boyfriend into her bed, and then tried to deny it."

"Spewing more lies, Zondra?" Dakota slipped her hand into Hamilton's. So caught up in the conversation, he hadn't seen her approach.

"No lies. Only facts."

"Facts like how I got a stunt role you wanted? What can I say? I had a better agent. It's been over twelve years. Get over it and move on."

"Just know I haven't forgotten...anything. One of these days someone is going to knock you off that throne you've placed yourself on."

"Well, it won't be you. Considering your fight scene on set yesterday, you couldn't punch your way out of a wall-less room."

Zondra glared at Dakota, a fire in her eyes that could demolish a skyscraper, but Hamilton had to give his woman credit. She sported her usual confident, almost arrogant expression while he prepared himself to break up a fight. But instead of saying more to Dakota, Zondra turned to him.

"Nice talking to you, handsome. Remember what I said." She walked away without a second glance.

Dakota sighed and leaned against him. "She hates me, and she's delusional. What did she say?"

"Nothing worth repeating." Hamilton lowered his head and kissed Dakota. He didn't believe a word Zondra said, and until Dakota gave him a reason not to trust her, he'd give her the benefit of the doubt.

"You and Sebastian looked pretty chummy. Friends?" Hamilton directed her away from the bar.

"Not hardly. More like acquaintances. He's interested in more, but I'm not. Jealous?"

Hamilton smiled down at her, recognizing the teasing in her voice. "Should I be?"

"Nope. I'm all yours, and so that there's no misunderstanding, that goes both ways. You're mine."

He laughed and wrapped his arms around her, kissing the top of her head. "Yes, ma'am. How about we go outside and get some air?" Hamilton asked close to her ear, and she shivered against him. "Cold?"

"No. You have that effect on me when you're this close. Now, when you say let's go out for some air, is that code for let's find a dark corner so you can get under my dress."

Hamilton chuckled and shook his head. "You little minx. As tempting as that is, the next time I have you will be in my bed. Tonight. But in the meantime, let's go check out the terrace and you can tell me why Sebastian Jeter was feeling you up."

She laughed. "Oh, you saw that, did you? Don't worry, baby. I don't care how rich and good-looking he is. You're the only man for me. Besides, he doesn't get my juices flowing the way you do."

Smiling and shaking his head, Hamilton led her across the room. They were near the terrace doors when Dakota slowed. He glanced at her before following her line of vision and then cursed under his breath.

"Hamilton, I swear I didn't know my father was going to be here." And of course, the man was headed in their direction. With a slight stagger in his walk, it was safe to assume he'd had a little too much to drink.

"I haven't talked to him in days. Last I heard he was on the west coast. I'll keep him away." Dakota tried to pull away, but Hamilton held on to her hand.

"No. I want you with me. Don't worry, I'll behave. Let's step outside." What he really wanted to do was avoid her father altogether. Less chance of an altercation.

Hamilton looked around to see if he could make eye contact with any of his guys and his gaze connected with Kenton's. Most of the team towered over the guests, making it easy for them to stay abreast of what was going on.

Hamilton gave a slight nod toward the terrace and Kenton started across the room. Angelo, the team leader for the night, was on the opposite side of the room but followed.

Hamilton didn't look to see if others took heed. His main concern now was to keep Wesley from causing a scene.

Shortly after he and Dakota stepped outside, Wesley burst out of the door.

Hamilton's pulse pounded in his ears. He noted a few people were already on the terrace or nearby. Wanting to put some distance between him and Wesley, he backed up, but Dakota's father wasn't having that. He charged toward them.

"What the hell are you doing with my daughter?"

"Dad, please. Just go back to the party."

"Not with—without you," her father said, his words slightly slurred. "I don't want you near this guy!"

Hamilton held tight to Dakota's hand. "Come on. Let's get out of here."

Wesley grabbed her arm, pulling her back, shocking her and Hamilton. "Don't touch her!"

"Dad, stop it!" Dakota said through gritted teeth and pulled away. "You don't get to tell me what to do. Now go back to the party."

Wesley moved around Dakota with the speed of a man half his age and pointed his finger at Hamilton's face.

"You stay away from her!"

"Listen, Wesley. I don't want any trouble," Hamilton said, anger knotting inside of him, especially when Wesley grabbed Dakota's arm, yanking her out of Hamilton's grasp.

"I will ki—kill you if you come near her again."

Dakota gasped. "Dad! Stop it."

"I'm not let—letting you go with that—that rapist!"

Something snapped inside of Hamilton. His fist plowed into Wesley's face.

"Hamilton, no!" Dakota shrieked and he felt her pull on the tail of his jacket, but it was too late. He practically lifted Wesley off of his feet and slammed him against the house. Seeing the man's nose gushing blood only made Hamilton punch him again.

Screams pierced the air and there was a flurry of movement, but Hamilton couldn't stop the fury raging through him. For years he wanted to shut this man up. To stop him from spewing lies and making his life a living hell.

He brought his arm back again, but before he could hit Wesley, someone grabbed Hamilton from behind.

"That's enough!" Angelo locked Hamilton's arms behind him and pulled him back, while Kenton held onto Wesley. Other members of the team formed a human wall around them, effectively blocking them from view.

Breathing hard and struggling to get his bearing, Hamilton's heart nearly stopped at the shock on Dakota's face.

Wesley shook out of Kenton's hold. "Get off me! I want that man arrested," he sputtered, wiping his bloody face with the sleeve of his suit jacket.

More security poured through the double doors, ushering people back into the house and away from the scene.

"Let's go," Angelo grumbled, tightening his hold. Hamilton knew the drill. They had procedures for dealing with unruly guests. He just never expected to be one of them. Considering the night had started out perfect, now everything he had worked for might be trashed because of one stupid mistake.

"Hamilton," Dakota called out and he stopped, but Angelo shoved him forward.

"Sorry, man. You know the routine," Angelo said, forcing Hamilton away from the scene.

He knew, but Dakota didn't. "Make sure one of you is with her at all times."

"Already done."

"Kenton! Move or so help me you're going to be the one needing protection!" Hamilton heard Dakota say. He almost felt sorry for the man. He might be over six feet tall and two-hundred-plus pounds, but he was no match for that little firecracker.

"God...what have I done?" Hamilton mumbled, thinking about the ramifications of punching Wesley.

"For starters, you just pummeled the woman's father. Way to make an impression on her family." Angelo had released him, but stayed close, escorting him around the outside of the home to the guest house the owners had allowed his guys to use.

Hamilton didn't respond. Dakota meant everything to him and he wouldn't lose her because of Wesley. Hopefully, she knew both of them well enough to give him the benefit of the doubt of any lies her father spewed. If not, Wesley would regret crossing him.

*

"Move out of the way!" Dakota roared, frustration and fear at war within her. She had to get to Hamilton, but Kenton blocked her every move, grasping her wrists when she swung at him again.

"Would you stop? I don't want to hurt you," Kenton said in a low rumble.

If she wasn't so pissed, she might've laughed. Clearly, he didn't know who he was dealing with. If he wasn't a friend of Hamilton's and worked for him, she would've already laid his ass out.

"Dakota, I promise he's okay," Kenton said, still holding onto her.

Torn by conflicting emotions, she stopped fighting him, her body deflating like a nail-punctured tire. What the hell had just happened? How had her perfect evening turned to shit in an instant?

"Where's Angelo taking him?" Her voice cracked and she cleared her throat, refusing to let Kenton see how much the last five minutes had upset her.

"We had to remove him from the scene. Protocol. But trust me, Ham won't leave here without you."

Knowing he was right, Dakota bit her bottom lip to get her emotions under control. Hamilton was a gentle man, and it shocked her to see him lose his temper. But who could blame him? Being called any kind of name could ignite a fight, but *rapist?* That was...

"If I release you, do you promise not to punch me again? I'm pretty sure you left a bruise on my chest," Kenton said. Dakota heard the humor in his words, but at the moment she felt more like crying than laughing.

"Yeah." She nodded and he let her go.

"Don't worry about Hamilton. He'll be fine, and once I get clearance I'll take you to him. All right?"

Dakota rubbed her forehead, trying to pull herself together. "Okay," she said absently and turned to her father.

He was sitting on one of several wood benches that lined the terrace and faced a pond. Someone had given him a few towels, ice, and a bottle of water. Dakota was pretty sure Hamilton hadn't hit him as hard as he could have. The first punch, maybe—but had he put all his weight behind the second one, her father probably would've been unconscious.

The bleeding had stopped, so it was safe to say his nose wasn't broken, but the left side of his face looked as if he had run into a door several times. And knowing him, he had refused medical attention.

At a loss, she stood there for a moment. Except for Kenton and another one of Atlanta's finest, whose name she couldn't recall, Dakota and her father were the only people left on the terrace. He had a lot of explaining to do. There was no way Hamilton had ever forced himself on a woman, but there had to be a good reason why her dad accused him of such a heinous crime.

"Do you need a doctor?" she asked as she approached him. She might've been confused and frustrated, but that didn't mean she didn't care about his well-being.

He waved her off with the bloody towel in his hand. "I'll be fine. But Dee Dee, you have to stay away from him," Wesley said.

"Why?" She folded her arms across her chest to ward off the chill in the air. It was a beautiful spring night, but the drama of the past few minutes had cast a dark cloud over the evening. "Why would you say something like that to him, especially here?" Thankfully, the commotion hadn't taken place inside the house where most of the attendees had been.

Her father huffed out a breath and didn't respond.

"Tell me!" she shouted, anger bubbling inside of her at his silence. "What is wrong with you? You can't just go around accusing someone of something like that."

"It's complicated."

"Complicated?" she snapped. "I'll give you complicated if you don't tell me why you accused my boyfriend of rape."

"Boyfriend? You can't be serious."

"I'm dead serious. Now start talking."

After a long hesitation, he said, "I can't discuss it."

"Dad!"

"Dad?" someone gasped, and Dakota swung around. Sebastian was standing in the doorway, shock written on his face as he darted across the threshold. "Wesley *Bradford* is your father?"

Kenton was in front of Sebastian before he could take another step. "We're asking everyone to stay inside until further notice."

"Not until I make sure Dakota is all right. Dakota?" He tried peering around Kenton, but the bodyguard was wider and a few inches taller than him.

"I'm fine, Sebastian. Please just give us a moment."

"All right, but Dakota...find me when you're ready to leave and I'll see you home."

"She already has a ride home," Kenton said before Dakota could respond, a hardness in his tone. She couldn't see his face, but considering how rigid his back was, and the fact Sebastian didn't say another word, the actor got the point.

Dakota hadn't noticed her at first, but the woman who'd been with Sebastian earlier tried to push past Kenton.

"Wesley!"

Kenton and the other bodyguard held them both off.

"That's Alexia. Let her through. She's one of my clients," Wesley explained.

"I don't care who she is. We're not done here," Dakota shouted, but then reined in her anger, knowing she wouldn't get far with her father if she didn't calm down. "I want answers, Dad, and I want them now. You might have ruined Hamilton's reputation and career by saying what you said and I want to know why."

"Dakota, this is not the time."

She plopped her fisted hands on her hips. "Are you serious right now? You just called him a rapist in front of everyone and now you suddenly don't want to tell me why? Oh no, you're going to talk; otherwise, you and I are done!"

When he still didn't speak, she started to move away but he reached for her hand. "Please, Dee Dee. I love you, sweetheart. I can't lose you, but you have to trust me on this. You need to stay away from him."

"Not until you tell me why."

Again, her father went mute and Dakota wanted to scream. Why wouldn't he tell her? For the life of her she couldn't understand why he and Hamilton couldn't be in the same room, and neither wanted to talk about whatever happened.

Dakota ran her hands down her face, fighting back tears as a nauseating sense of despair settled in her gut. God knew she loved her father, but she couldn't go on like this. He'd been manipulating her life one way or another for as long as she could remember. There was no way in hell she was letting him sabotage what she had with Hamilton.

Torment ate at her from the inside. She didn't want to lose her father, but she was tired of getting caught up in his mess. But when she turned to face him, to tell him just that, a thought sparked in her mind.

"What does Hamilton have on you?"

Despite the puffiness of his face, surprise sparked in his eyes. That was it. Hamilton had something on him. Whatever it was had to be huge if her father was prepared to let her walk out of his life.

"I guess it's safe to say you won't be pressing charges against him for what happened tonight."

He licked his lips before dropping his gaze. "No."

Dakota should be happy for that news, but that only meant that whatever happened was worse than she could imagine. Wesley Bradford lived to make people squirm, make them pay whether they deserved it or not. For him to suddenly back down wasn't normal.

"Dad, I'm really trying here. I want you and I to rebuild our relationship, but you're making it very difficult. I never know when to believe you, and now…" She released a shaky breath and swallowed. "If you can't be straight with me, you and I…we're never going to have what we used to have."

Wesley stood, staggering a bit. He used the bloody towel to dab at his nose, which wasn't bleeding as bad. "Honey, I want the same thing, but this subject is off-limits. It's none of your business."

"Tonight, you made it my business!" She seethed, her body vibrating with pent-up anger as she fought to get her breathing under control. They stood facing each other for several seconds, neither willing to back down.

"Dee Dee…"

"Since you won't tell me what you did, I guess we have nothing else to say to each other." Her voice broke on the last part. "Take care of yourself, Dad." Dakota looked away, tears blurring her vision, but she batted her eyes and swallowed, determined to keep them at bay.

When she glanced up, Kenton was standing on the edge of the terrace. He gestured with a slight nod in the direction where Angelo had taken Hamilton.

A tightness in her chest kept Dakota from taking a step forward. She wanted to see Hamilton, but she knew that once she turned away from her father, that was it. She was done fighting with him.

As if sensing her anguish, Kenton moved toward her. Another tear slipped down her cheek before she could catch it. He looked so uncomfortable and she felt like crap trying to keep herself together. Working with men most of the time, she maintained her tough-girl exterior, but right now she just didn't have it in her.

"Let's go, stuntwoman." Kenton looped a long arm around her shoulders and pulled her close to his side, comforting her. Just what she needed. "You know, I might have to get workman's comp for the beating you put on me," he cracked.

Dakota snorted. "Whatever. You shouldn't be such a wimp," she said, drying her cheeks with the back of her hand. She really liked Kenton. He was quickly becoming the big brother she always wanted.

Chapter Twenty

Hamilton gazed out the floor-to-ceiling window in the living room of the guest house, trying to organize his thoughts while staring into the night. His mind was all over the place. How could he have lost control like that? Acting like a damn animal, and for what? Wesley wasn't worth losing everything for. Punching the man in public had to be the stupidest thing Hamilton had ever done. And to lose control in front of his guys made the situation that much worse.

Damn. I messed up.

He placed his hands on the window frame and lowered his head as a maddening growl bubbled inside of him. His thoughts continued to crash into each other.

Wesley.

Atlanta's finest.

The party.

Dakota.

Pushing away from the window, he shoved his hands into the front pockets of his pants and blew out a frustrated breath. He had to tell her everything. Dakota meant too much to him to stay silent any longer. It was ironic how he'd tried keeping his distance from her when they first met; now he couldn't imagine his life without her.

She belonged to him, and he belonged to her.

He had to fix this.

Two quick raps against the door caused him to turn just as it opened and Kenton strolled in, leaving Dakota standing just beyond the threshold.

"Need anything else?" Kenton asked.

Hamilton stared at Dakota as she eased further into the living room. "No. Thanks for everything, man."

"You got it."

After Kenton closed the door, officially leaving the two of them to talk, Hamilton wasn't sure where to start.

Their gazes locked for the longest moment, but Dakota stayed rooted in place. She said nothing, and the space between them filled with a heavy tension, only made Hamilton more anxious. She always had something to say. Normally. Then again, this situation wasn't normal.

He ambled toward her and a new anguish seared his heart witnessing the pain in her eyes. Had Wesley told her? Did she believe her father's nonsense? Tears swam in her honey-brown orbs and Hamilton blamed himself. He should have never allowed Wesley to make him angry enough to lash out.

"I'm sorry," Hamilton said, his voice catching. "Baby, I am so sorry for everything. I didn't mean to embarrass you or ruin your evening. I also had no intention of hitting your father. I never want to do anything to hurt you."

She shook her head. "You did what anyone would've done under the circumstances. He deserved to be knocked on his ass. I'm sorry I asked you to come with me tonight, knowing there could've been a chance he'd show up. I don't know what he did to you, but…" she said on a sob and Hamilton pulled her into his arms before she could finish.

Apparently, Wesley hadn't told her.

"I know what my father is capable of and I'm sorry if he hurt you in any way," she mumbled against his chest.

Heart swelling at her words, Hamilton placed a kiss on top of her head and held her tighter. She had no idea how much it meant to hear she trusted him. Believed in him. After

Jackie's betrayal, he hadn't trusted another woman with his heart.

Until now.

Until Dakota.

"Come on, let's talk."

After leading Dakota to the upholstered sofa, he handed her a few tissues from the Kleenex box sitting on the end table.

"Thanks."

Hamilton leaned forward, his elbows on his knees as he decided where to start. "Ten years ago, when I was still a cop, me and my partner responded to a disturbance at your father's penthouse."

"Let me guess—an industry party."

Hamilton nodded.

"I hate his parties. Wealthy, grown people who act as if they don't have good sense," she said.

"Exactly. The anonymous caller, the person who called about the disturbance, mentioned there was underaged drinking, prostitution, and people doing drugs. We wanted to get the crowd under control, as well as question everyone. There were just so many people, we had to call for backup. Some of his guests were questioned on the spot, while those who were uncooperative had to be taken to the station."

Dakota shook her head, still not seeming surprised by any of what he was telling her.

"As we slowly cleared the apartment, I went back through and double-checked the bedrooms in the back of the unit."

"Were you looking for more people?"

Hamilton nodded. "As well as drugs. I didn't have a search warrant, but if I saw any contraband—drugs or anything like that in plain sight—we could collect it as evidence."

"Did you find anything?"

"I did, but I had a bigger problem." Hamilton released an unsteady breath. Telling this story was like reliving that night all over again. Embarrassment and anger warred within him even after so many years.

"When I reached the bedroom, a woman, Avery Day, was standing in the middle of the floor with a drink in her hand."

"Whoa. Wait. You met Avery Day? The actress who OD'd a few years ago?"

Hamilton nodded and sighed. "Yeah, she was in her early twenties and wasn't as well-known back then. Anyway, I was told the rooms had been cleared, and I didn't know where she came from. When I started questioning her, it was apparent she was drunk and high on something. One minute, she was acting normal and the next, she was like a different person. Erratic, yelling, and then back to normal."

"What happened?" Dakota prompted, placing a reassuring hand on his arm.

"She started coming on to me, making indecent suggestions and...I should've walked out of there at that moment or got another cop in there with me. But I figured I could deal with her. Young, cocky, and stupid, I stayed, putting myself in a compromising position before realizing it."

Hamilton rung his hands as his stomach churned and his pulse inched up. He had always considered himself a smart man but recapping what happened that night felt like he was discussing someone else. Someone who didn't have the intuition that he prided himself on now.

"Before I could leave the room, Avery dropped her robe and was completely naked. Then she started freaking out and screaming."

"Oh, Hamilton."

"I hurried out of the room, but it wasn't quick enough. Your father was one of the ones who'd been handcuffed, with the intention of taking him to the station for not cooperating. When I stepped into the hallway, one of the cops was there with Wesley."

"God...I can just imagine what happened next."

"Long story short, Wesley asked Avery what happened, and on the spot, she concocted the sexual assault story. Between Avery's acting abilities—even while high—and your father's insistence that I was a rapist, they made a bad situation worse. Within twenty-four hours the story hit the media and my world spun out of control. It became my word against hers. Wesley led the lynch mob, spewing lies whenever there were cameras and microphones in his face. I was crucified before evidence could be gathered."

Spasms of anxiousness erupted inside of Hamilton as memories of the day he told Jackie the same story came to mind. She hadn't believed him. Hadn't stuck by him.

Hamilton stood, unable to stay seated any longer as an anxious energy clawed through him. That time in his life felt like the end, like he would never recover from the humiliation.

"Much of the population loathed cops, even today. So, people were quick to believe the worst about me. A lowly cop taking advantage of an up-and-coming actress. Even if it hadn't been determined that she'd had sex with several partners that night, it was still my word against hers until the tests proved otherwise."

Silence filled the room and Hamilton didn't know what Dakota was thinking as she stared down at the crumpled tissue in her hand.

"When we ran into Jackie earlier, is this the incident that you were talking about that destroyed your relationship?"

"Yes. So concerned about what others said and thought, Jackie made herself sick with worry, choosing to believe everyone but me. Which wasn't good since she was six months pregnant with Dominic and it was a high-risk pregnancy. When all of this came out, her blood pressure was off the charts and she'd already been suffering from anxiety."

Dakota shook her head. "This whole situation had to be awful for you both."

"One of the worst times in my life, and Jackie would probably agree. She went into labor three months

170

prematurely, and I don't think I've ever prayed that hard in my life."

The day his son was born had been the happiest and the scariest day Hamilton had ever experienced. His precious gift had to fight to live.

"Thankfully, Dom was a fighter."

Hamilton told Dakota about his suspension during the investigation and the months that followed. After sharing with her, it felt as if a weight had been lifted from his shoulders. Maybe this time he would finally be able to lay the past to rest.

"How were you cleared?"

"Laz." Hamilton chuckled. "That man has saved my life a few times. He has more connections than anyone I know. He had gotten the word out to some of his informants that he was looking for anything on Avery. Weeks later, one of his CIs was at a bar and contacted Laz when he saw her in a back room shooting up coke with some guys. They caught her. The detectives had already been trying to gather evidence against her claims regarding me, assuming she might have a history of doing the same to others. Before the drug bust, they didn't have anything on her."

"Did she confess to lying about you?"

"Not right away. Eventually, she recanted her story, saying that she'd been high and had screamed rape to get Wesley's attention since he'd been ignoring her most of the night. I guess they'd been sleeping together."

Dakota's brows scrunched. "You gotta be kidding me. She almost ruined your life to get my father's attention? That's crazy... but I think I do remember something about this. I was in California at the time. Did they throw her in jail?"

"She was arrested for making a false accusation and was sentenced to five years, but barely did one. For the drug charge, she got a few years of probation and had to agree to drug treatment. But it was your father who kept the shit going. He said Avery had been coerced into admitting fault and that I had indeed forced myself on her. He still believes I assaulted the woman."

Leaning against the wall near the fireplace, Hamilton watched as Dakota walked over to him.

"My father has done some awful things, which is partly why we've always had a rocky relationship," she said, embracing Hamilton. "But this...I'm so sorry for what you went through. Thank you for telling me."

"I wish I would've told you sooner. Then maybe things wouldn't have gotten out of hand tonight." Hamilton didn't know that for sure, but at least Dakota wouldn't have been blindsided by Wesley's accusation.

"What happened once your name was cleared?"

"I resigned. My reputation was shot, and I was mentally and emotionally spent."

"I can imagine."

"Jackie and I had split by this time, but I was responsible for a baby. That's when I got hired on at the club, but I still needed closure. The only way I could get some type of justice was to file a civil lawsuit. I sued Avery and your father for defamation and won."

"That's good, but considering how large my dad is living, you probably didn't sue him for enough money."

Hamilton couldn't help but smile, grateful she believed him. Financially, he made out okay with the lawsuit. He received enough to set aside for Dominic's education, and he had invested the rest.

"I just thought of something. I tried to get my father to tell me what you had on him, and he wouldn't say."

"As per the settlement agreement, neither of them could continue accusing me or discussing the accusations of that night again."

"Or?"

"Or I could drag them back to court."

That was the last thing Hamilton wanted. As long as nothing came of the night, such as anything ending up in the paper or online, he didn't want to take Wesley back to court. He wanted to forget the incident ever happened.

Hamilton cradled Dakota against him. "Tired?" he asked.

"Very, it's been an emotionally exhausting night." She lifted her head and looked at him. "I just want to get out of these clothes and snuggle up with you...and then maybe sleep for a week."

Hamilton leaned down and kissed her sweet lips. "Sounds like a plan. Let's go home."

She smiled up at him. "I like the way that sounds."

"Yeah, me too."

Hamilton called Angelo to make sure everything was handled and that he could leave. According to him, Wesley had already left, not wanting any cops involved, and he hadn't wanted to be questioned by anyone about the incident.

That made two of them.

Chapter Twenty-One

Dakota released a wistful sigh when Hamilton opened the door to his house, and she strolled through the mudroom and into the bright kitchen. Weeks ago, when he first invited her to his place, she had immediately felt at home, loving how warm and inviting it was. The four-bedroom, two-story house didn't necessarily look like a bachelor's pad with its gourmet kitchen, traditional furnishings, and tan, beige, and brown color scheme. No, it looked more like a home for a family.

"Are you hungry?" Hamilton asked as he placed his keys on top of the stainless-steel refrigerator and undid his tie. He had worn a tailored, navy-blue suit that she hadn't seen him in before, but he looked as handsome and powerful as usual.

"No, I'm good. Just ready to go to bed," Dakota said. It had been a long day, and she was a little tired, but what she wanted most was to be hugged up to him. The night's events were still messing with her head. Knowing her father had something to do with Hamilton leaving the police force partly because of shame and lack of support was disappointing. Wesley was a proud man, even when wrong. No doubt the lawsuit put a chink in his superior attitude, only escalating the animosity he had toward Hamilton.

It had been an emotional evening for all of them. And right now, Dakota just wanted to set all thoughts aside and love on her man.

As if reading her mind, Hamilton reached for her hand, pulled her into his arms, and kissed the top of her head. She inhaled slowly. His masculine scent, a combination of sandalwood and citrus, surrounded her, bringing her a level of peace that she could only get from him.

"Let's go upstairs." With his arm around her, he shut off the downstairs lights and guided her to his bedroom. When he flipped the light switch, the room was illuminated by one of the bedside lamps.

Yep, feels like home.

Dakota kicked off her four-inch heels, glad to set her feet free. When she set her wrap and small clutch purse in a nearby chair, she watched as Hamilton started undressing. He shrugged out of his suit jacket and dress shirt, laying them on top of her belongings.

"Though I love this dress, I want you out of it," he said gruffly, and moved behind her, placing feathery kisses along the side of her neck and down to her bare shoulder. She had only worn the gray chiffon outfit once, and tonight it had done what she wanted it to do. It left Hamilton speechless, as she knew it would. He had said that the sheer-looking strapless white dress that stopped just above her knees made her look like a royal goddess. And all night he had made her feel like one.

Hamilton slowly unzipped the back of the dress and he loosely held the garment as it slid down her body. Dakota stepped out of it, leaving her in only a white thong.

"Damn, baby. You are truly a sight. I wanted to take my time with you tonight, but looking the way you do, that's going to be hard." He laid the dress across the chair. Wrapping his arms around her, he pulled her against him and gripped her ass, then squeezed. "You have the most incredible body..." His words trailed off as he littered kisses along her neck, nipping, licking and then she felt a light pinch and knew he was marking her. She didn't care. She was his, and her body belonged to him and only him.

His large hands slid slowly up her body and Dakota's eyes drifted closed. Her head fell back, giving him more access to her neck. He made her feel so good, so desired. Luscious heat soared through her veins as she soaked up the pleasure of what his mouth and hands were doing to her. She would never tire of the way he stroked every inch of her.

"Let's take this to the bed." With little effort, he lifted her and Dakota wrapped her arms around his neck, and her legs went around his waist. Cupping the back of his head, her mouth covered his. He urged her lips open with the thrusting of his tongue, forcing a groan out of her as he carried her across the room.

Hamilton eased her onto the king-sized bed, unwilling to take his mouth from hers. She might've started the kiss, but he quickly took over. The tenderness of his tongue, exploring the inside of her mouth, sent currents of desire roaring through her body.

"Mmm, you look good and you taste even better. Let me get out of my clothes," Hamilton murmured against Dakota's lips but was slow to pull away. When he finally lifted his head, he straightened and tugged on the back collar of his T-shirt and yanked it off. He tossed it to the floor, and the rest of his clothes quickly followed.

Each time Dakota saw his naked body, she reveled in how perfect it was. Muscles, not like a body builder's, but like a man who worked out regularly and took care of himself, bulged with every move he made. Dakota's gaze went lower. His long, thick shaft stood at attention, and she squeezed her thighs together as her sex pulsed, anticipating having him deep inside of her.

Oblivious or not caring that she was gawking at his dick, Hamilton grabbed a couple of condoms from his drawer and laid them on top of the nightstand. He eventually turned and caught her staring, but then his gaze raked over her body, assessing every inch of her, and landing on her tiny panties. It was as if he was seeing her for the first time. She had never been self-conscious about how she looked, and the lust brimming in his eyes only heightened her desire for him.

Before climbing onto the bed, his hand did a slow glide down the center of her body and didn't stop until he reached the top of her panties. Dakota lifted slightly, and Hamilton slid them over her hips and down her legs, dropping them to the floor.

He shook his head as if in awe, appreciation of what laid before him written on his face. Dakota smiled. When he looked at her like that, she felt beautiful, desirable and devilish. She cupped her breasts, squeezing them together and slowly running the pads of her thumbs over her pert nipples. She loved teasing him. The fire in his eyes glowed and the deep, sensual growl rumbling from his chest was like that of a predator, ready to pounce on his prey.

"You make me crazy, but I refuse to let your antics rush me." He climbed onto the bed and swatted her hands away, replacing them with his own. Hovering above her, he palmed the sides of her breasts pushing them together before pulling one of her nipples into his mouth. Dakota's back arched into him as he paid the same homage to the other. The heat between her thighs blossomed with the way his tongue swirled around her hardened bud. "Tonight, I'm taking my time with you," he mumbled against her heated skin.

Yeah...we'll see, she thought, knowing that with the way her body responded to him, they might have to get a quickie out of the way and then slow things down.

"You. Smell. So. Damn. Good." Between each word, he planted kisses on her chest, between her breasts and lingered when he reached her belly button. The touch of his mouth on her skin sent a tantalizing shiver through her. With each dip of his tongue and the way he caressed her, the night's events slowly faded into the background. Though she loved what he was doing, tonight she wanted him to feel how much he meant to her. Wanted him to know how loved he was.

Catching him off guard, she twisted her body and flipped him onto his back, then straddled him. The surprise on his face, with his eyes rounded and his mouth hanging open, was comical but Dakota didn't give him a chance to speak. Her mouth covered his with greediness as her perky nipples brushed against his solid chest. He cupped her face between his hands and their tongues sparred with each other, sending her need for him to new heights.

Hamilton deepened the kiss, and their sexual moans filled the quietness of the room. Dakota was laying on top of him, her hands on his head as she rubbed her body over his. When his hard length brushed against her sex, a quiver raked over her flesh. He made her feel so damn good.

Hamilton moaned a growl against her mouth, moments before his hands slid to her butt, his fingers digging into her skin to stop her from gyrating against him. Dakota knew she was playing with fire since his shaft was close enough to slide easily into her, but she couldn't stop.

"You either grab a condom, or I won't be responsible for my next move," he said gruffly, his heated gaze boring into her as the head of his penis bumped against her slick folds.

Yeah, they'd take it slow next time. Dakota snatched up the foil packet, and within seconds he had sheathed himself. Hamilton entered her in one smooth motion, and her eyes slammed closed.

Oh yes. She loved being on top. Not only because she was a control freak, but this way she could feel every inch of his shaft inside of her.

Bracing her hands on his chest, heat sizzled along her spine as she rode him, squeezing and rotating her hips with each move. Hamilton held her thighs loosely, as he moved beneath her, matching her stroke for stroke.

"Ah, Da—Dakota," he rasped, his jaw tightening and his eyes were barely open. His moves grew more intense, but all of a sudden, he stopped. She squeaked, caught by surprise when he flipped her onto her back and started up again. His powerful thrusts were turbulent as he thumped in and out of her, plunging deeper with every move.

Dakota fisted the bed sheets, her muscles tightening around his shaft as he pushed into her. Faster. Harder. She could barely catch her breath as her climax grew within reach. He felt too damn good.

"*Hamilton*," she breathed but cried out her pleasure when gripped by an orgasm. The flames of passion roared through her body, tapping every nerve ending along the way, sending her hurtling over the edge.

Hamilton was right behind her, his body jerking violently as his explosive release rocked them both. He collapsed on top of her, panting hard and mumbling something she couldn't make out.

"That was...wow." Dakota wrapped her arms around him struggling to get air into her lungs, but exhilaration soared through her body. Minutes later, energized for the next round, she nibbled on Hamilton's earlobe.

"I know what you're doing. You're insatiable," he wheezed.

"Maybe, but you can handle me."

He slowly lifted his head. "If not, I plan to give it one helluva try."

*

An hour later, Hamilton watched Dakota sleep, a sense of rightness falling over him. He knew his feelings for her were getting serious, but it was more than that. He had fallen in love with her. He didn't know when it happened, but what he felt was stronger than anything he'd ever experienced.

I love you. The words rattled inside his head, but he hadn't spoken them yet. He was madly and passionately in love with this woman, but he didn't want to tell her before she had drifted off to sleep. He hadn't wanted her to think that what he felt was only about sex.

The moonlight peeking through cast just enough light for him to make out her soft features and enhance her beauty. Dakota wasn't just gorgeous on the outside, but her internal beauty shone through, making him fall even deeper for her. He loved spending time with her. Loved how well she got along with his son, and more than anything, Hamilton loved how she made him feel. Dakota wasn't a woman who needed a man, but she made him feel as if he was the most important person in her life.

I love you.

He placed a kiss on her forehead. Soon. He'd tell her soon.

Chapter Twenty-Two

"What do you think?" the makeup artist asked when she turned Dakota's chair around to face the mirror.

Dakota turned her head left and right, impressed by the transformation. Given the long dark curly wig with reddish highlights and the way the artist had made up her face, she looked like a different person. At a quick glance, she and the lead actress could be twins.

"I think you're very good at what you do."

"Why, thank you. I try." The redhead beamed at Dakota, her diamond stud nose ring glittering under the lights.

At the last minute, the director decided to add a fight scene in which he needed Dakota's expertise. It wasn't a big scene, but it would give her an opportunity to show off some of her karate moves. For the past week, she and Homer had been getting along better. He had done a one-eighty in regards to his negative attitude toward her. She wasn't sure what changed, but it made working with him more tolerable.

With one last look in the mirror, Dakota said her goodbyes and exited the makeup trailer.

"How's it going?"

Dakota turned to see Sebastian leaning against the outside of the trailer. Handsome with a Larenz Tate type of swagger, but taller, Sebastian was quickly becoming one of Hollywood's drool-worthy heartthrobs.

"Hey there. I didn't know they were working on your scenes today," she said, accepting a hug from him. He always smelled so good but hugging him was starting to feel weird. He seemed to hold on longer than necessary these days.

"Actually, I just stopped by to talk to Homer for a minute and figured I'd say hello to you before I left." He fell into step with her as she walked to the trailer that she was sharing with a few other actresses.

"How's it been working with him?" she asked.

"Not too bad. Being family, he kinda has to be nice to me."

"Family? I had no idea you two were related."

"He's my uncle. Actually, I have a few family members in the industry, but it's not something we broadcast. Don't want anyone thinking I get special treatment. Speaking of family, I was surprised to learn that Wesley is your father. Why haven't you mentioned it?"

Dakota shrugged. "Like you are regarding your family in the business, it's not something I discuss. Besides, most people already know."

"I didn't know."

"Are you looking for a new agent?" she asked, wondering what difference it made that she and Wesley were related. She hoped he wasn't about to ask her for an introduction or a favor regarding her father. They still weren't on speaking terms. It had been almost a week since the afterparty and Dakota had been spending most of her spare time with Hamilton and Dominic, her two favorite guys.

"No, he's Alexia's agent."

"Oh, the woman you were with at the party?"

Sebastian nodded. "I tried to get her to go with someone different, no offense to your father, but she insists he's the best. She's a model but wants to get into acting."

Dakota couldn't deny that her dad was the best at what he did. "He'll do right by her if she's any good and serious about working."

"Well, I don't like him and I surely don't trust him with her."

Dakota couldn't say much about his feelings for her father. People either worshiped the ground he walked on because of his negotiating abilities, or they hated him. Which was why it would be impossible to narrow down the enemies who would send him threatening letters.

"Are you and Alexia dating?" she asked. She didn't really care, but Sebastian flirted with anyone in a skirt, and she wondered.

"Nah, we're just friends. I'm holding out for you."

Dakota looked at him sideways. "I hope you're kidding."

"I'm serious. I'm heading back to Cali in a few weeks, but I was hoping that you and I could spend some time together." He brushed the back of his fingers down her bare arm and a creepy sensation skittered through her body. Dakota moved out of reach. That touch was a little too intimate for her liking.

"I already told you at the party, I'm seeing someone."

"I didn't get the impression that it was serious."

She stopped walking and turned fully to him. "Why would you say that?"

"Because the guy let you roam around the party alone." He leaned in and lowered his voice. "If you were mine, I wouldn't let you out of my sight."

Dakota snorted and started back on her trek to the trailer. "Then it's good I'll never be yours. I don't like any man hovering over me."

Except for maybe Hamilton...a little, she thought. Thinking of him reminded her that she'd be seeing him in a few hours. He promised to stop by to check out her motorcycle scene. She wasn't sure which made her more excited, finally getting to ride a Ducati 1098S or having her man watch her in action.

"So, all of this time you've been flirting with me, was what? You being nice?" Sebastian asked defensively. Clearly, she had bruised his oversize ego.

Glad she had arrived at her trailer, Dakota was ready to end this conversation. "It wasn't flirting, and yes, I was being nice. I'm sorry if I gave you the impression that I was interested in something more. I'm very happy with the man I'm with. Very happy."

He stopped abruptly. "Well, I doubt it'll last."

Dakota frowned. "What's that supposed to mean?"

He turned and walked off without a backward glance.

"Yet another reason why I'm not interested in your narcissistic ass," she mumbled and headed into the trailer.

It was conversations like that one that had her thinking more about leaving the industry. Dealing with self-absorbed people was getting old and doing stunts for a living wasn't as appealing. Besides, this movie project was almost done and she was scheduled to head to Vegas and start her next assignment in a month. Dakota couldn't even imagine leaving Hamilton.

She shook the thought free. No, she wouldn't worry about that until the time came. Right now, she needed to focus on kicking some ass.

*

Hamilton stood next to his brother, Justin, watching as Dakota prepared for her motorcycle scene. She'd had a fight scene earlier, which he wasn't able to catch, but he was glad he made it to this one.

Her goal was to nail the motorcycle stunt in one shot in hopes of getting out of there early. According to her, it was the only day they could do the scene due to several streets being blocked off in the normally high-traffic area. Hamilton was hoping for the same since he also had the rest of the day free.

Dakota snagged his attention when she revved the engine of a custom Ducati 1098S and took off down the street before slowing and circling back. She looked like a total badass on the sleek black bike that was accented in chrome with a matching helmet. The black leather jumpsuit she was wearing added to the fierce look.

"Your woman has nerves of steel, man. I can't imagine doing half the stunts she's performed on this project," Justin said, admiration ringing in his voice. "How much did she tell you about this stunt?"

The question immediately put Hamilton on edge. "Not much. She just said that she'd be riding a motorcycle like one she wanted to purchase one day. I guess she's been planning to test drive one but hadn't yet."

"With the way she's handling that machine, no one would ever know she hadn't ridden it before."

As the words left Justin's mouth, Dakota did a wheelie, riding a short distance with the front wheel of the bike off the ground. Considering the act was illegal on city streets, he hoped it wasn't something she did outside of being on a movie set.

Justin chuckled. "Now she's just showing off, probably for you."

Hamilton's pulse thumped loudly in his ear and his chest tightened as she popped another wheelie. When the front tire hit the ground, she sped down the street at top speed, then slowed and turned around only to do it again. This woman was going to be the death of him. He didn't want her showing off. He just wanted her safe.

"This will be the last time I come and watch her do a stunt," he said to Justin. "My heart can't take this shit."

Justin laughed and pounded him on the back, then gripped his shoulder. "Well, brace yourself, bro. You're in for a treat."

If Hamilton hadn't promised Dakota that he'd be watching, he would've got the hell out of there right then. Now he was glad that Jackie had already had plans for Dominic. Otherwise, he would've brought his son to the set. Hamilton didn't need the kid fantasizing about motorcycle stunts.

"Do they usually have firefighters on the set?" He had noticed the firetruck parked at the end of the set along with an ambulance. "I can't remember seeing them the day Dom was here."

Justin shook his head. "Only when we're dealing with fire and explosives."

Hamilton's pulse inched higher. "Please tell me that's for another scene and not Dakota's."

Justin flashed another grin, and Hamilton wanted to march across the street and pull Dakota off the bike. Instead, he stood by watching as they gave her final instructions. He was too far away to hear the exchange, but she eventually gave a thumbs-up to the crew.

"Okay, here we go," Justin announced.

Hamilton held his breath thinking that he needed to talk to Dakota about looking for a different career. Knowing she did this type of work was one thing. Seeing her in action was something altogether different.

He half listened as his brother gave him a rundown of the stunt, saying something about the barn, ramp, and a haystack on the back end. From where they stood, Hamilton could barely see the starting point of the set, but he had a decent view and could watch most of the scene play out.

Dakota got into place and revved the engine several times before taking off. Anxiousness roared inside Hamilton, and his hands fisted. He watched the woman he loved fly down the street as if she had a death wish. Keeping her body low, Dakota blended in with the bike and seemed to be going twice as fast as when she was practicing. His pulse rate inched a little higher when she disappeared inside the barn. Seconds later, the front of the bike appeared and...

Boom!

Hamilton startled and his heart slammed against his chest when the bike flew through the air. Dakota was thrown twenty feet, barely missing some of the crew members.

"Oh, shit! Something went wrong!" Justin yelled.

Hamilton took off in a sprint, and an icy fear twisted inside his body as he raced down the street. Smoke billowed around the area making it difficult to see, but he kept moving. He had to get to her. He had to make sure she was okay. Emergency personnel and crew members had already leaped into action and the set was a flurry of activity.

Please...please...please... Let her be okay.

By the time he reached her, she was surrounded by practically everyone on the set.

"Dakota! Dakota!" Hamilton screamed, barely recognizing his own voice as panic rioted within him and he pushed his way through the crowd.

"Stay back! Give us some room," an EMT yelled, forcing the crowd back, but Hamilton couldn't stay away. He had to get to her. He had to make sure she was okay.

"Dakota!" he screamed over and over, still trying to get around everyone.

"Ham!" his brother yelled, holding tight to the tail of Hamilton's shirt, trying to keep him from getting any closer.

"I have to get to her. I have to—"

"Stop it!" Justin grabbed him around the waist with both arms in a tackle, practically lifting him off the ground and moving him away from the crowd. "Chill, man! You gotta keep your head. Let them do their job."

Hamilton continued pushing against his brother, unable to help himself. "I have to..." His voice hitched when he caught sight of her lying on the ground, his heart lodging in his throat. "Oh, God, she's not moving. She's not moving! I have to get to her! Dakota!" he screamed louder.

She had to hear him. He needed her to hear him.

I can't lose her. God, I can't lose her.

Chapter Twenty-Three

Head pounding, eyes burning, and suffering from a sore throat, Hamilton sat in the hospital's waiting room, surrounded by his parents and his oldest brother Chris. Not wanting Hamilton to be alone, Justin had made the calls to get them there for support. He appreciated them, but all he felt at the moment was numbness.

Like he wanted answers, he was sure OSHA—the Occupational Safety and Health Association—would do a thorough investigation into what went wrong on the set. According to Justin, there should've been a three-second delay with the explosion, and nothing should've happened until Dakota had cleared the barn. Had she not landed on the edge of the haystack, the accident could've been fatal. As it was, Hamilton still didn't know if she would pull through.

He swallowed hard and glanced down the long hallway where hospital personnel and visitors milled about, torment eating at him from the inside out. He hated hospitals. The smells, beeping machines, the bursts of screams, people crying for loved ones. All of it. It was the last place he ever wanted to be, and now he'd been waiting two hours and still hadn't heard anything from doctors.

A suffocating sensation tightened his throat and he rubbed his neck, willing himself to relax, but he couldn't.

Every few minutes his mind took him back to the accident, and the explosion that literally rocked him. Dakota could have been killed. That realization scared him to death.

"She's going to be fine," Hamilton's mother, Irene, said. She was sitting in the chair next to him, her hand moving in circular motions, rubbing his back the way she used to do when they were kids. "She's a fighter. I could tell when you brought her to the house last weekend. She's tough and stubborn."

"Beyond stubborn," Hamilton added stoically. He just prayed that attribute got her through this.

Dakota and his mother had hit it off immediately. He hadn't realized it before but seeing them together brought out the fact that they were so similar in personality. Both were strong-willed, feisty, and had a similar sense of humor. It had been years since he'd taken a woman home to meet his folks, and they were beyond thrilled to know he was serious about someone. Especially someone they liked upon first meeting. Of course, his mother was already hearing wedding bells and fantasizing about getting more grandchildren. Specifically, a granddaughter since she already had three grandsons.

Right now, Hamilton would give anything to spend the rest of his life with Dakota. She was it for him. If...no, *when* they got through this, he wasn't wasting time with a long courtship or a long engagement. The accident was a good reminder that life was short, and he had no intention of wasting any time in making her his wife.

Hamilton's phone vibrated and he dug it from his pocket to see Jackie's number on the screen.

"I'll be back," Hamilton said to his family and moved a short distance away from the waiting area.

"Hello?"

"Hi, Dad. How's Dakota? Is she still in the hospital?"

Hamilton had called Dominic to let him know that he and Dakota wouldn't be able to pick him up for dinner because she'd gotten hurt at work. Hamilton hadn't supplied much detail, not wanting to upset Dominic who loved Dakota almost as much as he did.

"Yeah, son. The doctors are still running tests, but I'll call you when I have a little more information. All right?"

"Okay...but can I come and see her? She won't mind and I promise I won't get in the way."

Hamilton closed his eyes and pinched the bridge of his nose trying to ward off the emotion swirling within him. "Not today, but we'll see what the doctors say about her having visitors."

"You always say, we'll see. The doctor won't mind if I see her. I can just tell them that she's gonna to be my other mom. Can I come, Dad? Huh? Can I?"

Hamilton's eyes snapped opened and he frowned. Where the hell had that come from? "What are you talking about, son?"

Silence filled the phone-line and Hamilton wondered if the call had dropped.

"Dominic?"

"Yes?"

"What makes you think Dakota's going to be your other mother?"

"When Antonio's dad got married, Antonio said he has two moms now. When you and Dakota get married, she's going to be my other mom. Please, Dad. Can I come to the hospital? She'll be glad to see me. She says I brighten her day. Please."

Hamilton sighed and leaned against the wall, unsure of how to address the marriage and mom comment. They hadn't discussed the possibility, but not much got past Dominic, and a blind person could see how much Hamilton loved Dakota.

"We'll see, Dom," Hamilton finally said. "Let me talk to the doctors first. Okay?"

They talked for a few minutes longer, well Dominic talked and Hamilton listened. His son's running monologue was like a healing balm for Hamilton's tattered emotions. But when he saw Laz down the hall speaking to Chris, Hamilton cut the conversation short and headed toward his friend.

"You look like shit," Laz said before giving him a brotherly hug. "Heard anything yet?"

Hamilton shook his head. "No. Were you able to reach Wesley?" The studio had Dakota's emergency contact information and promised to call her father, but Hamilton asked Laz to also try to reach him. They might not like the guy, but Hamilton knew he'd want to know about Dakota and the accident. He had also contacted Tymico and left a message for her.

"Yeah, I found him. He's in Miami, but said he'll get the first flight out."

"Mr. Crosby?" a doctor called out, looking around before calling the name again. Hamilton snapped to attention and hurried toward him.

"Yes, I'm Hamilton Crosby. How is she?" he said in a rush, a wave of anxiousness crashing inside his gut, as he stood before the doctor desperate for answers.

"I'm Doctor Saarni, the attending physician. Ms. Bradford is in recovery," he said, using Dakota's birth name.

Hamilton listened, his blood pressure rising as the doctor listed Dakota's injuries including a concussion, fractured ribs, a punctured lung, a broken arm and a host of bruises. Had it not been for the extra cushioning in the helmet, the special material of the jumpsuit, the other protective gear, and that haystack near the barn, Hamilton knew she'd be dead.

Invincible. She often joked that she was invincible.

"Ms. Bradford is in critical but stable condition. It was a good thing she wore all of the protected gear. The only burn she received was on her left wrist, the space between where the glove stopped and the sleeve of her biker suit met. She's a very lucky young lady. Right now, she's heavily sedated, but should be awake in a few hours."

"Can I see her?"

After a slight hesitation, the doctor said, "Once we get her settled into a room, I'll have a nurse come out and get you."

Shaken up, Hamilton nodded, then filled his family in on what he'd just learned. He suggested they head out since he planned to stay at the hospital. His brother offered to bring him back food and some clothes that could get him through the next day or two since Hamilton had already decided that he wasn't leaving the hospital without her.

When he pushed open the door to Dakota's room, his breath lodged in his throat and apprehension scraped along his nerves. He'd seen his share of injuries and even dead bodies, but this…this was too close to home. This was his woman laying up in the bed with a tube coming out of her chest and arms, monitors beeping, the unnerving sound amping up his unease.

Moving closer to the bed, he assessed her with a critical eye, remembering how the doctor said that she was very lucky. Hamilton knew that. He'd been there. He saw the way she had been thrown through the air. There were so many variables that had played into saving Dakota's life and he was just grateful he hadn't lost her.

He leaned in close, his mouth inches from hers. He wasn't sure if she could hear him, but just in case. "I love you, Dakota. I love you so damn much and I need you. Baby, I need you to fight. I need you well."

He placed a kiss on her forehead and pulled a chair as close to the bed as he could get it. He didn't know exactly when she would wake up, but he planned to be there when she did.

*

Hours later, Hamilton stood and stretched his arms high above his head in an effort to work out the stiffness in his back. The day had been long, but he was hopeful that Dakota would open her beautiful eyes and talk to him. Even throughout their work day, they tried to make time to check in with each other, and he realized how much he missed hearing her voice. Hearing her laugh. Hearing what craziness would come out of her mouth.

He took in her sleeping form. She hadn't twitched, hadn't moved, nothing. At one point he had to ask the nurse if she was really okay. The staff had been in and out for most of the day, assuring him that she was stable and that they expected a full recovery.

Hamilton wanted so badly to wake her, but the doctor explained that she needed her rest and needed time to heal.

The room's door swung open and he straightened, stiffening the moment Wesley burst into the room.

"What are you doing in here?" Wesley snapped.

Hamilton sighed. He had mentally prepared himself for this moment, but this guy was like an irritating gnat. "You really want to do this here, Wesley, knowing your daughter was almost killed?"

The older man had the decency to look ashamed. He glanced at the bed and gasped at the sight of Dakota.

"Oh my, God. Look at her." He covered his mouth with his hand as he moved closer to the bed. "H—how could... She's been riding motorcycles for fifteen years. I don't understand how this could've happened. She knows how to handle herself." His voice cracked on the last word.

Standing on the opposite side of the bed, Hamilton explained what he witnessed on the movie set and the little that he knew at the moment. Everyone wanted answers, but that would take time.

"Somebody's going to pay for this. What type of half-assed security measures did they have in place? Wait until I get a hold of her agent, and Homer," he said of the director. That snagged Hamilton's attention as he recalled Dakota mentioning the number of enemies her father had in the industry. But there was no way the director would intentionally sabotage his project. Would he?

Wesley continued to drone on as if he forgot he wasn't the only one in the room. Hamilton had learned a long time ago that if you let someone talk, without interrupting, you could often get more answers than if you asked questions.

"That guy always had it in for me. Probably took his frustrations out on my child, making her do those ridiculous stunts," Wesley mumbled to himself, pacing in the tight space next to the bed. Then he stopped and stood over Dakota, getting visibly emotional. "How many times did I tell her to quit? I told her that those damn stunts were going to get her killed! She didn't listen. She never listens! Now, look at her." Wesley swiped at his damp face, then rubbed the back of his neck.

Hamilton wasn't sure what to say. He didn't like that Dakota put herself in danger every day, but he also knew that she could lose her life just walking down the street. Was he uncomfortable with what she did for a living? Yes, but he respected the fact that she was doing something she loved.

"You can grab that chair over there," Hamilton said, nodding to the only other seating in the room near the window. He had vowed to Dakota that he would learn how to live in the same world as Wesley.

Might as well start now.

"Thanks, but I won't be staying," Wesley said, clearing his throat and suddenly looking a little uncomfortable. "I just wanted to see her, and to tell her... Never mind, I'll call the nurses station periodically to check on her."

Hamilton shoved his hands into his front pants pockets, surprised her father hadn't planned to stick around. "Why don't you at least stay until she wakes up. I'm sure she'd want to see you." Dakota missed him but was too stubborn to try and make peace with her father.

"She's not happy with me right now, and I don't want to cause her any undue stress." Wesley glanced at him but quickly looked away.

One of them had to be the bigger man. If Wesley thought Hamilton would lash out or throw punches while Dakota was laid up, he didn't have to worry about that.

Dakota meant everything to him and he wanted to do whatever necessary to try and get along with her father.

"Listen, Wes, about what happened at the par—"

Wesley lifted his hand. "Don't. I know I was out of line that night, but my feelings for you remain the same. I know you did something with Avery and there's nothing you can say that would change my mind on the subject. You don't deserve my daughter, but if she's too blind to see that for herself, there's nothing I can do or say to change her mind."

Despite the twinge of annoyance sparking inside of him, Hamilton refused to stoop to the man's level. "I'm sorry you feel that way, but I'm not going anywhere. I love your daughter."

After the words were out of his mouth, Hamilton realized he'd told her father how he felt, before he could officially tell Dakota. Telling her how much he loved her while she was asleep didn't count, but the satisfaction of throwing Wesley off his high horse brought him pleasure.

Teeth clenched, Wesley glared at him. "She'll learn soon enough what type of man you are."

"Trust me. She already knows the type of man I am."

A knock sounded on the door and Tymico peeked in. "Hi." She glanced from Hamilton to Wesley. "Is it okay if I come in?"

"Of course, sweetheart," Wesley said before Hamilton could respond. He met her halfway and pulled her into a hug. "Dakota's still sleeping, but the nurse I talked to a few minutes ago said she's going to be fine."

Tymico nodded and slipped out of Wesley's arms and approached Hamilton.

"Thank you for calling me. I was on a flight coming from Florida and just got back a short while ago. I'm so sorry. I know this has to be hard for you. Let me know if there's anything I can do." She hugged him.

Hamilton thought it was interesting that they both had been in Florida but didn't comment. "Thank you, and thanks for stopping by."

"Of course. She's my best friend," Tymico said in a choked voice as she approached the bed. Hamilton stepped back to give her room. "Dee, what have you done?"

Hamilton observed as the woman held Dakota's hand, tears sliding down her cheek as she encouraged her friend to get better soon. Dakota might've thought that Wesley was the only family she had, but Hamilton could see how much Tymico loved her.

"I'm going to leave," Wesley said to no one in particular and kissed Dakota on the cheek.

"Leave?" Tymico frowned. "Bradford, don't you want to stick around at least until she wakes up?"

Bradford? Hamilton didn't know Dakota's friend well, but he was a little surprised that she referred to Wesley by his last name.

"I wish I could stick around, but I—I need to get going. Are you planning to stay with Dakota awhile?" Wesley asked, ignoring Hamilton.

Tymico bit down on her bottom lip, still holding Dakota's hand, but looked at Hamilton. "Do you mind if I stick around?"

"Of course not," he said. "I'm sure Dakota would want that. I'll walk Wesley out and give you some time with her."

Wesley frowned, but said his goodbyes to Tymico and walked out with Hamilton right behind him.

"Just so we're clear," Hamilton said the moment the door closed. "I'm here for the long haul. Might as well get used to seeing me with your daughter. We can either try to get along or—"

"Just because you're sniffing around Dakota doesn't mean there will ever be anything between you and me. She's going to come to her senses one day and when she does, I'll be right there to gloat."

Hamilton watched the man stroll down the hallway in his thousand-dollar suit and an I-own-this-place swagger. He might intimidate those in his world, but Wesley needed to think again if he thought he could make Hamilton go away. *Not gonna happen. I'm here to stay.*

Chapter Twenty-Four

"What's wrong, baby?" Hamilton asked. He sat on the side of the bed, the back of his fingers caressing her cheek.

Dakota closed her eyes, amazed at how well he knew her, how he picked up on her moods even before she acknowledged them herself. She'd been in the hospital for a week and didn't remember much about the first few days, but Tymico filled her in on what Hamilton wouldn't. Such as how he hadn't left her side the whole time, except to use the bathroom, stretch his legs, and talk to his son. Even then he didn't leave without making sure either Wesley was there, or a member of his family, or Tymico, was in the room.

"Dakota?"

She opened her eyes and met Hamilton's gaze. "I need to get out of here." Dakota had never been good at sitting around. That wasn't her. And laying in a hospital bed, barely able to move without pain, was getting old. "I know the doc said I'll probably be able to leave in a couple of days, but can you break me out of here today?"

A slow smile tipped the corner of his lips and Dakota's heart turned over in her chest. God, this man could brighten her world with just a smile.

"What? You want to do like a prison break or something?"

"Yeah, can you help a sista out?" she cracked. "Better yet, get Laz here. I know he can pull some strings and help me break out of this joint."

Hamilton laughed. "You're starting to sound like Dominic. Laz is his go-to person for doing things I wouldn't approve of."

"Smart kid."

"Yeah, too smart," he said and turned serious. He moved in close, only a breath away, and gave her a soul-stirring kiss. Dakota didn't know what she had done to deserve this sweet gentle man, but she was so thankful. She wouldn't have been able to get through the last few days of excruciating pain, frustration and tears without him.

Hamilton pulled back and sifted his fingers through her hair, smoothing it down. "I told you this days ago, but just in case you didn't hear me, I want you to know how much I love you. I love you so damn much, Dakota."

"Hamilton, stop trying to make me cry." She blinked back tears. "I don't remember you saying those words, but I felt...I feel your love for me, and I love you even more. I love you so much." She touched his face with her good hand, loving the feel of the scruff on his cheek from not shaving a few days.

"It killed me seeing you lying here in pain, knowing there was nothing I could do to make you feel better."

"You did make me feel better. I'll admit the left side of my body still feels like one huge throbbing nerve. But I don't even want to think about what it would've been like going through this without you by my side. Pulling for me. Standing by me. Loving me. I will forever be grateful to you."

They kissed again and Dakota knew at that moment that they would have a long life together. No way was she living the rest of her days without this man.

"I'm giving up stunt work," she announced.

Hamilton sat on the side of the bed but said nothing. Shortly after she was coherent and able to talk without dealing with shortness of breath, they had discussed the accident. He joked about tying her to a chair to keep her from risking her life again, but she knew he wouldn't stop her from doing what she loved.

"I've had enough," Dakota continued. "I have had plenty of scrapes and bruises over the years, even broke my leg and wrist once. But this time is different. This time scared me."

"I'll support whatever you decide, and I have to be honest. I'm glad you're thinking about quitting. I can't handle seeing you hurt and in pain."

"Do you know what you want to do instead?"

"I have some ideas, but nothing concrete yet."

Her agent informed her that production had been shut down on the movie set during the investigation, but Dakota had already decided not to return. Technically, the motorcycle stunt was her last scene as per her contract, and if the footage they had wasn't enough, they'd just have to find someone else. She couldn't go back. If they wanted to sue her for breach of contract, she'd deal with it.

"Well, you can think about next steps after you're out of here." After a quick peck on the lips, Hamilton stood from the bed and walked across the room to the table where his cell phone was sitting. He typed something into it before setting it back down and returning to her. "You look tired."

"I am a little." And her bruised hip bone was starting to throb again.

As if reading her, Hamilton said, "Before you take more pain meds, I have a surprise for you."

"A surprise? Wha—" The door swung open before she could ask, and Dominic walked in. Dakota scooted up and Hamilton hurried over to adjust the pillows behind her. "There's my sunshine. Dom, I've missed you."

Dominic stood near the door, his backpack dragging on the floor as he took in all of the equipment. According to Hamilton, Dominic had been begging to see her for days. Dakota felt the same way. Her favorite guys had become such an important part of her life. She didn't want to go days without seeing either of them.

"Dom, can I get a hug?" she asked, hoping to prompt him forward. For a minute it looked as if he was going to start crying or bolt from the room, but then he moved toward her.

"Dakota," Hamilton started in that warning tone he'd been using since she'd been in the hospital. "You're still healing. No lifting. No pulling. No—"

"I know, I know. More rules, but I need a hug...and not just your hugs," she said, smiling at Dominic who stopped at the side of the bed.

"What they do to you? What's all this stuff? Are you going to die?" he asked, in that serious tone that she'd grown to love.

Dakota chuckled and her heart swelled. She missed talking with him. "No, sweetheart. I'm going to be fine, but I'm anxious to see the plans for the tree house. Your father told me that you started working on them."

He lit up at the mention of the project they'd concocted during one of their outings a couple of weeks ago

"Guess what?" he said excitedly and started to climb on the bed.

"Dom, not on the bed," Hamilton said.

"It's okay," Dakota said, patting the right side of the mattress, and Dominic climbed up. "Once you give me a hug, then I need you to tell me everything. What'd I miss?"

He hugged her quickly, even added a sweet kiss to her cheek. "Grandpa made a picture of the tree house. Wanna see it?"

"Of course. I hope he didn't start building it without me."

"No. I told him we have to supervise. It's going to be big. Oh, and it's gonna have a pole inside of it so we can slide down it like firemen. Or we can use the ladder or maybe we can just jump off the balcony."

Dakota heard Hamilton groan and she smiled. He'd made it clear that going forward, he didn't want her anywhere near danger or risking her life for anything. Apparently, he was going to have to give his son the same speech.

Dakota settled back as Dominic hopped from one topic to the next. She hated being in the hospital, but as long as she had Hamilton and Dominic, it didn't matter where she was.

"Are you coming to my birthday party?" Dominic asked, explaining that it would be at his grandparents' house.

"I wouldn't miss it," Dakota responded, ignoring how Hamilton folded his arms across his chest, not looking too pleased. She loved him, but not even he, or the constant pain invading her body, would keep her from Dominic's birthday party. He wasn't her son, but she loved him as if he were.

Thirty minutes later there was another knock on the door.

"Look who I found in the hallway," her father said as he walked in, followed by Tymico. They paused upon seeing Dominic laying on the bed next to Dakota. He had kicked off his shoes and laid down beside her ten minutes into their conversation.

"Let me guess. This must be Dominic," Tymico grinned and waved at Hamilton on her way to the bed.

"Yep, the one and only," Dakota said, smiling down at Dominic who was looking a little shy. "Dom, this is my best friend, Ms. Tymico. Actually, she's more like a sister. Ty, this is Dominic, Hamilton's son."

She shook his hand. "It's a pleasure to meet you, Dominic. Dee talks about your all the time."

"She does?"

"Yep, but she didn't tell me you were so cute."

Dominic smiled shyly and sifted through his backpack as if he were actually looking for something. "Thanks."

"And, Dom, this is my father, Mr. Bradford." Dakota didn't miss her father's disapproving look, though he wore one of his fake smiles.

"Hi," Dominic said shyly and shook the hand Wesley extended.

"All right, Dom. Let's give Dakota and her guests some privacy," Hamilton said.

"But I'm not finished telling her about the turtle Mom let me get. Her name is Dee." He grinned at Dakota and she burst out laughing.

"You named your turtle after me? I'm flattered."

"I was going to name it Dakota, but Dad said there could only be one Dakota."

Her gaze slid to Hamilton's and he winked at her. *This man... God, I love him.*

"Let's go, Dom," he said, ignoring Dominic's protests as he gathered his shoes and they left the room.

"You're involved with a man who has a child?"

Dakota shrugged, immediately regretting the move when she felt a twinge in her back. Today had been the longest she'd sat up for any long period of time, and now she was starting to feel the effect.

"What can I say? I have a big heart. I fell in love with a man who has a child, and I love my father who accuses people of heinous crimes, despite their innocence."

"Don't sass me, young lady."

"Yes, *sir*," Dakota mocked, struggling not to laugh. She was finally feeling like herself, at least mentally.

"Okay, do I have to referee you two?" Tymico said, her hands on her hips. "Or maybe I should hang outside if you're going to do your usual arguing."

"Nah, you can stay. I don't feel like arguing."

"So how are you feeling, honestly?"

"I feel good." She and Tymico chatted while Wesley stared out the window. As they caught up, Dakota thought about how much she missed their girl talk. They'd been seeing less and less of each other since Dakota got her own place, and they both were dating.

Tymico glanced at her watch. "Okay, I have to head out. I just wanted to stop by and check on you before I fly out this evening." Tymico hugged her carefully. "I'll call you tomorrow."

"Thanks, sis. I appreciate you stopping by."

"No problem. Now no arguing when I leave," Tymico said before strolling out of the room.

"I didn't expect to see you today, Dad."

"I figured since you're being discharged tomorrow, we should probably talk logistics about what you want moved from your apartment to the house."

Dakota frowned. "What house?"

"What do you mean, what house? Our house. The house you grew up in. That's where you'll be recovering. Between the housekeeper and—"

"I'm not moving in with you." She and Hamilton had discussed living arrangements for the next few weeks, at least until she was back on her feet. Dakota never slept over on the days Hamilton had Dominic, but during her recovery, she would stay in Hamilton's guest room whenever Dominic stayed the night. "Dad, I've already made arrangements."

"You're going to be shacking up with that guy?" he asked, disgust lacing his words.

"Says the man who has had several live-in lovers. I'm grown. Like what you do is your business, what I do is mine. But thanks for the offer."

"Dakota, you're being unreasonable. I worry about you. It's best if you stay with me. Besides, you said you forgave me for my behavior at the party, but you're still keeping me at arm's length."

"Don't try to put this on me," she said, her hand on her chest. They had removed the chest tube, but there were moments where it still seemed hard to get air into her lungs. "I do forgive you for embarrassing me, but that has nothing to do with this situation. You're trying to force me to do something I don't want to do."

"I want you home, so you can heal."

Dakota laid her head on the pillow, feeling a little tired. "I appreciate your offer, but I'm not moving back home."

"Yes, you are."

"Dad, please. Let's not do this. Why can't you just respect my decision? I'll be staying with Hamilton for a little while, and that's all I'm going to say on the subject."

"You are my child and I want you with me. How dare you put that—that has-been cop before—"

"Get out." Dakota lifted her head and kept her voice low. Anger seized her body, despite her trying to remain calm. Her father didn't budge, his arms folded across his chest in defiance. "I said, get out!" she yelled.

Hamilton burst through the door, a nurse right behind him.

"What's wrong?" he asked, standing next to the bed. "You're shaking."

"Dakota, are you in pain?" the nurse asked

"Yes, and I—I want him out of here. He won't leave."

"What the hell, man?" Hamilton growled and moved to the side of the bed where her father was standing.

"H—Ham," Dakota warned, praying there wouldn't be a repeat of the fight he and her father had weeks ago.

"Babe, I'm not going to touch him. I just can't understand how a man who claims to love his daughter, can see you're in distress, and not do anything." He shook his head, looking disgusted. "You gotta go, Wesley."

Her father looked from Hamilton to her, before storming out of the room.

While the nurse checked her blood pressure, Dakota chanced a glance at Hamilton who was rubbing her hand, watching her as if daring her to move.

"Your blood pressure is 153/105. I'll get you something for the pain, but right now, try to relax," the nurse said before leaving the room.

"I shouldn't have let him get me riled up."

"And I should've stayed in here."

She told him about the conversation and her disappointment when her father didn't leave when she asked him to.

"I can't figure that guy out. I know you want a relationship with him, but Dakota, I can't help but wonder if he has your best interest at heart."

She didn't respond, not knowing what to say. Her dad was complicated. He wanted what he wanted and everyone else's feelings be damned.

Once the nurse returned and Dakota took the pain medication, she tried to block out the argument with her father. He was so adamant about her staying with him, and she wondered why. What was he up to? Was he just trying to keep her from Hamilton, or was he up to something else?

Chapter Twenty-Five

"Dinner was delicious, and the flowers and candles were a nice touch, too," Dakota said, gushing over the long-stemmed roses and the four tapered candles illuminating the dining room table. "I didn't know you were such a romantic."

Hamilton shrugged. "What can I say? I'm a man of many talents."

"Mmm," she moaned, flashing that sexy smile that always sent blood rushing to the lower part of his body. "I can't wait to experience some more of your talents."

"If you're referring to the talents I think you're referring to, not gonna happen. At least not until you heal a little more."

She was moving around better, but her ribs and left hip were still bothering her. The cast on her left arm was now covered in Dominic's drawings.

"I'm not made of china, Hamilton."

"I know, babe, but I want you at a hundred percent. Or at least close to it before we indulge in strenuous activities."

She huffed out a breath, not looking too pleased, but she didn't argue. That told Hamilton all he needed to know. She wasn't physically ready for sex.

He stood, blew out the candles and reached for her hand. "Come with me."

"Where are we going?"

"To the family room. Since we've had dinner and dessert, I figured maybe we could do a little slow dancing. Very slow if you're up for it."

That brought a smile to her face. "Wow, you're really pouring it on thick tonight. I'd love to dance with you."

Seconds later, the smooth melody of Eric Benét's "Spend My Life With You" poured through the speakers and Hamilton eased Dakota into his arms, careful of her bruised ribs. He missed being able to hold her like he usually did, feeling her body snuggled against his. Dancing with her now only reinforced what he already knew. He wanted to hold her like this for the rest of his life.

Before the end of the song, Hamilton slowly pulled away.

Dakota looked at him confused. "What? Did I step on your feet or something?"

He chuckled, she was such a lightweight, he probably wouldn't have noticed even if she had. "No. I just needed to get something." He strolled over to the bookshelf and grabbed the velvet box that he'd hidden. Returning to Dakota, he dropped down on one knee.

"Oh my..." she gasped, her hands going to her mouth.

"It takes some people years to know when they've found the right one. It took me a couple of days at a safe house to know you were someone special, and a couple of months to know that I want to spend the rest of my life with you. Baby, I love you. Will you do me the honor of being my wife?"

With a hand on her chest and glossy eyes, Dakota nodded. "Yes, yes I'll marry you! Oh my God, Hamilton!" she shrieked, laughing through her tears.

He stood and wrapped her in his arms but loosened his grip when she winced.

"Sorry." He kissed her and slipped the halo diamond ring with rubies along the sides onto her finger.

"It's so beautiful," she whispered in awe. "I had no idea."

"I know we've joked about how it'll be when we're married and have kids. But I love you too much to let another day go by without showing you that I'm serious about our future together. I'm looking forward to spending the rest of my life with you."

"I feel the same way, but I hope you don't want a long engagement. You know I'm a little impatient."

"A little?" He laughed. "Within twenty-four hours of being together at the safe house, you were talking about us getting married. I'd say you're also a little presumptuous and demanding."

"Don't forget intuitive, smart, and persistent."

"Right, and I love everything about you." And he already knew there wouldn't be a dull moment in their marriage.

"And I love you more."

Hamilton lowered his mouth to hers, claiming her lips. The pounding of his heart, in anticipation of his proposal, finally quieted and he lost himself in their kiss. He looked forward to their future, knowing that this time, he had chosen the person who was made for him.

*

Two days later, Dakota leaned against the railing of Hamilton's parents' deck, unable to stop glancing at her engagement ring. There were moments she still couldn't believe that they were getting married. They hadn't set a date, but they both agreed that it would be in the next few months. Neither of them wanted anything big, and though Dakota hadn't suggested it yet, she hoped Hamilton wouldn't mind going to the courthouse.

She looked out over the backyard at kids laughing, playing and running around. It was Dominic's birthday and his party was as lively as he promised it would be. He'd been talking about the event for weeks, and she loved seeing how happy he was.

"Dakota, do you need anything? Maybe something else to eat or drink," Irene, Hamilton's mother, asked when she stepped out of the house carrying an infant.

"No, thank you. I'm fine. Your family has been catering to me from the moment I walked through the door. For a minute, I thought your daughter-in-law was going to cut up my meat for me."

The older woman laughed and smile lines crinkled around eyes that were so similar to Hamilton's. She was a beautiful woman, with salt and pepper hair pulled into a ponytail that hung down her back, and blemish-free skin the color of milk chocolate. According to Hamilton, she was in her seventies, but she looked much younger than her years.

"You gave all of us a scare, especially Hamilton. We're just glad to have you here with us."

"Yeah, I scared myself. Thanks for everything you all have done for me. I really appreciate the support."

Irene waved her off. "That's what family does. Isn't that right, Miracle?" she said to the baby in her arms who was Mason's youngest child. He and his wife London, along with their children, had arrived a few minutes earlier.

"How old is she?" Dakota asked, rubbing the baby's hand and eliciting a sweet little smile from her.

"She's almost five months."

"Did I hear right, that Mason has four kids under the age of four?"

Irene laughed. "Yes, girl. He was trying to talk London into having enough children to make up a basketball team. They're close with three boys and this little cutie-pie. Their set of twins just turned two, and the oldest will be four in a couple of months. Needless to say, they have their hands full."

"Yes, they do." Dakota couldn't imagine having four kids, especially that close together in age.

"You're wonderful with Dominic. Do you want children?" Irene asked slyly.

Dakota laughed. She and Hamilton had announced their engagement before Dominic's friends arrived at the party. His family didn't look surprised, and right away, his mother and daughters-in-law started talking weddings.

210

"I love children, and I'm hoping to have a couple," Dakota said.

"Good. I have three grandsons who I adore, but I'm holding out hope for a granddaughter I can spoil. In the meantime, I get to practice with this little one."

"Mama, telephone," Chris, Hamilton's older brother, called out from the patio door.

"Be right there," she said over her shoulder. "Dakota, if you need anything, just holler."

"Will do. Thanks."

Shortly after Irene left, Jackie strolled up the deck stairs.

"I'm glad you were able to make it," she said, standing next to Dakota and leaning her hip against the railing.

"Thanks. I wouldn't have missed it. Dominic is a special little boy."

Jackie smiled, staring out into the backyard where Dominic was running with a water gun, chasing one of his friends. "Yeah, he's the best thing that's ever happened to me."

They stood in silence for a while, and for the first time in a long time, Dakota was at a loss for conversation. What did one say to her fiancé's ex-fiancée?

"I hear congratulations are in order," Jackie said without looking at Dakota. "Dominic told me that you and Hamilton are getting married."

"Yes. We haven't set a date yet, but it will be soon," Dakota said not knowing what else to say and feeling a bit awkward.

"Hamilton's a great guy, and I wish you both the best."

Okay, I didn't see that coming.

"Thank you. That really means a lot."

She smiled and it seemed genuine. "Just don't make the same mistakes I made. Loyalty is important to him. Every day I regret not believing in him enough. Not trusting him when I knew he was trustworthy, and not standing by him when he needed me the most."

Dakota stared at the woman as realization dawned on him.

"You still love him, don't you?" She wasn't sure, but Dakota felt something deep in her gut, listening to the woman's words.

"I'll always love him. He's the father of my child."

Dakota nodded, knowing it was more than that, but didn't harp on the topic. Hamilton was easy to love and she couldn't blame the woman for still having feelings for him. She was just glad to know that she didn't have to worry about Hamilton's commitment to her.

She glanced across the yard where he was sitting, talking to a couple of other dads. Every so often, like now, their gazes would connect and that usual warm, fuzzy feeling that she only experienced with him engulfed her.

"I don't think he ever looked at me the way he looks at you," Jackie said, turning her attention to Dakota. "I can tell he really loves you."

Dakota smiled, thinking about the conversation she and Hamilton once had at Club Masquerade when they were just getting to know each other. She'd always wanted to be in a relationship where others looking in could see the love she had for her mate and vice versa. She just never thought that fantasy would come to fruition.

*

Hamilton, sitting at one of the tables near the pool, glanced across the yard at the house. He couldn't help wondering what Jackie was saying to Dakota. He had watched his ex approach her, pretty sure she wouldn't start any drama during Dominic's party, but not positive.

"Aren't you a little concerned that your fiancée is talking to your ex?" Laz asked, setting a plate of food down on the table before sitting in the seat next to Hamilton. "You should be closer, just in case you have to pull them off of each other."

"I'm not worried. They both love Dominic too much to do anything that would ruin his party."

"Yeah, if you say so. Women are unpredictable. One minute you think you know them, and the next they throw you a curveball that makes you question your own damn name."

Hamilton laughed. "Did something happen between you and the prosecutor?"

His friend bit into a hamburger and frowned. "This ain't about me. We're talking about you and your women."

"I don't have women. I have a woman. As in one. You're the person who came over here talking about unpredictable women."

"Whatever, just drop it," Laz said testily, only making Hamilton laugh more. His friend didn't have to say anything. His attitude said it all. Attorney Ramsey had gotten to him and he probably didn't know what to do with his feelings for her.

Hamilton looked up just as Justin came through the back gate, making a beeline for them. "I was wondering when he'd show up," Hamilton said, knowing his brother wouldn't miss Dominic's party.

"Damn, he looks like he's about ready to hurt somebody," Laz stated.

Hamilton stood, thinking the same thing. "What's up, bro? I was wondering where you were. Everything all right?"

"It wasn't an accident," Justin said in a rush, his breaths coming in short spurts as if he had just run a marathon. "Somebody fucked with my equipment on the movie set, making the back portion of the barn explode too soon."

Hamilton's pulse pounded in his ear and a surge of fear seeped into his body. He stared at his brother, trying to wrap his mind around what Justin was *really* telling him. "Are you saying that someone *intentionally* tried to hurt Dakota?" His gaze slid to where she was standing on the deck.

"I'm saying the movie set is now considered a crime scene."

Hamilton ran his hand over his head, a sense of foreboding gripping him tighter than a straitjacket ever could.

213

Tons of thoughts bombarded his mind. He had to get Dakota some protection.

"I know you have questions, and I'll tell you everything I know, but first I need to let Shelby know I'm here," Justin said of his fiancée.

"Okay...um...don't say anything to Dakota yet," Hamilton stammered, shocked by the news.

Justin nodded and walked away as if a boulder weighed him down. He had every reason to be worried since his rigging company was in jeopardy. But right now, all Hamilton could think about was that someone might've been trying to kill Dakota. Did this have anything to do with her father?

"Before you jump to conclusions, you don't know if Dakota was the intended target. Maybe someone was trying to disrupt production," Laz said.

"Maybe, but I'm not taking any chances. Until I know otherwise, I'm having someone on her 24/7, and I'm going to need your help on this. I need any information you can get your hands on."

"Ham, you know that's Dunwoody," Laz said of the suburb that was north of Atlanta. "That's out of my jurisdiction."

"That's never stopped you before!" he bit out, sharper than intended, and huffed out a breath. "I'm sorry. I didn't—"

"No problem. I know you're worried about your woman. I'll get right on it and get back to you." Laz gathered his empty plate and tossed it in the trash before making his way over to Dominic.

Hamilton's attention went to Dakota, who was watching him from across the yard. She must have seen the shock on his face because her smile dropped and she started toward him. She'd been through so much lately, and now he had to explain that her father's sins might have caught up with her.

He pulled his cell phone from his pocket and called his office.

"Hello," their executive assistant answered on the second ring.

"Egypt, I have a situation."

Chapter Twenty-Six

"I can't believe someone sabotaged the bike and the explosion mechanism," Dakota said the moment the detectives left Hamilton's home. For the past hour, they'd asked her one question after another but hadn't been able to answer any of her questions. Like who would do something like this? Did they have any suspects?

They had nothing. No fingerprints. No DNA. No idea who could've tampered with the oil drain plug. The worst part was, she couldn't remember anything after entering the barn that day.

Hamilton returned to the living room after walking the detectives out, looking as frustrated as Dakota felt. He, Kenton, and Angelo had sat quietly during the questioning, but it was as if she could hear the wheels in their heads turning. Tossing thoughts around, but not sharing.

"Do you want me to get Egypt to get a safe house together?" Angelo asked Hamilton.

"No," Dakota said before he could respond. "I'm not hiding. I want this over with. So, if I need to be the bait to—

"Oh, hell no," Hamilton growled, a scowl marring his handsome face. She was standing in the living room and he came over and stood in front of her. "You will not intentionally put yourself at risk, Dakota. We've already talked about this. Until further notice, you'll have at least two of us with you always. I don't want you going *anywhere* by yourself. Understand?"

She jammed her hands onto her hips and glared right back at him. "Oh, so you're going to treat me like a prisoner? Make me stay inside or escort me to the bathroom whenever I have to use it?"

"If that's what it takes to keep you safe, yeah." He released a dramatic sigh and rubbed his hand over his head. He grasped the front of her shirt and pulled her toward him. "Listen, baby. I almost lost you a few weeks ago. I can't go through that again. I need you safe and in one piece. Okay?"

Now she was the one sighing. "All right. I'll follow your lead, and I'm sorry. I don't mean to seem ungrateful that you guys are looking out for me. I just don't want to be cooped up or have you hovering over me, but I'll try to cooperate."

She kissed him, hoping to lighten his mood some. He'd been uptight since the day before when Justin told him what was going on.

"Okay, this is all very touching, but this lovey-dovey crap is making me uncomfortable," Kenton grumbled and strolled into the kitchen. He poured himself a cup of coffee.

"There you go being a wimp again," Dakota teased, glad he was there. She often used him as her comic relief. "Can you pour me a cup, too?"

"I have to watch your six and cater to you? I'm starting to wonder if that cast on your arm is real, or if you're using it to get me to do everything for you. Ham, you guys aren't paying me enough."

"Yeah, yeah, yeah. Just keep her safe, and in the meantime, pour me a cup of coffee, too."

"Make that three," Angelo piped in.

"Coming right up."

"I was thinking about something while the detectives were here. You mentioned that your father has been in LA for a while. Is that normal? Does he usually travel for weeks at a time?"

"The last couple of months, he has. At first, I didn't think much of it, but now I wonder if he's staying on the move because of the threats," Dakota said and sat in one of the dining room chairs to drink her coffee.

"I think it's odd that he keeps firing his security detail." Kenton sat across from her, placing a pack of cookies that she bought earlier in the middle of the table.

"And I'm wondering if he knows who's after him and just isn't saying," Hamilton added.

"These last couple of years, I feel like I don't even know my father. He's been hiding something, but I don't know what, and I don't know why."

"I know we're thinking that the accident might be connected to Wesley, but we can't rule out that it might not be," Hamilton said. Though he'd been more shaken by the news than she was when Jason told him, he had been her rock. She didn't want them hovering over her all day and night, but she also didn't want to cause him any undue stress.

"I know the detectives are following up with your father regarding the threats he's been getting, but is it possible that you have an enemy?" Angelo asked.

"Anything's possible, but I can't think of anyone."

"I saw you put Sebastian Jeter on the list of people you spoke to the day of the accident," Hamilton said. "When did you see him?"

"He was waiting for me outside of the makeup trailer before I did the fight scene." Dakota took a sip of her coffee and noticed the look he and Kenton exchanged. "What?"

"Why didn't you tell me? I saw the way he was all over you at the party. Has he ever threatened you or made you feel uncomfortable?" Hamilton asked, that serious edge in his tone that he used with Lester the night at the club.

Dakota reflected on his question before responding. She told them about Sebastian's relationship to Homer, the director, and how Sebastian didn't like Wesley. She felt Hamilton stiffen when she mentioned being uncomfortable

218

with the way Sebastian hugged her, but he didn't say anything.

"What about Zondra?" Hamilton asked. "I didn't see her name on your list."

"She only had a couple of scenes with this production and I didn't even think about her."

"Even though she threatened you that night of the party? And didn't you mention that you ran into her one day at your father's office?"

Dakota frowned, recalling the encounter with Zondra at the party when she said something about not forgetting anything.

"And what about that food truck guy, Lester? Have you seen him since that night at the club?"

"I saw him a few days after that incident, but I haven't been to the food truck. I was afraid he might spit in my food or something."

Hamilton nodded. "That's probably a good idea to stay away from him."

"Well, it doesn't matter now since I won't be returning to the movie set. Also, with you guys acting as my shadows, people like Sebastian and Lester will probably stay clear of me anyway."

"Good," they all said in unison, and Dakota rolled her eyes. They had to find this person soon. Otherwise, she didn't know how long she could tolerate having bodyguards.

"Well, I'll get photos of these people and make sure anyone guarding you know who to look out for," Angelo said. Dakota hadn't noticed him typing into his phone.

For the next several minutes, they discussed logistics and schedules on who would guard her and when.

"One of us should try to sit in when the detectives interview some of these people. I know they already interviewed the director, some of the production crew and some of Justin's guys. But maybe we can get in on the rest," Hamilton suggested.

"I'll give them a call tomorrow to find out," Angelo offered.

"What about street cams?" Kenton asked, folding his thick arms across his chest. "The detectives didn't mention them, but it sounded like the set covered several city blocks. We might check to see if they pulled something from them."

"I put a call into Wiz right before the detectives showed up. He's going to see what he can pull and get back to us," Hamilton said, referring to Cameron "Wiz" Miller, one of the owners of Supreme Security who worked out of the Chicago office. Apparently, the guy was a tech guru and a computer genius.

"Will the city give him access to the cameras?" Dakota asked.

"If they don't, he'll hack into them," Hamilton said as if that was a normal occurrence. Dakota knew then that she didn't want to know how they got information to help with their work. She'd just trust that they all knew what they were doing.

She yawned, starting to feel the effects of the day. She'd cut back on some of the pain meds, despite still dealing with tender ribs and an achy hip. Each day she improved physically, but she found she still tired out faster than usual.

"Why don't you go and get some rest. I'll be up there shortly," Hamilton said and helped her out of the seat.

"I think that's a good idea. You guys have a good night."

Dakota couldn't wait to crawl into bed. She just hoped she slept better than she had the night before.

*

Stretched out on his king-sized bed, with his arm folded over his eyes, Hamilton debated on getting up. His body was exhausted, and frustration had been a constant companion in the last five days of knowing about the movie set problems.

Detectives were no closer in narrowing down suspects, and Dakota was starting to feel claustrophobic having security with her all the time. Hamilton didn't know who would be happier when this was all over: him, Dakota, or Kenton, who complained daily that she was wearing him out.

He smiled thinking about her. Though still a little sore, her recovery was coming along, and their living arrangement was working out. Except Dakota was missing her time with Dominic. Considering the threat on her life, she couldn't see him as often, which she hated. But today they would spend the day with him at Hamilton's parents' house, which added an extra layer of protection due to the land surrounding their place.

"Ham."

He glanced at the door where Dakota stood staring down at the cell phone in her hand and wearing an oversized T-shirt and yoga pants. That was another reason why he couldn't wait for the case to be solved. Before he had to get a security detail for her, she walked around the house in his shirts, looking way better in them than he did.

"Yeah, babe. What's up?"

"I think something is wrong." She glanced at him, worry marring her face.

Hamilton sat up. "What is it?"

She twisted her lower lip between her teeth and moved toward the bed and eased onto it, sitting next to him. "I got a text from my dad last night. Actually, it was at two o'clock this morning."

"And?"

"And besides the odd time that it was sent, the message seems a little cryptic."

Now she had Hamilton's full attention. "What does it say?"

"It says — *Just know I'll always love you.*"

Hamilton waited for her to say more, but when she didn't he prompted her. "What part seems cryptic?"

"All of it. He's never been the lovey-dovey type, to use Kenton's phrase. I've always known he loved me, but this," she held up the phone, "doesn't sound like him." She stood and groaned a little before rubbing her hip.

"Did you take anything for the pain today?"

"No. As long as I keep moving, it's not that bad."

Hamilton slipped into his boxer briefs and the jeans lying on the floor next to the bed. "You think someone has Wesley's phone?"

"I don't know, but…I think something is wrong. Well, I don't really know, but I just have this feeling."

Hamilton rarely ignored his gut or what most people considered intuition. So, he'd take hers seriously as well.

"Didn't you talk to him yesterday when he got back to town? Did he sound strange?"

"It was the day before, and no, he sounded like his usual self, but we only talked for five minutes. I'm still keeping my conversations with him short."

"Well, maybe you should call him."

She rubbed her forehead and sighed.

"Come here." Hamilton pulled her into his arms and placed a kiss on the side of her head. "If you're staying away from your father because of me, don't. I'd never try to come between you two, no matter how I feel about him. You're the one I love. Nothing he can say or do will ever change that."

"Aw, you say the sweetest things, and I love you, too."

"Call your father. I'm gonna hop in the shower. When I'm done, we can head out. Dominic is already at my folks' place, and I'm thinking we can eat breakfast there to kick off the day."

"Sounds like a plan."

After a quick kiss, Hamilton released her and headed to the bathroom. For Dakota's sake, he hoped Wesley was all right.

Chapter Twenty-Seven

"I'm sorry we had to change the plans," Dakota said from the back seat of the SUV, while Hamilton and Kenton occupied the front seat. They'd been using one of Supreme's vehicles since Hamilton felt it was safer for transporting her around, and Dakota was quickly beginning to enjoy being chauffeured.

"It's all right," Hamilton said and turned onto her father's street.

Dakota had called Wesley's home number, expecting his live-in housekeeper to answer, but she didn't, which wasn't unusual. Since he'd been traveling more, he didn't need the help around the house. But when she tried his cell phone and the call went immediately to voicemail, she knew something wasn't right. He never turned his phone off and if he was on another call, he always clicked over to at least tell her that he'd call her back.

Hamilton turned into the long driveway of Wesley's estate.

"My dad never leaves the gate open."

"Maybe he had to make a quick run and didn't bother with it," Kenton said.

"The gate is always locked."

Dakota rubbed her clammy hands together, concern vibrating through her body. Hamilton followed her instructions along the winding driveway that always seemed to go on forever. Her father had purchased the home shortly before she started high school. At first, Dakota was in love with the seventy-five-hundred-square-foot home. It had everything a teenager could want, including a huge game room, theater, large pool and tennis courts. She and her friends pretty much had full run of the home. Yet, after a while, the estate seemed too big. Too cold.

"You grew up here?" Hamilton asked once the huge house finally came into view. The home was surrounded by trees on the acre lot, and they couldn't see the neighbors.

"Yes, for a few years before I left for California."

"Still, seems pretty big for two people," Kenton said, peering out the window.

Hamilton drove around the circular drive and stopped near the front cobblestone walkway until Dakota instructed him to park on the side of the house.

"Actually, there were four of us. Me, my dad, my grandmother and we had a live-in housekeeper. Dakota scanned the exterior, not noticing anything out of place but that anxiousness she felt earlier was stronger than ever.

They climbed out of the truck, and Hamilton slid his 9mm into the back waistband of his pants. He and Kenton were always prepared for anything, but Dakota hoped their extra precautionary routine wasn't necessary.

"Remember what I said." Hamilton held her hand, and they headed to the side entrance. "You do as I say, otherwise you'll have to stay in the truck until we check things out."

"Yeah, yeah, I got it."

She dug her keys from her pocket and unlocked the door that led into the kitchen.

"Dad?" Dakota called out, looking around the eating area and attached sunroom.

"Does he usually leave the alarm off?" Hamilton asked, staying close to her while Kenton ventured down the hallway that led to the mudroom and the four-car garage.

"No, not even when he's in for the night. It usually beeps whenever someone opens a door or a window."

"Which it didn't do," Hamilton noted, sounding concerned.

"Dad, are you here?" Every nerve in Dakota's body was wound tighter than a snare drum. She had no idea what they would find and wondered if maybe she should've stayed in the truck.

"Three cars and a truck in the garage. Does that sound right?" Kenton asked when he returned to the kitchen.

"Yes."

"Let's split up," Hamilton suggested. He and Kenton pulled out their guns, keeping the weapons at their sides. "Dakota, you're with me."

She and Hamilton checked the office, theater, and a guest room before heading to the second floor, leaving Kenton to finish clearing the first floor. Not much scared Dakota, but fear of what they would find had her gripping the back of Hamilton's shirt, forcing him to stop.

"Babe, we can leave. I can get the cops in here just in case some—"

"No. No, I'm okay. Do you want to split up?"

"You're not leaving my sight." His words were low and fierce. Did he sense the same panic building in her? That something was very wrong? She tried drumming up the same calm she used when preparing for stunts, but her body pulsed with anxiety, and a sense of foreboding surrounded her.

Hamilton eased up the stairs. As instructed, Dakota stayed close to him. They had almost reached the top landing when he stopped abruptly.

"Shit," he whispered as Dakota bumped into his back. She grabbed hold of his T-shirt to keep from falling until he reached around and pulled her to his body.

"I need to get you out of here."

The sudden fear in his eyes set off warning bells in her mind. Catching her off guard, his arm went around her waist and he started to lift her, but she jerked away. The moment she did, Dakota spotted her father lying in the hallway. Her heart stopped. A pool of blood painted the white carpet beneath him.

"Daddy!" she screamed. Her pulse pounded loudly in her ear as she fell to the floor next to him. "Wh—what happened?" she cried, shocked to see him lying there. There was so much blood...

Hamilton checked his pulse.

"Is he..." she choked out, unable to say more as the gunshot wound in his bloody chest jumped out at her like a neon sign.

"Barely."

She swiped at the warm tears streaking down her cheeks, her heart racing faster than a locomotive. *Who would do this?* "We have to do something."

Hamilton leaped into action, taking off his black T-shirt, leaving him wearing only his undershirt. "We need to keep pressure on his wound," he said, using the fabric to stem the loss of blood from Wesley's chest.

Kenton seemed to appear out of nowhere, a cell phone to his ear as he talked to a 911 operator saying something about needing an ambulance, and mentioning a break-in. According to what he was telling the person on the phone, someone had entered through the patio door. As he talked, he kept moving, slipping in and out of bedrooms on the second floor, his gun at his side.

Dakota trembled with fear, her teeth chattering as if she was in freezing weather. All the while Hamilton and Kenton remained calm as if finding a bloody body and checking a house was an everyday occurrence.

"There's another body in the master bathroom," Kenton announced, pocketing his phone. "I checked the whole house. Whoever was here is gone. And who is Brad?"

"Wh—what?" Dakota asked slowly, an ominous sense of unrest seeping into her soul. "Why do y—you ask?"

Hamilton looked at her, seeming to be thinking the same thing, but said nothing as he continued to keep pressure on her father's wound.

"On the bathroom mirror, it says—I love you, Brad."

Dakota didn't even feel herself move. Before she knew it, she was racing down the hall, a wave of panic pushing her forward as she prayed her thoughts were wrong. *Please, God, don't let it be her. Please don't...*

Before she reached the master bathroom, Kenton's strong arms were around her, lifting her off her feet.

"Let me go!" she screamed and jabbed her elbow back with force. He cursed when she connected with his stomach. His grip loosened just enough for her to scurry away, and she stumbled to the bathroom.

Please, don't let it be...

"No!" The ear-piercing scream ripped from her throat and Dakota dropped to her knees. Tears blurred her vision as a stab of pain impaled her heart. "God, no!"

Her stomach lurched at the sight of the hole in the center of her friend's head, and before she could make it to the toilet, she doubled over. The contents of her stomach spilled from her mouth as sobs racked her body.

Tymico. Oh, God, Tymico.

Chapter Twenty-Eight

A suffocating sensation tightened Hamilton's throat at the retching sounds filtering down the hall. Dakota's gut-wrenching cries soon followed. He couldn't get to her fast enough. By the time he reached the bathroom, Kenton was just covering Tymico's body with a sheet, and Dakota was doubled over on the floor.

Careful of what he touched, Kenton snatched up a wad of tissue from the tissue box on the counter. He handed them to Hamilton, who quickly wiped Dakota's mouth.

"Toss the bedroom and the office," Hamilton mumbled under his breath to Kenton. They needed to search as many rooms as possible before the cops arrived, but he could already hear the sirens getting closer.

Hamilton carried Dakota out of the room. He couldn't even imagine what type of hurt she was experiencing. When they set out that morning to check on Wesley, he never expected they'd walk in on anything like this.

"I got you, baby," he whispered, taking Dakota into a different bathroom. Limp in his arms, he worried she wouldn't recover from this shock. Sitting on a cushioned bench, Hamilton held her against him while he wiped her face. "I'm so sorry," he murmured over and over, unable to come up with anything else to say.

"H—how could he? How could he do this to Ty…to me?" She cried harder. This time her sobs cutting through Hamilton like a samurai sword, and there wasn't a damned thing he could do to comfort her. He had no idea how he would get her through this.

A short while later, Hamilton heard Kenton let in the cops and EMTs. If he thought he'd had a long day the other night when the detectives stopped by his house, it would be nothing compared to what they were about to go through now.

*

It was almost eight o'clock in the evening before Hamilton had a chance to debrief with his guys as they huddled in his home office. He and Kenton had filled Mason and Angelo in on some of the details, but they all were curious to learn what Kenton had dug up during his quick search of Wesley's home. One thing was clear—Wesley and Tymico were having an affair.

"What did you find?" Hamilton asked Kenton, who pulled several folded pieces of paper from his pockets.

"I was able to go through the dresser drawers and the closet in the bedroom, as well as the desk drawers before the cops arrived."

"And do we know for sure Wesley's wounds weren't self-inflicted?" Mason asked as they all skimmed over the letters that Kenton laid on the desk.

"I'm pretty sure they weren't; besides, there was no weapon near him," Kenton said. "I also found this photo with one of the threats." He handed the picture, old and crinkled with yellowing on the edges, to Angelo. The letter, he gave to Hamilton.

It's time you paid for taking her from me was spelled out with letters that were cut from a newspaper or magazine.

"That doesn't look like Wesley. Do you know who the woman is?" Angelo asked Hamilton, handing him the photo.

He shook his head. It was hard to make out the man or the woman, but he agreed the guy didn't look like Wesley.

"Was there an envelope or something that could give us an idea of when this letter and photo were sent or received?" Hamilton asked.

"Nope. The letters were shoved haphazardly into his bottom desk drawer, and that one was sitting on top with the photo folded inside of it.

"So, at some point, Wesley had to know who was threatening him," Mason concluded.

"And the bastard didn't care enough to tell Dakota. I just don't get that guy. The moment he found out, he should've told somebody, especially her in light of the accident."

Last Hamilton had heard, Wesley was in surgery. He had offered to take Dakota to the hospital, but she didn't want to go, especially after they had to inform Tymico's mother of what happened.

Hamilton held up the photo. "When we figure out who these people are, then we'll know who we need to track down."

He just hoped it was soon because he didn't know how much more Dakota could handle.

*

Hours later, Dakota lay curled up in the center of Hamilton's huge bed, feeling as if she'd just gone five rounds with Ronda Rousey. Every part of her body hurt, but it was her heart that she didn't think would ever heal.

No matter how she played the scenario they'd walked in on that morning, nothing made sense. She had more questions than answers and it made her sick to know that her father and best friend were seeing each other behind her back.

But it was her father she was most angry with. Tymico was vulnerable to men as it was, and she would've been no match for the charm her father could inflict.

I love you, Brad.

The words on the bathroom mirror, written in lipstick, would forever haunt her.

I knew something wasn't right, but why hadn't Tymico said anything?

The door to the bedroom opened seconds later.

Hamilton sat on the side of the bed. Without speaking, his fingers sifted through her hair, pushing bangs from her face. One of the many things she loved about him was his ability to know when not to say anything. He wasn't a big talker anyway, but she knew his silence had more to do with him not knowing what to say.

What could he say? The whole situation was jacked up.

"Thank you for being here for me," she said, her voice strained.

"I will always be here for you." Hamilton bent down and his lips brushed hers, and she batted away the tears threatening to fall. Dakota couldn't remember the last time she'd cried so much, especially when she went with Hamilton to tell Tymico's mother about what happened. The woman fainted, and they thought they'd have to take her to the emergency room when she finally did come around. Heartbroken didn't begin to describe the pain of losing her only child. Like Dakota, she had no idea Tymico had been seeing Wesley but had heard her daughter mention a Brad numerous times.

Brad. Hearing the name had angered Dakota all over again. Tymico had shortened Bradford, Wesley's last name, knowing Dakota would never figure out who she was referring to.

Just another way to deceive me.

"I heard from the hospital. Your father is out of surgery but in critical condition. Do you want to go and see him?"

"No." She wasn't ready. She didn't know if she'd ever be ready. "You knew, didn't you?"

Hamilton frowned. "Knew what?"

"About my father and Ty."

Closing his eyes, he tilted his head back and sighed. "Not exactly. I watched their interaction each time they visited you at the hospital." He looked at her. "They seemed a little too friendly. I thought maybe something was going on with them, but I didn't know for sure. It didn't even dawn on me to mention their behavior to you since we haven't seen or heard much from either of them since you've been here."

Dakota turned onto her back, groaning when her hip connected with the mattress.

How had she missed it? As soon as the thought popped into her mind, she remembered that day at her father's office. There were probably other signs, but there's no way she would've thought about them being together.

Hamilton kicked off his shoes and climbed onto the bed, pulling her to him. "How about you eat something. I'm sure you'll feel better if you do."

Her stomach chose that moment to growl. She hadn't eaten since breakfast, over twelve hours ago, and was a little hungry. "Okay, but I want one of those ginormous burgers from Bad Daddy's and I want Kenton to go and get it."

Hamilton laughed. "Good luck with that. After you elbowed him, I don't think you're going to be able to ask him to do anything for you for a long time. I'm just glad it was him you hit and not me."

Dakota smiled for the first time in hours. "Yeah, I guess I do owe him an apology. Maybe he'll forgive me if I treat him to a burger."

"That would probably work since there's not much he wouldn't do for food." Hamilton tilted to his side and pulled something from the back pocket of his pants. A photo. "Do either of them look familiar?"

Dakota stared at it for the longest time. "That's my mother when she was younger. I've never seen this picture before, but she looks younger than I am now. Who's the guy? Considering how hugged up they are, I'd say they were pretty close."

"We're not sure, but Kenton found that picture with another threatening letter your father received. Actually, there have been a lot of letters, but that was the only photo."

"I assume that once we figure out who the guy is, then we'll know who's been threatening him and who might've killed Tymico."

"That's what we're thinking."

"That means at some point, my dad knew who was behind the threats, huh?"

Hamilton nodded and placed a kiss on her temple. She didn't have to say what she was thinking, because she was sure he already knew. This was just one more secret her father had kept from her. Had he told her, maybe then Hamilton and his team or the cops would've been able to catch this guy.

"What can you tell me about your parents?"

"Not much. If I remember right, they actually met in California and moved here shortly before I was born."

"Was your mother in the entertainment industry? Maybe an actress?"

Dakota frowned. "I don't think so. I think she was still in college when they met. You think that guy is someone in the industry?"

"I do. Wiz has a facial recognition app, but the photo is too damaged for him to do anything with. He also mentioned that, normally, it works best with digital images or video."

"I guess we'll have to go and see my father one day since he might be the only one who can give us answers."

"Yeah, as soon as he's coherent, we'll go to the hospital."

Dakota wasn't looking forward to that visit, but she wanted this nightmare to be over.

She tilted her head up to look at Hamilton who was staring down at her. "The day after we're able to put all of this behind us, I wanna get married."

A slow smile spread across his sexy mouth. "That works for me. I'll be ready."

Chapter Twenty-Nine

"Are you sure you can handle this?" Hamilton asked Dakota. They were at the hospital to visit Wesley, but Hamilton hadn't thought it a good idea to come right after leaving Tymico's funeral. Dakota had been a wreck, but he hadn't been able to talk her out of coming.

"Yes, I want to know who killed my best friend and who tried to kill me."

Wesley had been in the hospital five days, and after two surgeries he was expected to make a full recovery. According to the nurse, this was the first day he'd been awake for any long period of time.

"Somehow the black clothes seem appropriate for this visit. Wouldn't you say?" Dakota mumbled, still angry with her father. The only reason she was there was because she needed answers.

"We shouldn't be too long," Hamilton said to Kenton who had been keeping a short distance behind them.

"Take your time. I'll be out here."

Hamilton pushed open the door, and it wasn't until they were in the middle of the room did they realize Wesley wasn't alone.

"Homer, I didn't expect to see you here," Dakota said and approached a guy who Hamilton had seen previously but couldn't place where.

Homer, Homer, who was...the director. The movie director.

All types of warning bells went off inside Hamilton's head. Was this guy responsible for the threats, murder and attempted murder of Dakota? At six feet tall, with salt and pepper hair, olive skin, and a medium build, Homer could be the guy in the photo, but Hamilton wasn't sure. He'd only seen him from a distance once.

Hamilton glanced at Wesley. He was as pale as a corpse, and Hamilton was pretty sure it had nothing to do with all the blood he'd lost days ago. When his attention went back to Homer, the man was watching him. Hamilton didn't know what he saw on his face, but before he could react, Homer wrapped his arm around Dakota's neck and pulled her to him.

"Scream and you die," he said to her in a lethal tone, a gun pointed at her temple. Then Homer looked at Hamilton. "Come any closer and I *will* kill her."

Hamilton lifted his hands out in front of him. "Okay, okay. Let's calm down. We don't want any trouble. Just let her go."

The man backed up to the window, the gun held steady in his hand. It was clear he was comfortable with the weapon.

"Please...don't...do this. Take...me," Wesley rasped.

"Dakota, did your father ever tell you how he met your mother?"

"No," she said, barely above a whisper.

"Figures. I'm sure he didn't want you to know he stole her from me. Katrina was my life. She was the woman I was supposed to marry and have children with. We were all friends and Wes knew how I felt about her. He didn't care. He only cared about himself."

"I didn't know. He shouldn't have done that to you." Dakota's words were calm, but Hamilton could hear the catch in her voice.

"Wes moved her to Atlanta, far away from me when her home was in LA. She loved California and he forced her to leave. And his selfishness and greediness are what eventually killed her."

"No," Wesley said. "We were…in love. She was…everything…to me."

Hamilton didn't want to make any sudden moves, and he prayed Dakota wouldn't either. Homer's gun was now against her throat. One wrong move and she'd be gone.

"Homer, I know you're angry with Wesley, but this is not how to get back at him. Dakota hasn't wronged you. Leave her out of this."

"I vowed that I would make him pay for what he did to me. For who he took from me. The only way he'll know my pain is if I take something just as precious from him."

"You already did that when you killed his girlfriend, Tymico," Hamilton said.

Homer shook his head vigorously and Hamilton hated he brought Ty's name into the conversation. The last thing he wanted was to upset this man.

"That was an accident. I didn't know she was there. She just…she wasn't supposed to be there. She wouldn't have gotten hurt if it weren't for Wes."

"I'm sorry," Wesley said, his voice weak. "I didn't mean to… Homer is right. We all spent time together. Every weekend. Me, him, and Kat… She and I fell in love. We didn't mean to hurt anyone. It just happened, and *she's* the one who wanted to move to Georgia."

"You're ly—"

"Please don't hurt my daughter," Wesley cut into Homer's words.

Hamilton kept his attention on Dakota as she stared into his eyes. He didn't see fear. All he saw was love. This woman was his, and her bravery never ceased to amaze him. She was planning something, and he knew they only had one shot.

"Homer, if you kill her, you won't be getting back at Wesley. She doesn't belong to him. She's mine, and I love her as much as you loved Katrina. Please, don't do this. Don't take her from me."

The man looked at Hamilton as if he was considering his words, and his arm relaxed around Dakota. She might not be one hundred percent, and she still had a cast on her arm, but he'd been watching her each day getting stronger and stronger. She could take the guy, but he didn't want her risking her life.

"I'm sorry," Homer said. "You look at her the way I used to look at my Katrina, but I have to do this. Wesley doesn't deserve Dakota."

"I agree, but—"

"Katrina was perfect," Homer said to Dakota. "Even more beautiful than you are. Every day I saw you on the set, I thought of her. I dreamed of her, but your father—"

"Homer, we all agree, Wesley was wrong, but if you kill Dakota, you're killing the woman I love. The woman I plan to marry. The woman who will be the mother of my children."

Dakota blinked several times and Hamilton eased his hand behind his back.

"Kiai!" she yelled, and elbowed Homer in the stomach, then slammed her foot down his shin.

"Get down!" Hamilton yelled and whipped out his gun. Dakota dived to the floor, and he pulled the trigger. A single shot to the head and Homer crumbled to the floor.

Kenton burst through the door, and within minutes, the room was flooded with hospital personnel and security. Hamilton had only one focus.

"Dakota," he breathed, his heart hammering in his chest when he didn't immediately see her. Then she came into view. Sidestepping around those in the room, she hurried to him, practically falling into his arms.

"It's over, baby. It's all over," he said.

*

The next day, Dakota stepped away from Hamilton and stood near her father's bed, afraid of the anger still brewing inside of her. The day before had been one nightmare after another. First attending her best friend's funeral, which had been one of the hardest things she'd ever done. And then having a man hold her at gunpoint because of feeling he'd been wronged by Wesley. Dakota was done. If it hadn't been for needing closure on some of the horrors that she'd been experiencing lately, she wouldn't there.

She didn't know if she'd ever be able to forgive her father.

"I can wait outside," Hamilton said.

"No," Dakota and Wesley said in unison.

"I need to apologize," Wesley said to Hamilton, which shocked Dakota. "I'm sorry for everything I put you and your family through. Back then…and even recently, I was angry and cocky."

He paused and glanced away. Dakota wasn't sure she wanted to hear more, afraid that whatever he said would make her like him even less. None of them spoke until her father continued.

"Avery made a fool of me, sleeping with other men while we were in a relationship. That night, when I heard her screaming as you walked out of my bedroom," he said to Hamilton, who still hadn't spoken, "I really believed you had done something to her. But later, when I found out she had slept with others that night, I was angry. I went after you to avoid humiliation. Wanting…needing to believe that you had forced yourself on her. I know what I've done is unforgivable, but I really am sorry. I'll do whatever I can to make amends."

Dakota shook her head. *"Unbelievable.* You just keep…disappointing me," she choked out, swallowing hard to keep from bursting into tears. "Why now? Why the change of heart?"

"I've made so many mistakes. It's time I right some of my wrongs."

Dakota didn't respond immediately, but she felt that time had come and gone a long time ago.

"I asked you several times if you knew who was sending you the threats. Each time you said no."

"Dee Dee, I swear to you. I didn't know until the middle of the night...before the shooting. Tymico and I were planning to talk to you about us the next morning, which was also when I intended to tell you about Homer." Tears bloomed in his eyes and he batted them away. "I had no idea he would break into the house and..."

Dakota tried not to get emotional, wanting to believe he was telling her the truth about everything. She just didn't know what to believe.

"How long...how long were you seeing Ty?"

"Almost five months."

"Why? Why her? Why my best friend...my sister?" Dakota choked out, determined not to cry, but each time she thought about how she would never see Tymico again, a stab of pain pierced her heart.

"It just happened. We ran into each other at the airport. She was working, on a flight that I was on heading to California. When we landed, I invited her to dinner."

Dakota remembered that. Tymico had called her that night and told her that she'd ran into Wesley and that they'd hung out. Dakota hadn't thought anything of it. They were family. She remembered joking with Tymico, telling her that she should've chosen a more expensive restaurant to get Wesley to take her to. Never thinking that the two of them would eventually be sleeping together.

"We bumped into each other periodically, and we always had a good time whenever we were together."

"Why didn't either of you tell me? Why sneak around?"

"She wanted to tell you, but I...I just couldn't. I didn't want you to think I was some dirty old man or that I was using her."

Instead, Dakota thought he was so much worse than that.

"I know you probably won't believe me, but I loved her, Dee Dee," he said, his voice full of emotion before tears leaked from his eyes. "I really loved her. I never intended to fall in love with her."

Dakota wondered if he realized that the two women he claimed to love were dead, partly because of him. She didn't have the energy to point that out.

"I'm sorry for everything I put you through, both of you," Wesley said to her and Hamilton. "Please forgive me."

Dakota glanced at Hamilton who'd been silently watching her from across the room and wondered what he was thinking. When she returned her attention back to her father, he looked more exhausted than she felt. She had never been able to stay angry with him too long, but too much had happened in the last few days.

"I need time," she said.

He nodded. When he started struggling to keep his eyes open, they left him to sleep.

Dakota was so emotionally spent as they trudged out of the hospital, she could barely see straight. She and Hamilton didn't speak until they climbed into his truck.

"What are your thoughts regarding all that my father said?" Dakota asked. She rested her head on the headrest, barely able to keep her eyes open. "Do you believe he's really sorry for what he did to you? Do you think he was telling the truth about Ty?"

Hamilton stared out the front window and took so long to respond, Dakota thought he wouldn't, but then he said, "I feel like I've been vindicated. I didn't realize how much I needed for him to apologize, to admit he was wrong about me. I doubt we'll ever be friends, but I'm willing to let him into our lives for your sake."

Dakota wasn't there yet. There would always be a special spot in her heart for him because he was her father, but the trust had been shattered. It was going to take a long time for her to welcome him back into her life.

"I believed him when he said he loved Ty. He seemed genuinely distraught, both at losing her and hurting you. I'm not going to make excuses for your father, Dakota, but I will tell you something my mother said to me after I left Atlanta PD. She said you'll never be able to truly move on with your life without forgiveness."

As Hamilton pulled out of the parking lot, Dakota thought about the last few months of her life. Her days with Hamilton had been like a dream come true, but then some of the things she'd experienced lately were like living a nightmare.

You'll never be able to truly move on with your life without forgiveness.

"I have to forgive my father because I don't want anything to hinder the life you and I are planning to build together."

Hamilton held her hand and squeezed. "I'll be right here to support you. I guess right now, though, we should head home since we have a wedding to plan."

Dakota smiled, feeling so blessed and excited about her future with this wonderful man.

"Have I told you lately how much you mean to me?"

Hamilton brought her hand to his lips and kissed the back of it. "I think you might've mentioned it a time or two, but I'll never get tired of hearing it. And I hope you know how much I love you."

"Yeah, I do." She grinned. "We're going to have an amazing life together. I can't wait!"

Epilogue

Three days later...

Excitement bubbled inside of Dakota as they stood in Judge Wallace's chambers. He was officiating their wedding; a wedding Dakota thought wouldn't happen for another few weeks due to poor planning. They hadn't considered that they'd need an appointment to get married at the courthouse.

But as usual, Hamilton saved the day. He had provided security for the Judge earlier in the year and had called in a favor the day before. Now here they were, with Laz, Kenton, and Dominic as their witnesses.

"Now by the power vested in me by the City of Atlanta, I pronounce you husband and wife. You may kiss your bride."

"I've been waiting all day for this moment." Hamilton's strong hands went around her waist and he pulled her close. When their lips touched, pleasure ricocheted through Dakota's body and a burst of fireworks shot off in her head. Hamilton had kissed her plenty of times, made love to her mouth like no one else, but this...this time was different. This time she was kissing her husband, the man she planned to spend the rest of her life with.

"Ugh, they always do this," Dominic grumbled, and Dakota broke off the kiss, unable to hold back her laughter. She never knew what was going to come out of his mouth.

"This is what married people do," Hamilton said, staring into Dakota's eyes. "I'm going to be kissing my *wife* all day, every day for the rest of my life. So, get used to it, kid."

Once they finished the paperwork and thanking the judge, their small wedding party filed out of the judge's chamber. They hadn't told anyone, except Laz and Kenton their wedding plans, but intended to have a large reception in a couple of months.

Since Dominic still had trouble keeping secrets, they hadn't told him the wedding plans until they arrived at the courthouse.

"Man, wait until you fall in love. You're going to be just like your dad," Laz said, draping his arm around Dominic's shoulder as they strolled toward the courthouse exit.

"I'm never kissing a girl. I don't care if she is pretty."

They all laughed.

"Yeah, you say that now," Kenton jumped in, walking on the other side of Dominic. "Trust me, in a few years—"

"In about twenty years," Hamilton corrected.

Kenton grinned and shook his head. "Okay, in twenty years, Dom, you won't be able to keep the girls off of you."

Dakota listened as they all went back and forth, telling Dominic what he could expect in the future. Dakota couldn't ever remember being so happy. She had finally married the man of her dreams and couldn't wait to start their life together. The only thing that would have made her wedding day perfect was if her best friend would've been there. She never imagined getting married without Tymico by her side.

As for Wesley, he was still in the hospital and Dakota made an effort to start her journey to forgiveness by visiting him daily. They actually talked without arguing, which was an improvement. She made arrangement for him to have a live-in nurse until he was fully recovered. Once she returned from her honeymoon, she planned to continue her frequent visits.

They had a long way to go in rebuilding their relationship, but she was optimistic that it could happen.

"I'll go and get the SUV," Kenton said, slipping on his sunglasses.

"And I see someone I know. I'll catch up with you guys a little later," Laz announced and headed down the hallway toward a tall, black woman wearing a gorgeous gray power suit, looking like a total boss.

"Who is that?" Dakota whispered.

Hamilton grinned as he stared after his friend. "That would be Journey Ramsey. An attorney Laz is in love with. He just doesn't know it yet."

Dakota nodded slowly, looking forward to learning more details about the woman. Maybe while they were on their honeymoon, she could pry more information out of Hamilton. They planned to spend a couple of days at a hotel in downtown Atlanta, and then on Saturday, they were leaving for a week-long stay in Orlando. Dominic didn't know it yet, but they were surprising him and his best friend with a trip to Disney World.

"So that was really your wedding?" Dominic asked Dakota, frowning. "That doesn't look like a wedding dress," he said of the floral sleeveless dress that she'd chosen that was both sexy, yet modest. "And aren't you supposed to go to a church? There wasn't even any music. Why did..."

"And it begins," Hamilton said under his breath as Dominic followed them outside, asking one question after another, not caring if he got an answer.

Dakota burst out laughing. This was the beginning of her new life and she was happier than she ever thought possible.

"You know you're stuck with us now, right?" Hamilton said, stealing another kiss.

"I know." She grinned. "And you two are the best thing that's ever happened to me. I can't wait to start this new chapter in our lives."

"Me too, baby. Me too."

*

If you enjoyed this book by Sharon C. Cooper, consider leaving a review on any online book site, review site or social media outlet.

Join Sharon's Mailing List

To get sneak peeks of upcoming stories and to hear about giveaways that Sharon is sponsoring, go to **https://bit.ly/1Sih6ol** to join her mailing list.

A Dose of Passion (Harlequin Kimani – Contemporary Romance)
Model Attraction (Harlequin Kimani – Contemporary Romance)
A Passionate Kiss (Bennett Triplets Series)

Made in the USA
Las Vegas, NV
12 October 2021